CW00485249

UNHURRIED TALES

MY FAVOURITE NOVELLAS

RUSKIN BOND

ALEPH

ALEPH BOOK COMPANY
An independent publishing firm
promoted by ***Rupa Publications India***

First published in India in 2017
by Aleph Book Company
7/16 Ansari Road, Daryaganj
New Delhi 110 002

ISBN: 978-93-86021-88-5

3 5 7 9 10 8 6 4 2

Printed by Parksons Graphics Pvt. Ltd., Mumbai

CONTENTS

INTRODUCTION

C. R. Mandy, who published much of my early work in the *Illustrated Weekly of India* back in the 1950s, once called the novella a 'literary dachshund', the dachshund being a breed of dog with a long body and very short legs, and the novella being a long short story which isn't quite long enough to be called a novel!

Publishers in general are prejudiced against novellas. They cost almost as much as novels to be produced, and if the book buyer has to pay the same for a short novel as for a long one he tends to feel cheated.

I wrote *Time Stops at Shamli* in 1956, shortly after *The Room on the Roof* was published, and I couldn't find anyone to publish it. Twenty thousand words long just wasn't the right length. My typescript was finally lost in the post, but a carbon copy (there were no Xerox machines in those days) had found its way into P. Lal's Writers Workshop in Calcutta, and he put it away and forgot about it, and eventually I forgot about it too. About thirty years later, when he was cleaning out his office, he came across my typescript and very kindly sent it back to me.

That must be a record of sorts for a manuscript to be 'under consideration'.

Well, in 1987, David Davidar, who had just launched the first Penguins in India, asked me to send him some of my work, and I immediately bombarded him with hundreds of stories, short and long, including the unpublished 'Shamli'. And to cut a long story short, he made *Time Stops at Shamli* the title of one of my collections, and till today, thirty years later, it remains one of my most successful books.

So much for my first novella.

There have been many over the years, but here I must pause and inform the reader why I like this literary form, both as a writer and as a reader myself. To begin with, the words 'novel' and 'novella' both come from the Italian novella storia, meaning 'new story'. Both respectable literary forms. But then you have the 'novelette' which, according to the Oxford English Dictionary, is 'a short romantic novel regarded as not very well written'. I presume the Mills and Boon writers, and others of their ilk, fall into this category. 'Not very well written'. I shudder at the thought of ever having to write one. I grew up reading all sorts of books, but the romantic novelette was not among them.

An eminent literary critic has defined the short novel or novella as a narrative genre that 'demands compositional economy, homogeneity of conception, concentration in the analysis of character, and strict aesthetic control'. This sounds rather pompous—in fact, it is pompous—and if I'd read those lines before setting out to write, I would not have had the temerity to write anything. But writing is all about breaking the rules, not tamely following them and over the years I have enjoyed my writing simply because I haven't bothered over much with 'aesthetic control', whatever that may be.

There are many great writers who have written outstanding novellas, and these are a few of them. *The Lifted Veil* by George Eliot, *On the Eve* by Ivan Turgenev, *Death in Venice* by Thomas Mann, *The Immoralist* by André Gide, *The Aspern Papers* by Henry James, *Heart of Darkness* by Joseph Conrad, *The Blue Hotel* by Stephen Crane, *Red Leaves* by William Faulkner, *The Gioconda Smile* by Aldous Huxley, *Sally Bowles* by Christopher Isherwood, *Decline and Fall* by Evelyn Waugh, *The Old Man and the Sea* by Ernest Hemingway, *Of Mice and Men* by John Steinbeck.

The list could go on to fill several pages. These are simply a few personal favourites. And I can't forget the short novels that I read as a boy and that set me off on my own literary journey: H. G. Wells' *The Invisible Man*, R. L. Stevenson's *Dr Jekyll and My Hyde* and *The Ebb Tide;* Sterne's *Sentimental Journey* and Mary Shelly's *Frankenstein.*

Looking back on my long literary journey, I can see that I gave priority to the writing of short stories and essays; but that was because

I was in constant need of a regular monthly income, which only shorter work could bring me. Whenever I had the luxury of two or three months free of these financial pressures, I would indulge in a longer work—a long short story or a novella. Hence, *Time Stops at Shamli* and *Bus Stop, Pipalnagar*; *The Sensualist* and *A Handful of Nuts*; *Maharani* and *Tales of Fosterganj* and several of my childhood novels. I loved writing these longer pieces of fiction because it allowed me to develop my characters and stories in an unhurried way. That's why this book is entitled *Unhurried Tales*.

I wrote *The Blue Umbrella* as a children's story, but when a friend read it in manuscript form he said, 'I loved it. Why don't you turn it into a children's story?'

'It's a children's story,' I said.

'Yes, I see that now,' he said. 'It could be both things…'

I wrote *The Blue Umbrella* in a few days. Everything in it rang true—the time, the place, the girl! The characters and the incidents first fell into place as I went along, without any attempt to invent a plot or point a moral. And yet it makes a point. And Binya and her blue umbrella have been my bestseller for the last forty years.

Angry River was a longer work when I first wrote it. Once again, there was the old problem of length. 'It's not long enough for us to publish as an adult novel,' said Julia MacRae, an editor with Hamish Hamilton. 'But if you make it even shorter, we can do it as a children's book.'

And that's what happened.

I have been a little hard on leopards in *Night of the Leopard* and *Tales of Fosterganj*. My apologies to the big cats. Leopards usually mind their own business, and will leave you alone if you leave them alone. But just occasionally one of them gets a taste of human flesh, fancies the flavour, and wants more of it.

Tales of Fosterganj has a leopard, as well as a lizard and a mysterious black bird, but they are overshadowed by various odd characters such as Sunil the pickpocket, the down to earth Mr Foster (a descendant of Bonnie Prince Charlie), and a strange couple who live in a crumbling old palace on the outskirts of a hill station. These characters and the incidents they set off give the story a picaresque quality.

I have always wanted to write a picaresque tale and in *Tales of Fosterganj* I have indulged myself. Please forgive me.

Ruskin Bond

Landour, Mussoorie
October 2017

TIME STOPS AT SHAMLI

The Dehra Express usually drew into Shamli at about five o'clock in the morning at which time the station would be dimly lit and the jungle across the tracks would just be visible in the faint light of dawn. Shamli is a small station at the foot of the Shivalik hills and the Shivaliks lie at the foot of the Himalayas, which in turn lie at the feet of God.

The station, I remember, had only one platform, an office for the stationmaster, and a waiting room. The platform boasted a tea stall, a fruit vendor, and a few stray dogs. Not much else was required because the train stopped at Shamli for only five minutes before rushing on into the forests.

Why it stopped at Shamli, I never could tell. Nobody got off the train and nobody got on. There were never any coolies on the platform. But the train would stand there a full five minutes and the guard would blow his whistle and presently Shamli would be left behind and forgotten...until I passed that way again.

I was paying my relations in Saharanpur an annual visit when the night train stopped at Shamli. I was thirty-six at the time and still single.

On this particular journey, the train came into Shamli just as I awoke from a restless sleep. The third-class compartment was crowded beyond capacity and I had been sleeping in an upright position with my back to the lavatory door. Now someone was trying to get into the lavatory. He was obviously hard pressed for time.

'I'm sorry, brother,' I said, moving as much as I could to one side.

He stumbled into the closet without bothering to close the door.

'Where are we now?' I asked the man sitting beside me. He was smoking a strong aromatic bidi.

'Shamli station,' he said, rubbing the palm of a large calloused hand over the frosted glass of the window.

I let the window down and stuck my head out. There was a cool breeze blowing down the platform, a breeze that whispered of autumn in the hills. As usual there was no activity except for the fruit vendor walking up and down the length of the train with his basket of mangoes balanced on his head. At the tea stall, a kettle was steaming, but there was no one to mind it. I rested my forehead on the window ledge and let the breeze play on my temples. I had been feeling sick and giddy but there was a wild sweetness in the wind that I found soothing.

'Yes,' I said to myself, 'I wonder what happens in Shamli behind the station walls.'

My fellow passenger offered me a bidi. He was a farmer, I think, on his way to Dehra. He had a long, untidy, sad moustache.

We had been more than five minutes at the station. I looked up and down the platform, but nobody was getting on or off the train. Presently the guard came walking past our compartment.

'What's the delay?' I asked him.

'Some obstruction further down the line,' he said.

'Will we be here long?'

'I don't know what the trouble is. About half an hour at the least.'

My neighbour shrugged and throwing the remains of his bidi out of the window, closed his eyes and immediately fell asleep. I moved restlessly in my seat and then the man came out of the lavatory, not so urgently now, and with obvious peace of mind. I closed the door for him.

I stood up and stretched and this stretching of my limbs seemed to set in motion a stretching of the mind and I found myself thinking: 'I am in no hurry to get to Saharanpur and I have always wanted to see Shamli behind the station walls. If I get down now, I can spend the day here. It will be better than sitting in this train for another hour. Then in the evening I can catch the next train home.'

In those days I never had the patience to wait for second thoughts and so I began pulling my small suitcase out from under the seat.

The farmer woke up and asked, 'What are you doing, brother?'

'I'm getting out,' I said.

He went to sleep again.

It would have taken at least fifteen minutes to reach the door as people and their belongings cluttered up the passage. So I let my suitcase down from the window and followed it on to the platform.

There was no one to collect my ticket at the barrier because there was obviously no point in keeping a man there to collect tickets from passengers who never came. And anyway, I had a through-ticket to my destination which I would need in the evening.

I went out of the station and came to Shamli.

Outside the station there was a neem tree and under it stood a tonga. The pony was nibbling at the grass at the foot of the tree. The youth in the front seat was the only human in sight. There were no signs of inhabitants or habitation. I approached the tonga and the youth stared at me as though he couldn't believe his eyes.

'Where is Shamli?' I asked.

'Why, friend, this is Shamli,' he said.

I looked around again but I couldn't see any sign of life. A dusty road led past the station and disappeared into the forest.

'Does anyone live here? I asked.

'I live here,' he said with an engaging smile. He looked an amiable, happy-go-lucky fellow. He wore a cotton tunic and dirty white pyjamas.

'Where?' I asked.

'In my tonga, of course,' he said. 'I have had this pony for five years now. I carry supplies to the hotel. But today the manager has not come to collect them. You are going to the hotel? I will take you.'

'Oh, so there's a hotel?'

'Well, friend, it is called that. And there are a few houses too and some shops, but they are all a mile from the station. If they were not a mile from here, I would be out of business.'

I felt relieved but I still had the feeling of having walked into a town consisting of one station, one pony and one man.

'You can take me,' I said. 'I'm staying till this evening.'

He heaved my suitcase into the seat beside him and I climbed in at the back. He flicked the reins and slapped his pony on the buttocks and, with a roll and a lurch, the buggy moved off down the dusty forest road.

'What brings you here?' asked the youth.

'Nothing,' I said. 'The train was delayed. I was feeling bored. And so I got off.'

He did not believe that but he didn't question me further. The sun was reaching up over the forest but the road lay in the shadow of tall trees—eucalyptus, mango and neem.

'Not many people stay in the hotel,' he said. 'So it is cheap. You will get a room for five rupees.'

'Who is the manager?'

'Mr Satish Dayal. It is his father's property. Satish Dayal could not pass his exams or get a job so his father sent him here to look after the hotel.'

The jungle thinned out and we passed a temple, a mosque, a few small shops. There was a strong smell of burnt sugar in the air and in the distance I saw a factory chimney. That, then, was the reason for Shamli's existence. We passed a bullock cart laden with sugarcane. The road went through fields of cane and maize, and then, just as we were about to re-enter the jungle, the youth pulled his horse to a side road and the hotel came in sight.

It was a small white bungalow with a garden in the front, banana trees at the sides and an orchard of guava trees at the back. We came jingling up to the front veranda. Nobody appeared, nor was there any sign of life on the premises.

'They are all asleep,' said the youth.

I said, 'I'll sit in the veranda and wait.' I got down from the tonga and the youth dropped my case on the veranda steps. Then he stooped in front of me, smiling amiably, waiting to be paid.

'Well, how much?' I asked.

'As a friend, only one rupee.'

'That's too much,' I complained. 'This is not Delhi.'

'This is Shamli,' he said. 'I am the only tonga in Shamli. You may not pay me anything, if that is your wish. But then, I will not take you back to the station this evening. You will have to walk.'

I gave him the rupee. He had both charm and cunning, an effective combination.

'Come in the evening at about six,' I said.

'I will come,' he said with an infectious smile. 'Don't worry.' I waited till the tonga had gone round the bend in the road before walking up the veranda steps.

The doors of the house were closed and there were no bells to ring. I didn't have a watch but I judged the time to be a little past six o'clock. The hotel didn't look very impressive. The whitewash was coming off the walls and the cane chairs on the veranda were old and crooked. A stag's head was mounted over the front door but one of its glass eyes had fallen out. I had often heard hunters speak of how beautiful an animal looked before it died, but how could anyone with true love of the beautiful care for the stuffed head of an animal, grotesquely mounted, with no resemblance to its living aspect?

I felt too restless to take any of the chairs. I began pacing up and down the veranda, wondering if I should start banging on the doors. Perhaps the hotel was deserted. Perhaps the tonga driver had played a trick on me. I began to regret my impulsiveness in leaving the train. When I saw the manager I would have to invent a reason for coming to his hotel. I was good at inventing reasons. I would tell him that a friend of mine had stayed here some years ago and that I was trying to trace him. I decided that my friend would have to be a little eccentric (having chosen Shamli to live in), that he had become a recluse, shutting himself off from the world. His parents—no, his sister—for his parents would be dead—had asked me to find him if I could and, as he had last been heard of in Shamli, I had taken the opportunity to enquire after him. His name would be Major Roberts, retired.

I heard a tap running at the side of the building and walking around found a young man bathing at the tap. He was strong and well built and slapped himself on the body with great enthusiasm. He had not seen me approaching so I waited until he had finished bathing and had begun to dry himself.

'Hallo,' I said.

He turned at the sound of my voice and looked at me for a few moments with a puzzled expression. He had a round cheerful face and crisp black hair. He smiled slowly. But it was a more genuine smile than the tonga driver's. So far I had met two people in Shamli and they were both smilers. That should have cheered me, but it didn't. 'You have come to stay?' he asked in a slow, easy-going voice.

'Just for the day,' I said. 'You work here?'

'Yes, my name is Daya Ram. The manager is asleep just now but I will find a room for you.'

He pulled on his vest and pyjamas and accompanied me back to the veranda. Here he picked up my suitcase and, unlocking a side door, led me into the house. We went down a passageway. Then Daya Ram stopped at the door on the right, pushed it open and took me into a small, sunny room that had a window looking out on to the orchard. There was a bed, a desk, a couple of cane chairs, and a frayed and faded red carpet.

'Is it all right?' said Daya Ram.

'Perfectly all right.'

'They have breakfast at eight o'clock. But if you are hungry, I will make something for you now.'

'No, it's all right. Are you the cook too?'

'I do everything here.'

'Do you like it?'

'No,' he said. And then added, in a sudden burst of confidence, 'There are no women for a man like me.'

'Why don't you leave, then?'

'I will,' he said with a doubtful look on his face. 'I will leave...'

After he had gone I shut the door and went into the bathroom to bathe. The cold water refreshed me and made me feel one with the world. After I had dried myself, I sat on the bed, in front of the open window. A cool breeze, smelling of rain, came through the window and played over my body. I thought I saw a movement among the trees.

And getting closer to the window, I saw a girl on a swing. She was a small girl, all by herself, and she was swinging to and fro and singing, and her song carried faintly on the breeze.

I dressed quickly and left my room. The girl's dress was billowing in the breeze, her pigtails flying about. When she saw me approaching, she stopped swinging and stared at me. I stopped a little distance away.

'Who are you?' she asked.

'A ghost,' I replied.

'You look like one,' she said.

I decided to take this as a compliment, as I was determined to make friends. I did not smile at her because some children dislike adults who smile at them all the time.

'What's your name?' I asked.

'Kiran,' she said. 'I'm ten.'

'You are getting old.'

'Well, we all have to grow old one day. Aren't you coming any closer?'

'May I?' I asked.

'You may. You can push the swing.'

One pigtail lay across the girl's chest, the other behind her shoulder. She had a serious face and obviously felt she had responsibilities. She seemed to be in a hurry to grow up, and I suppose she had no time for anyone who treated her as a child, I pushed the swing until it went higher and higher and then I stopped pushing so that she came lower each time and we could talk.

'Tell me about the people who live here,' I said.

'There is Heera,' she said. 'He's the gardener. He's nearly a hundred. You can see him behind the hedges in the garden. You can't see him unless you look hard. He tells me stories, a new story every day. He's much better than the people in the hotel and so is Daya Ram.'

'Yes, I met Daya Ram.'

'He's my bodyguard. He brings me nice things from the kitchen when no one is looking.'

'You don't stay here?'

'No, I live in another house. You can't see it from here. My father is the manager of the factory.'

'Aren't there any other children to play with?' I asked.

'I don't know any,' she said.

'And the people staying here?'

'Oh, they.' Apparently Kiran didn't think much of the hotel guests.

'Miss Deeds is funny when she's drunk. And Mr Lin is the strangest.'

'And what about the manager, Mr Dayal?'

'He's mean. And he gets frightened of the slightest things. But Mrs Dayal is nice. She lets me take flowers home. But she doesn't talk much.'

I was fascinated by Kiran's ruthless summing up of the guests. I brought the swing to a standstill and asked, 'And what do you think of me?'

'I don't know as yet,' said Kiran quite seriously. 'I'll think about you.'

As I came back to the hotel, I heard the sound of a piano in one of the front rooms. I didn't know enough about music to be able to recognize the piece but it had sweetness and melody though it was played with some hesitancy. As I came nearer, the sweetness deserted the music, probably because the piano was out of tune.

The person at the piano had distinctive Mongolian features and so I presumed he was Mr Lin. He hadn't seen me enter the room and I stood beside the curtains of the door, watching him play. He had full round lips and high, slanting cheekbones. His eyes were large and round and full of melancholy. His long, slender fingers hardly touched the keys.

I came nearer and then he looked up at me, without any show of surprise or displeasure, and kept on playing.

'What are you playing?' I asked.

'Chopin,' he said.

'Oh, yes. It's nice but the piano is fighting it.'

'I know. This piano belonged to one of Kipling's aunts. It hasn't been tuned since the last century.'

'Do you live here?'

'No, I come from Calcutta,' he answered readily. 'I have some business here with the sugarcane people, actually, though I am not a businessman.' He was playing softly all the time so that our conversation was not lost in the music. 'I don't know anything about business. But I have to do something.'

'Where did you learn to play the piano?'

'In Singapore. A French lady taught me. She had great hopes

of my becoming a concert pianist when I grew up. I would have toured Europe and America.'

'Why didn't you?'

'We left during the war and I had to give up my lessons.'

'And why did you go to Calcutta?'

'My father is a Calcutta businessman. What do you do and why do you come here?' he asked. 'If I am not being too inquisitive.'

Before I could answer, a bell rang, loud and continuously, drowning the music and conversation.

'Breakfast,' said Mr Lin.

A thin dark man, wearing glasses, stepped nervously into the room and peered at me in an anxious manner.

'You arrived last night?'

'That's right,' I said. 'I just want to stay the day. I think you're the manager?'

'Yes. Would you like to sign the register?'

I went with him past the bar and into the office. I wrote my name and Mussoorie address in the register and the duration of my stay. I paused at the column marked 'profession', thought it would be best to fill it with something and wrote 'author'.

'You are here on business?' asked Mr Dayal.

'No, not exactly. You see, I'm looking for a friend of mine who was last heard of in Shamli, about three years ago. I thought I'd make a few inquiries in case he's still here.'

'What was his name? Perhaps he stayed here.'

'Major Roberts,' I said. 'An Anglo-Indian.'

'Well, you can look through the old registers after breakfast.'

He accompanied me into the dining room. The establishment was really more of a boarding house than a hotel because Mr Dayal ate with his guests. There was a round mahogany dining table in the centre of the room and Mr Lin was the only one seated at it. Daya Ram hovered about with plates and trays. I took my seat next to Lin and, as I did so, a door opened from the passage and a woman of about thirty-five came in.

She had on a skirt and blouse which accentuated a firm, well-rounded figure, and she walked on high heels, with a rhythmical swaying of the hips. She had an uninteresting face, camouflaged with lipstick, rouge and powder—the powder so thick that it had become embedded in the natural lines of her face—but her figure compelled admiration.

'Miss Deeds,' whispered Lin.

There was a false note to her greeting.

'Hallo, everyone,' she said heartily, straining for effect. 'Why are you all so quiet? Has Mr Lin been playing *The Funeral March* again?' She sat down and continued talking. 'Really, we must have a dance or something to liven things up. You must know some good numbers, Lin, after your experience of Singapore nightclubs. What's for breakfast? Boiled eggs. Daya Ram, can't you make an omelette for a change? I know you're not a professional cook but you don't have to give us the same thing every day, and there's absolutely no reason why you should burn the toast. You'll have to do something about a cook, Mr Dayal.' Then she noticed me sitting opposite her; 'Oh, hallo,' she said, genuinely surprised. She gave me a long appraising look.

'This gentleman,' said Mr Dayal introducing me, 'is an author.'

'That's nice," said Miss Deeds. 'Are you married?'

'No,' I said. 'Are you?'

'Funny, isn't it,' she said, without taking offence, 'no one in this house seems to be married.'

'I'm married,' said Mr Dayal.

'Oh, yes, of course,' said Miss Deeds. 'And what brings you to Shamli?' she asked, turning to me.

'I'm looking for a friend called Major Roberts.'

Lin gave an exclamation of surprise. I thought he had seen through my deception.

But another game had begun.

'I knew him,' said Lin. 'A great friend of mine.'

'Yes,' continued Lin. 'I knew him. A good chap, Major Roberts.'

Well, there I was, inventing people to suit my convenience, and people like Mr Lin started inventing relationships with them. I was too intrigued to try and discourage him. I wanted to see how far he would go.

'When did you meet him?' asked Lin, taking the initiative.

'Oh, only about three years back, just before he disappeared. He was last heard of in Shamli.'

'Yes, I heard he was here,' said Lin. 'But he went away, when he thought his relatives had traced him. He went into the mountains near Tibet.'

'Did he?' I said, unwilling to be instructed further. 'What part of the country? I come from the hills myself. I know the Mana and Niti passes quite well. If you have any idea of exactly where he went, I think I could find him.' I had the advantage in this exchange because I was the one who had originally invented Roberts. Yet I couldn't bring myself to end his deception, probably because I felt sorry for him. A happy man wouldn't take the trouble of inventing friendships with people who didn't exist. He'd be too busy with friends who did.

'You've had a lonely life, Mr Lin?' I asked.

'Lonely?' said Mr Lin, with forced incredulousness. 'I'd never been lonely till I came here a month ago. When I was in Singapore…'

'You never get any letters though, do you?' asked Miss Deeds suddenly.

Lin was silent for a moment. Then he said: 'Do you?'

Miss Deeds lifted her head a little, as a horse does when it is annoyed, and I thought her pride had been hurt, but then she laughed unobtrusively and tossed her head.

'I never write letters,' she said. 'My friends gave me up as hopeless years ago. They know it's no use writing to me because they rarely get a reply. They call me the Jungle Princess.'

Mr Dayal tittered and I found it hard to suppress a smile. To cover up my smile I asked, 'You teach here?'

'Yes, I teach at the girls' school,' she said with a frown. 'But don't talk to me about teaching. I have enough of it all day.'

'You don't like teaching?' I asked.

She gave me an aggressive look. 'Should I?' she asked.

'Shouldn't you?' I said.

She paused, and then said, 'Who are you, anyway, the Inspector of Schools?'

'No,' said Mr Dayal who wasn't following very well, 'he's a journalist.'

'I've heard they are nosey,' said Miss Deeds.

Once again Lin interrupted to steer the conversation away from a delicate issue.

'Where's Mrs Dayal this morning?' asked Lin.

'She spent the night with our neighbours,' said Mr Dayal. 'She should be here after lunch.'

It was the first time Mrs Dayal had been mentioned. Nobody spoke either well or ill of her. I suspected that she kept her distance from the others, avoiding familiarity. I began to wonder about Mrs Dayal.

Daya Ram came in from the veranda looking worried.

'Heera's dog has disappeared,' he said. 'He thinks a leopard took it.'

Heera, the gardener, was standing respectfully outside on the veranda steps. We all hurried out to him, firing questions which he didn't try to answer.

'Yes. It's a leopard,' said Kiran appearing from behind Heera. 'It's going to come into the hotel,' she added cheerfully.

'Be quiet,' said Satish Dayal crossly.

'There are pug marks under the trees,' said Daya Ram.

Mr Dayal, who seemed to know little about leopards or pug marks, said, 'I will take a look,' and led the way to the orchard, the rest of us trailing behind in an ill-assorted procession.

There were marks on the soft earth in the orchard (they could have been a leopard's) which went in the direction of the riverbed. Mr Dayal paled a little and went hurrying back to the hotel. Heera returned to the front garden, the least excited, the most sorrowful. Everyone else was thinking of a leopard but he was thinking of the dog.

I followed him and watched him weeding the sunflower beds. His face was wrinkled like a walnut but his eyes were clear and bright. His hands were thin and bony but there was a deftness and power in the wrist and fingers and the weeds flew fast from his spade. He had cracked, parchment-like skin. I could not help thinking of the gloss and glow of Daya Ram's limbs as I had seen them when he was bathing and wondered if Heera's had once been like that and if Daya Ram's would ever be like this, and both possibilities—or were they probabilities—saddened me. Our skin, I thought, is like the leaf of a tree, young and green and shiny. Then it gets darker and heavier, sometimes spotted with disease, sometimes eaten away. Then fading, yellow and red, then falling, crumbling into dust or feeding the flames of fire. I looked at my own skin, still smooth, not coarsened by labour. I thought of Kiran's fresh rose-tinted complexion; Miss Deeds' skin, hard and dry; Lin's pale taut skin, stretched tightly across his prominent cheeks and forehead; and Mr Dayal's grey skin growing thick hair.

And I wondered about Mrs Dayal and the kind of skin she would have.

'Did you have the dog for long?' I asked Heera.

He looked up with surprise for he had been unaware of my presence.

'Six years, sahib,' he said. 'He was not a clever dog but he was very friendly. He followed me home one day when I was coming back from the bazaar. I kept telling him to go away but he wouldn't. It was a long walk and so I began talking to him. I liked talking to him and I have always talked to him and we have understood each other. That first night, when I came home I shut the gate between us. But he stood on the other side looking at me with trusting eyes. Why did he have to look at me like that?'

'So you kept him?'

'Yes, I could never forget the way he looked at me. I shall feel lonely now because he was my only companion. My wife and son died long ago. It seems I am to stay here forever, until everyone has gone, until there are only ghosts in Shamli. Already the ghosts are here...'

I heard a light footfall behind me and turned to find Kiran. The barefoot girl stood beside the gardener and with her toes began to pull at the weeds.

'You are a lazy one,' said the old man. 'If you want to help me sit down and use your hands.'

I looked at the girl's fair round face and in her bright eyes I saw something old and wise. And I looked into the old man's wise eyes, and saw something forever bright and young. The skin cannot change the eyes. The eyes are the true reflection of a man's age and sensibilities. Even a blind man has hidden eyes.

'I hope we find the dog,' said Kiran. 'But I would like a leopard. Nothing ever happens here.'

'Not now,' sighed Heera. 'Not now... Why, once there was a band and people danced till morning, but now...' He paused, lost in thought and then said: 'I have always been here. I was here before Shamli.'

'Before the station?'

'Before there was a station, or a factory, or a bazaar. It was a village then, and the only way to get here was by bullock cart. Then a bus service was started, then the railway lines were laid and a station built, then they started the sugar factory, and for a few years Shamli was a town. But the jungle was bigger than the town. The rains were heavy and malaria was everywhere. People didn't stay long in Shamli. Gradually, they went back into the hills. Sometimes I too wanted to go back to the hills, but what is the use when you are old and have no one left in the world except a few flowers in a troublesome garden. I had to choose between the flowers and the hills, and I chose the flowers. I am tired now, and old, but I am not tired of flowers.'

I could see that his real world was the garden; there was more variety in his flower beds than there was in the town of Shamli. Every month, every day, there were new flowers in the garden, but there were always the same people in Shamli.

I left Kiran with the old man, and returned to my room. It must have been about eleven o'clock.

I was facing the window when I heard my door being opened. Turning, I perceived the barrel of a gun moving slowly round the edge of the door. Behind the gun was Satish Dayal, looking hot and sweaty. I didn't know what his intentions were; so, deciding it would be better to act first and reason later, I grabbed a pillow from the bed and flung it in his face. I then threw myself at his legs and brought him crashing down to the ground.

When we got up, I was holding the gun. It was an old Enfield rifle, probably dating back to the Afghan wars, the kind that goes off at the least encouragement.

'But—but—why?' stammered the dishevelled and alarmed Mr Dayal.

'I don't know,' I said menacingly. 'Why did you come in here pointing this at me?'

'I wasn't pointing it at you. It's for the leopard.'

'Oh, so you came into my room looking for a leopard? You have, I presume been stalking one about the hotel?' (By now I was convinced that Mr Dayal had taken leave of his senses and was hunting imaginary leopards.)

'No, no,' cried the distraught man, becoming more confused. 'I was looking for you. I wanted to ask you if you could use a gun. I was thinking we should go looking for the leopard that took Heera's dog. Neither Mr Lin nor I can shoot.'

'Your gun is not up-to-date,' I said. 'It's not at all suitable for hunting leopards. A stout stick would be more effective. Why don't we arm ourselves with lathis and make a general assault?'

I said this banteringly, but Mr Dayal took the idea quite seriously. 'Yes, yes,' he said with alacrity, 'Daya Ram has got one or two lathis in the godown. The three of us could make an expedition. I have asked Mr Lin but he says he doesn't want to have anything to do with leopards.'

'What about our Jungle Princess?' I said. 'Miss Deeds should be pretty good with a lathi.'

'Yes, yes,' said Mr Dayal humourlessly, 'but we'd better not ask her.'

Collecting Daya Ram and two lathis, we set off for the orchard and began following the pug marks through the trees. It took us ten minutes to reach the riverbed, a dry hot rocky place; then we went into the jungle, Mr Dayal keeping well to the rear. The atmosphere was heavy and humid, and there was not a breath of air amongst the trees. When a parrot squawked suddenly, shattering the silence, Mr Dayal let out a startled exclamation and started for home.

'What was that?' he asked nervously.

'A bird,' I explained.

'I think we should go back now,' he said. 'I don't think the leopard's here.'

'You never know with leopards,' I said, 'they could be anywhere.'

Mr Dayal stepped away from the bushes. 'I'll have to go,' he said. 'I have a lot of work. You keep a lathi with you, and I'll send Daya Ram back later.'

'That's very thoughtful of you,' I said.

Daya Ram scratched his head and reluctantly followed his employer back through the trees. I moved on slowly, down the little used path, wondering if I should also return. I saw two monkeys playing on the branch of a tree, and decided that there could be no danger in the immediate vicinity.

Presently I came to a clearing where there was a pool of fresh clear water. It was fed by a small stream that came suddenly, like a snake, out of the long grass. The water looked cool and inviting. Laying down the lathi and taking off my clothes, I ran down the bank until I was waist-deep in the middle of the pool. I splashed about for some time before emerging, then I lay on the soft grass and allowed the sun to dry my body. I closed my eyes and gave myself up to beautiful thoughts. I had forgotten all about leopards.

I must have slept for about half an hour because when I awoke, I found that Daya Ram had come back and was vigorously threshing about in the narrow confines of the pool. I sat up and asked him the time.

'Twelve o'clock,' he shouted, coming out of the water, his dripping body all gold and silver in sunlight. 'They will be waiting for dinner.'

'Let them wait,' I said.

It was a relief to talk to Daya Ram, after the uneasy conversations in the lounge and dining room.

'Dayal sahib will be angry with me.'

'I'll tell him we found the trail of the leopard, and that we went so far into the jungle that we lost our way. As Miss Deeds is so critical of the food, let her cook the meal.'

'Oh, she only talks like that,' said Daya Ram. 'Inside she is very soft. She is too soft in some ways.'

'She should be married.'

'Well, she would like to be. Only there is no one to marry her. When she came here she was engaged to be married to an English army captain. I think she loved him, but she is the sort of person who cannot help loving many men all at once, and the captain could not understand that—it is just the way she is made, I suppose. She is always ready to fall in love.'

'You seem to know,' I said.

'Oh, yes.'

We dressed and walked back to the hotel. In a few hours, I thought, the tonga will come for me and I will be back at the station. The mysterious charm of Shamli will be no more, but whenever I pass this way I will wonder about these people, about Miss Deeds and Lin and Mrs Dayal.

Mrs Dayal… She was the one person I had yet to meet. It was with some excitement and curiosity that I looked forward to meeting her; she was about the only mystery left in Shamli, now, and perhaps she would be no mystery when I met her. And yet… I felt that perhaps she would justify the impulse that made me get down from the train.

I could have asked Daya Ram about Mrs Dayal, and so satisfied my curiosity; but I wanted to discover her for myself. Half the day was left to me, and I didn't want my game to finish too early.

I walked towards the veranda, and the sound of the piano came through the open door.

'I wish Mr Lin would play something cheerful,' said Miss Deeds. 'He's obsessed with *The Funeral March*. Do you dance?'

'Oh, no,' I said.

She looked disappointed. But when Lin left the piano, she went into the lounge and sat down on the stool. I stood at the door watching her, wondering what she would do. Lin left the room somewhat resentfully.

She began to play an old song which I remembered having heard in a film or on a gramophone record. She sang while she played, in a slightly harsh but pleasant voice:

Rolling round the world
Looking for the sunshine
I know I'm going to find some day…

Then she played 'Am I Blue?' and 'Darling, Je Vous Aime Beaucoup'. She sat there singing in a deep husky voice, her eyes a little misty, her hard face suddenly kind and sloppy. When the dinner gong rang, she broke off playing and shook off her sentimental mood, and laughed derisively at herself.

I don't remember that lunch. I hadn't slept much since the previous night and I was beginning to feel the strain of my journey. The swim had refreshed me, but it had also made me drowsy. I ate quite well, though, of rice and kofta curry, and then feeling sleepy, made for the garden to find a shady tree.

There were some books on the shelf in the lounge, and I ran my eye over them in search of one that might condition sleep. But they were too dull to do even that. So I went into the garden, and there was Kiran on the swing, and I went to her tree and sat down on the grass.

'Did you find the leopard?' she asked.

'No,' I said, with a yawn.

'Tell me a story.'

'You tell me one,' I said.

'All right. Once there was a lazy man with long legs, who was always yawning and wanting to fall asleep…'

I watched the swaying motions of the swing and the movements of the girl's bare legs, and a tiny insect kept buzzing about in front of my nose…

'…and fall asleep, and the reason for this was that he liked to dream.'

I blew the insect away, and the swing became hazy and distant, and Kiran was a blurred figure in the trees…

'…liked to dream, and what do you think he dreamt about..?' Dreamt about, dreamt about…

When I awoke there was that cool rain-scented breeze blowing across the garden. I remember lying on the grass with my eyes closed, listening to the swishing of the swing. Either I had not slept long, or Kiran had been a long time on the swing; it was moving slowly now, in a more leisurely fashion, without much sound. I opened my eyes and saw that my arm was stained with the juice of the grass beneath me. Looking up, I expected to see Kiran's legs waving above me. But instead I saw dark slim feet and above them the folds of a sari. I straightened up against the trunk of the tree to look closer at Kiran, but Kiran wasn't there. It was someone else in the swing, a young woman in a pink sari, with a red rose in her hair.

She had stopped the swing with her foot on the ground, and she was smiling at me. 'It wasn't a smile you could see, it was a tender fleeting movement that came suddenly and was gone at the same time, and its going was sad. I thought of the others' smiles, just as I had thought of their skins: the tonga driver's friendly, deceptive smile; Daya Ram's wide sincere smile; Miss Deeds's cynical, derisive smile. And looking at Sushila, I knew a smile could never change. She had always smiled that way.

'You haven't changed,' she said.

I was standing up now, though still leaning against the tree for support. Though I had never thought much about the sound of her voice, it seemed as familiar as the sounds of yesterday.

'You haven't changed either,' I said. 'But where did you come from?' I wasn't sure yet if I was awake or dreaming.

She laughed as she had always laughed at me.

'I came from behind the tree. The little girl has gone.'

'Yes, I'm dreaming,' I said helplessly.

'But what brings you here?'

'I don't know. At least I didn't know when I came. But it must have been you. The train stopped at Shamli and I don't know why, but I decided I would spend the day here, behind the station walls. You must be married now, Sushila.'

'Yes, I am married to Mr Dayal, the manager of the hotel. And what has been happening to you?'

'I am still a writer, still poor, and still living in Mussoorie.'

'When were you last in Delhi?' she asked. 'I don't mean Delhi, I mean at home.'

'I have not been to your home since you were there.'

'Oh, my friend,' she said, getting up suddenly and coming to me, 'I want to talk about our home and Sunil and our friends and all those things that are so far away now. I have been here two years, and I am already feeling old. I keep remembering our home—how young I was, how happy—and I am all alone with memories. But now you are here! It was a bit of magic. I came through the trees after Kiran had gone, and there you were, fast asleep under the tree. I didn't wake you then because I wanted to see you wake up.'

'As I used to watch you wake up…'

She was near me and I could look at her more closely. Her cheeks did not have the same freshness—they were a little pale—and she was thinner now, but her eyes were the same, smiling the same way. Her fingers, when she took my hand, were the same warm delicate fingers.

'Talk to me,' she said. 'Tell me about yourself.'

'You tell me,' I said.

'I am here,' she said. 'That is all there is to say about myself.'

'Then let us sit down and I'll talk.'

'Not here,' she took my hand and led me through the trees. 'Come with me.'

I heard the jingle of a tonga bell and a faint shout. I stopped and laughed.

'My tonga,' I said. 'It has come to take me back to the station.'

'But you are not going,' said Sushila, immediately downcast.

'I will tell him to come in the morning,' I said. 'I will spend the night in your Shamli.'

I walked to the front of the hotel where the tonga was waiting. I was glad no one else was in sight. The youth was smiling at me in his most appealing manner.

'I'm not going today,' I said. 'Will you come tomorrow morning?'

'I can come whenever you like, friend. But you will have to pay for every trip, because it is a long way from the station even if my tonga is empty. Usual fare, friend, one rupee.'

I didn't try to argue but resignedly gave him the rupee. He cracked his whip and pulled on the reins, and the carriage moved off.

'If you don't leave tomorrow,' the youth called out after me, 'you'll never leave Shamli!'

I walked back through the trees, but I couldn't find Sushila.

'Sushila, where are you?' I called, but I might have been speaking to the trees, for I had no reply. There was a small path going through the orchard, and on the path I saw a rose petal. I walked a little further and saw another petal. They were from Sushila's red rose. I walked on down the path until I had skirted the orchard, and then the path went along the fringe of the jungle, past a clump of bamboos, and here the grass was a lush green as though it had been constantly watered. I was still finding rose petals. I heard the chatter of seven sisters, and the call of a hoopoe. The path bent to meet a stream, there was a willow coming down to the water's edge, and Sushila was waiting there.

'Why didn't you wait?' I said.

'I wanted to see if you were as good at following me as you used to be.'

'Well, I am,' I said, sitting down beside her on the grassy bank of the stream. 'Even if I'm out of practice.'

'Yes, I remember the time you climbed up an apple tree to pick some fruit for me. You got up all right but then you couldn't come down again. I had to climb up myself and help you.'

'I don't remember that,' I said.

'Of course you do.'

'It must have been your other friend, Pramod.'

'I never climbed trees with Pramod.'

'Well, I don't remember.'

I looked at the little stream that ran past us. The water was no more than ankle-deep, cold and clear and sparking, like the mountain stream near my home. I took off my shoes, rolled up my trousers, and put my feet in the water. Sushila's feet joined mine.

At first I had wanted to ask about her marriage, whether she was happy or not, what she thought of her husband; but now I couldn't ask her these things. They seemed far away and of little importance. I could think of nothing she had in common with Mr Dayal. I felt that her charm and attractiveness and warmth could not have been appreciated, or even noticed, by that curiously distracted man. He was much older than her, of course, probably older than me. He was obviously not her choice but her parents', and so far they were childless. Had there been children, I don't think Sushila would have minded Mr Dayal as her husband. Children would have made up for the absence of passion—or was there passion in Satish Dayal?... I remembered having heard that Sushila had been married to a man she didn't like. I remembered having shrugged off the news, because it meant she would never come my way again, and I have never yearned after something that has been irredeemably lost. But she had come my way again. And was she still lost? That was what I wanted to know…

'What do you do with yourself all day?' I asked.

'Oh, I visit the school and help with the classes. It is the only interest I have in this place. The hotel is terrible. I try to keep away from it as much as I can.'

'And what about the guests?'

'Oh, don't let us talk about them. Let us talk about ourselves. Do you have to go tomorrow?'

'Yes, I suppose so. Will you always be in this place?'

'I suppose so.'

That made me silent. I took her hand, and my feet churned up the mud at the bottom of the stream. As the mud subsided, I saw Sushila's face reflected in the water, and looking up at her again, into her dark eyes, the old yearning returned and I wanted to care for her and protect her. I wanted to take her away from that place, from sorrowful Shamli. I wanted her to live again.

Of course, I had forgotten all about my poor finances, Sushila's family, and the shoes I wore, which were my last pair. The uplift I was experiencing in this meeting with Sushila, who had always, throughout her childhood and youth, bewitched me as no other had ever bewitched me, made me reckless and impulsive.

I lifted her hand to my lips and kissed her on the soft of her palm.

'Can I kiss you?' I said.

'You have just done so.'

'Can I kiss you?' I repeated.

'It is not necessary.'

I leaned over and kissed her slender neck. I knew she would like this, because that was where I had kissed her often before. I kissed her on the soft of the throat, where it tickled.

'It is not necessary,' she said, but she ran her fingers through my hair and let them rest there. I kissed her behind the ear then, and kept my mouth to her ear and whispered, 'Can I kiss you?'

She turned her face to me so that we looked deep into each other's eyes, and I kissed her again. And we put our arms around each other and lay together on the grass with the water running over our feet. We said nothing at all, simply lay there for what seemed like several years, or until the first drop of rain.

It was a big wet drop, and it splashed on Sushila's cheek just next to mine, and ran down to her lips so that I had to kiss her again. The next big drop splattered on the tip of my nose, and Sushila laughed and sat up. Little ringlets were forming on the stream where the raindrops hit the water, and above us there was a pattering on the banana leaves.

'We must go,' said Sushila.

We started homewards, but had not gone far before it was raining steadily, and Sushila's hair came loose and streamed down her body. The rain fell harder, and we had to hop over pools and avoid the soft mud. Sushila's sari was plastered to her body, accentuating her ripe, thrusting breasts, and I was excited to passion. I pulled her beneath a big tree, crushed her in my arms and kissed her rain-kissed mouth. And then I thought she was crying, but I wasn't sure, because it might have been the raindrops on her cheeks.

'Come away with me,' I said. 'Leave this place. Come away with me tomorrow morning. We will go somewhere where nobody will know us or come between us.'

She smiled at me and said, 'You are still a dreamer, aren't you?'

'Why can't you come?'

'I am married. It is as simple as that.'

'If it is that simple you can come.'

'I have to think of my parents, too. It would break my father's heart if I were to do what you are proposing. And you are proposing it without a thought for the consequences.'

'You are too practical,' I said.

'If women were not practical, most marriages would be failures.'

'So your marriage is a success?'

'Of course it is, as a marriage. I am not happy and I do not love him, but neither am I so unhappy that I should hate him. Sometimes, for our own sakes, we have to think of the happiness of others. What happiness would we have living in hiding from everyone we once knew and cared for. Don't be a fool. I am always here and you can come to see me, and nobody will be made unhappy by it. But take me away and we will only have regrets.'

'You don't love me,' I said foolishly.

'That sad word love,' she said, and became pensive and silent.

I could say no more. I was angry again and rebellious, and there was no one and nothing to rebel against. I could not understand someone who was afraid to break away from an unhappy existence lest that existence should become unhappier. I had always considered it an admirable thing to break away from security and respectability. Of course, it is easier for a man to do this. A man can look after himself, he can do without neighbours and the approval of the local society. A woman, I reasoned, would do anything for love provided it was not at the price of security; for a woman loves security as much as a man loves independence.

'I must go back now,' said Sushila. 'You follow a little later.'

'All you wanted to do was talk,' I complained.

She laughed at that and pulled me playfully by the hair. Then she ran out from under the tree, springing across the grass, and the wet mud flew up and flecked her legs. I watched her through the thin curtain of rain until she reached the veranda. She turned to wave to me, and then skipped into the hotel.

The rain had lessened, but I didn't know what to do with myself. The hotel was uninviting, and it was too late to leave Shamli. If the grass hadn't been wet I would have preferred to sleep under a tree rather than return to the hotel to sit at that alarming dining table.

I came out from under the trees and crossed the garden. But

instead of making for the veranda I went round to the back of the hotel. Smoke issuing from the barred window of a back room told me I had probably found the kitchen. Daya Ram was inside, squatting in front of a stove, stirring a pot of stew. The stew smelt appetizing. Daya Ram looked up and smiled at me.

'I thought you had gone,' he said.

'I'll go in the morning,' I said, pulling myself up on an empty table. Then I had one of my sudden ideas and said, 'Why don't you come with me? I can find you a good job in Mussoorie. How much do you get paid here?'

'Fifty rupees a month. But I haven't been paid for three months.'

'Could you get your pay before tomorrow morning?'

'No, I won't get anything until one of the guests pays a bill. Miss Deeds owes about fifty rupees on whisky alone. She will pay up, she says, when the school pays her salary. And the school can't pay her until they collect the children's fees. That is how bankrupt everyone is in Shamli.'

'I see,' I said, though I didn't see. 'But Mr Dayal can't hold back your pay just because his guests haven't paid their bills.'

'He can if he hasn't got any money.'

'I see,' I said. 'Anyway, I will give you my address. You can come when you are free.'

'I will take it from the register,' he said.

I edged over to the stove and leaning over, sniffed at the stew.

'I'll eat mine now,' I said. And without giving Daya Ram a chance to object, I lifted a plate off the shelf, took hold of the stirring spoon and helped myself from the pot.

'There's rice too,' said Daya Ram.'

I filled another plate with rice and then got busy with my fingers. After ten minutes I had finished. I sat back comfortably, in a ruminative mood. With my stomach full I could take a more tolerant view of life and people. I could understand Sushila's apprehensions, Lin's delicate lying and Miss Deeds's aggressiveness. Daya Ram went out to sound the dinner gong, and I trailed back to my room.

From the window of my room I saw Kiran running across the lawn and I called to her, but she didn't hear me. She ran down the path and out of the gate, her pigtails beating against the wind.

The clouds were breaking and coming together again, twisting and spiralling their way across a violet sky. The sun was going down behind the Shivaliks. The sky there was bloodshot. The tall slim trunks of the eucalyptus tree were tinged with an orange glow; the rain had stopped, and the wind was a soft, sullen puff, drifting sadly through the trees. There was a steady drip of water from the eaves of the roof on to the window sill. Then the sun went down behind the old, old hills, and I remembered my own hills, far beyond these.

The room was dark but I did not turn on the light. I stood near the window, listening to the garden. There was a frog warbling somewhere and there was a sudden flap of wings overhead. Tomorrow morning I would go, and perhaps I would come back to Shamli one day, and perhaps not. I could always come here looking for Major Roberts, and who knows, one day I might find him. What should he be like, this lost man? A romantic, a man with a dream, a man with brown skin and blue eyes, living in a hut on a snowy mountain top, chopping wood and catching fish and swimming in cold mountain streams; a rough, free man with a kind heart and a shaggy beard, a man who owed allegiance to no one, who gave a damn for money and politics, and cities and civilizations, who was his own master, who lived at one with nature knowing no fear. But that was not Major Roberts—that was the man I wanted to be. He was not a Frenchman or an Englishman, he was me, a dream of myself. If only I could find Major Roberts.

When Daya Ram knocked on the door and told me the others had finished dinner, I left my room and made for the lounge. It was quite lively in the lounge. Satish Dayal was at the bar, Lin at the piano, and Miss Deeds in the centre of the room executing a tango on her own. It was obvious she had been drinking heavily.

'All on credit,' complained Mr Dayal to me. 'I don't know when I'll be paid, but I don't dare refuse her anything for fear she starts breaking up the hotel.'

'She could do that, too,' I said. 'It would come down without much encouragement.'

Lin began to play a waltz (I think it was a waltz), and then

I found Miss Deeds in front of me, saying, 'Wouldn't you like to dance, old boy?'

'Thank you,' I said, somewhat alarmed. 'I hardly know how to.'

'Oh, come on, be a sport,' she said, pulling me away from the bar. I was glad Sushila wasn't present. She wouldn't have minded, but she'd have laughed as she always laughed when I made a fool of myself.

We went around the floor in what I suppose was waltz time, though all I did was mark time to Miss Deeds's motions. We were not very steady—this because I was trying to keep her at arm's length, while she was determined to have me crushed to her bosom. At length Lin finished the waltz. Giving him a grateful look, I pulled myself free. Miss Deeds went over to the piano, leaned right across it and said, 'Play something lively, dear Mr Lin, play some hot stuff.'

To my surprise, Mr Lin without so much as an expression of distaste or amusement, began to execute what I suppose was the frug or the jitterbug. I was glad she hadn't asked me to dance that one with her.

It all appeared very incongruous to me: Miss Deeds letting herself go in crazy abandonment, Lin playing the piano with great seriousness, and Mr Dayal watching from the bar with an anxious frown. I wondered what Sushila would have thought of them now.

Eventually Miss Deeds collapsed on the couch breathing heavily.

'Give me a drink,' she cried.

With the noblest of intentions I took her a glass of water. Miss Deeds took a sip and made a face. 'What's this stuff?' she asked. 'It is different.'

'Water,' I said.

'No,' she said, 'now don't joke, tell me what it is.'

'It's water, I assure you,' I said.

When she saw that I was serious, her face coloured up and I thought she would throw the water at me. But she was too tired to do this and contented herself with throwing the glass over her shoulder. Mr Dayal made a dive for the flying glass, but he wasn't in time to rescue it and it hit the wall and fell to pieces on the floor.

Mr Dayal wrung his hands. 'You'd better take her to her room,' he said, as though I were personally responsible for her behaviour just because I'd danced with her.

'I can't carry her alone,' I said, making an unsuccessful attempt at helping Miss Deeds up from the couch.

Mr Dayal called for Daya Ram, and the big amiable youth came lumbering into the lounge. We took an arm each and helped Miss Deeds, feet dragging, across the room. We got her to her room and on to her bed. When we were about to withdraw she said, 'Don't go, my dear, stay with me a little while.'

Daya Ram had discreetly slipped outside. With my hand on the doorknob I said, 'Which of us?'

'Oh, are there two of you?' said Miss Deeds, without a trace of disappointment.

'Yes, Daya Ram helped me carry you here.'

'Oh, and who are you?'

'I'm the writer. You danced with me, remember?'

'Of course. You dance divinely, Mr Writer. Do stay with me. Daya Ram can stay too if he likes.'

I hesitated, my hand on the doorknob. She hadn't opened her eyes all the time I'd been in the room, her arms hung loose, and one bare leg hung over the side of the bed. She was fascinating somehow, and desirable, but I was afraid of her. I went out of the room and quietly closed the door.

As I lay awake in bed I heard the jackal's 'pheau', the cry of fear which it communicates to all the jungle when there is danger about, a leopard or a tiger. It was a weird howl, and between each note there was a kind of low gurgling. I switched off the light and peered through the closed window. I saw the jackal at the edge of the lawn. It sat almost vertically on its haunches, holding its head straight up to the sky, making the neighbourhood vibrate with the eerie violence of its cries. Then suddenly it started up and ran off into the trees.

Before getting back into bed I made sure the window was shut. The bullfrog was singing again, 'ing-ong, ing-ong', in some foreign language. I wondered if Sushila was awake too, thinking about me. It must have been almost eleven o'clock. I thought of Miss Deeds with her leg hanging over the edge of the bed. I tossed restlessly and then sat up. I hadn't slept for two nights but I was not sleepy. I got out of bed without turning on the light and slowly opening my door, crept down the passageway. I stopped at the door of Miss Deeds's room. I stood there listening, but I heard only the ticking of the big clock that might have been in the room or somewhere in the passage. I put my hand on the doorknob, but the door was bolted. That settled the matter.

I would definitely leave Shamli the next morning. Another day in the company of these people and I would be behaving like them. Perhaps I was already doing so! I remembered the tonga driver's words: 'Don't stay too long in Shamli or you will never leave!'

When the rain came, it was not with a preliminary patter or shower, but all at once, sweeping across the forest like a massive wall, and I could hear it in the trees long before it reached the house. Then it came crashing down on the corrugated roof, and the hailstones hit the window panes with a hard metallic sound so that I thought the glass would break. The sound of thunder was like the booming of big guns and the lightning kept playing over the garden. At every flash of lightning I sighted the swing under the tree, rocking and leaping in the air as though some invisible, agitated being was sitting on it. I wondered about Kiran. Was she sleeping through all this, blissfully unconcerned, or was she lying awake in bed, starting at every clash of thunder as I was? Or was she up and about, exulting in the storm? I half expected to see her come running through the trees, through the rain, to stand on the swing with her hair blowing wild in the wind, laughing at the thunder and the angry skies. Perhaps I did see her, perhaps she was there. I wouldn't have been surprised if she were some forest nymph living in the hole of a tree, coming out sometimes to play in the garden.

A crash, nearer and louder than any thunder so far, made me sit up in bed with a start. Perhaps lightning had struck the house. I turned on the switch but the light didn't come on. A tree must have fallen across the line.

I heard voices in the passage—the voices of several people. I stepped outside to find out what had happened, and started at the appearance of a ghostly apparition right in front of me. It was Mr Dayal standing on the threshold in an oversized pyjama suit, a candle in his hand.

'I came to wake you,' he said. 'This storm...'

He had the irritating habit of stating the obvious.

'Yes, the storm,' I said. 'Why is everybody up?'

'The back wall has collapsed and part of the roof has fallen in. We'd better spend the night in the lounge—it is the safest room. This is a very old building,' he added apologetically.

'All right,' I said. 'I am coming.'

The lounge was lit by two candles. One stood over the piano, the other on a small table near the couch. Miss Deeds was on the couch, Lin was at the piano stool, looking as though he would start playing Stravinsky any moment, and Dayal was fussing about the room. Sushila was standing at a window, looking out at the stormy night. I went to the window and touched her but she didn't look around or say anything. The lightning flashed and her dark eyes were pools of smouldering fire.

'What time will you be leaving?' she asked.

'The tonga will come for me at seven.'

'If I come,' she said, 'if I come with you, I will be at the station before the train leaves.'

'How will you get there?' I asked, and hope and excitement rushed over me again.

'I will get there,' she said. 'I will get there before you. But if I am not there, then do not wait, do not come back for me. Go on your way. It will mean I do not want to come. Or I will be there.'

'But are you sure?'

'Don't stand near me now. Don't speak to me unless you have to.' She squeezed my fingers, then drew her hand away. I sauntered over to the next window, then back into the centre of the room.

A gust of wind blew through a cracked windowpane and put out the candle near the couch.

'Damn the wind,' said Miss Deeds.

The window in my room had burst open during the night and there were leaves and branches strewn about the floor. I sat down on the damp bed and smelt eucalyptus. The earth was red, as though the storm had bled it all night.

After a little while I went into the veranda with my suitcase to wait for the tonga. It was then that I saw Kiran under the trees. Kiran's long black pigtails were tied up in a red ribbon, and she looked fresh and clean like the rain and the red earth. She stood looking seriously at me.

'Did you like the storm?' she asked.

'Some of the time,' I said. 'I'm going soon. Can I do anything for you?'

'Where are you going?'

'I'm going to the end of the world. I'm looking for Major Roberts, have you seen him anywhere?'

'There is no Major Roberts,' she said perceptively. 'Can I come with you to the end of the world?'

'What about your parents?'

'Oh, we won't take them.'

'They might be annoyed if you go off on your own.'

'I can stay on my own. I can go anywhere.'

'Well, one day I'll come back here and I'll take you everywhere and no one will stop us. Now is there anything else I can do for you?'

'I want some flowers, but I can't reach them,' she pointed to a hibiscus tree that grew against the wall. It meant climbing

the wall to reach the flowers. Some of the red flowers had fallen during the night and were floating in a pool of water.

'All right,' I said and pulled myself up on the wall. I smiled down into Kiran's serious, upturned face. 'I'll throw them to you and you can catch them.'

I bent a branch, but the wood was young and green and I had to twist it several times before it snapped.

'I hope nobody minds,' I said, as I dropped the flowering branch to Kiran.

'It's nobody's tree,' she said.

'Sure?'

She nodded vigorously. 'Sure, don't worry.'

I was working for her and she felt immensely capable of

protecting me. Talking and being with Kiran, I felt a nostalgic longing for childhood—emotions that had been beautiful because they were never completely understood.

'Who is your best friend?' I said.

'Daya Ram,' she replied. 'I told you so before.'

She was certainly faithful to her friends.

'And who is the second best?'

She put her finger in her mouth to consider the question, and her head dropped sideways.

'I'll make you the second best,' she said.

I dropped the flowers over her head. 'That is so kind of you. I'm proud to be your second best.'

I heard the tonga bell, and from my perch on the wall saw the carriage coming down the driveway. 'That's for me,' I said. 'I must go now.'

I jumped down the wall. And the sole of my shoe came off at last.

'I knew that would happen,' I said.

'Who cares for shoes,' said Kiran.

'Who cares,' I said.

I walked back to the veranda and Kiran walked beside me, and stood in front of the hotel while I put my suitcase in the tonga.

'You nearly stayed one day too late,' said the tonga driver. 'Half the hotel has come down and tonight the other half will come down.'

I climbed into the back seat. Kiran stood on the path, gazing intently at me.

'I'll see you again,' I said.

'I'll see you in Iceland or Japan,' she said. 'I'm going everywhere.'

'Maybe,' I said, 'maybe you will.'

We smiled, knowing and understanding each other's importance. In her bright eyes I saw something old and wise. The tonga driver cracked his whip, the wheels creaked, the carriage rattled down the path. We kept waving to each other. In Kiran's hand was a spring of hibiscus. As she waved, the blossoms fell apart and danced a little in the breeze.

Shamli station looked the same as it had the day before. The same train stood at the same platform and the same dogs prowled beside the fence. I waited on the platform till the bell clanged for the train to leave, but Sushila did not come.

Somehow, I was not disappointed. I had never really expected her to come. Unattainable, Sushila would always be more bewitching and beautiful than if she were mine.

Shamli would always be there. And I could always come back, looking for Major Roberts.

BUS STOP, PIPALNAGAR

I

My balcony was my window on the world.

The room itself had only one window, a square hole in the wall crossed by two iron bars. The view from it was rather restricted. If I craned my neck sideways, and put my nose to the bars, I could see the end of the building. Below was a narrow courtyard where children played. Across the courtyard, on a level with my room, were three separate windows belonging to three separate rooms, each window barred in the same way, with iron bars. During the day it was difficult to see into these rooms. The harsh, cruel sunlight filled the courtyard, making the windows patches of darkness.

My room was very small. I had paced about in it so often that I knew its exact measurements. My foot, from heel to toe, was eleven inches long. That made my room just over fifteen feet in length; for, when I measured the last foot, my toes turned up against the wall. It wasn't more than eight feet broad, which meant that two people was the most it could comfortably accommodate. I was the only tenant but at times I had put up at least three friends—two on the floor, two on the bed. The plaster had been peeling off the walls and in addition the greasy stains and patches were difficult to hide, though I covered the worst ones with pictures cut out from magazines—Waheeda Rehman, the Indian actress, successfully blotted out one big patch and a recent Mr Universe displayed his muscles from the opposite wall. The biggest stain was all but concealed by a calendar that showed Ganesh, the elephant-headed god, whose blessings were vital to all good beginnings.

My belongings were few. A shelf on the wall supported an untidy pile of paperbacks, and a small table in one corner of the room supported the solid weight of my rejected manuscripts and an ancient typewriter which I had obtained on hire.

I was eighteen years old and a writer.

Such a combination would be disastrous enough anywhere, but in India it was doubly so; for there were not many papers to write for and payments were small. In addition, I was very inexperienced and though what I wrote came from the heart, only a fraction touched the hearts of editors. Nevertheless, I persevered and was able to earn about a hundred rupees a month, barely enough to keep body, soul and typewriter together. There wasn't much else I could do. Without that passport to a job—a university degree—I had no alternative but to accept the classification of 'self-employed'—which was impressive as it included doctors, lawyers, property dealers, and grain merchants, most of whom earned well over a thousand rupees a month.

'Haven't you realized that India is bursting with young people trying to pass exams?' asked a journalist friend. 'It's a desperate matter, this race for academic qualifications. Everyone wants to pass his exam the easy way, without reading too many books or attending more than half a dozen lectures. That's where a smart fellow like you comes in! Why would students wade through five volumes of political history when they can buy a few model-answer papers at any bookstall? They are helpful, these guess-papers. You can write them quickly and flood the market. They'll sell like hot cakes!'

'Who eats hot cakes here?'

'Well, then, hot chapattis.'

'I'll think about it,' I said; but the idea repelled me. If I was going to misguide students, I would rather do it by writing second-rate detective stories than by providing them with readymade answer papers. Besides, I thought it would bore me.

II

The string of the cot needed tightening. The dip in the middle of the bed was so bad that I woke up in the morning with a stiff back. But I was hopeless at tightening bed-strings and would have to wait until one of the boys from the tea shop paid me a visit. I was too tall for the cot, anyway, and if my feet didn't stick out at one end, my head lolled over the other.

Under the cot was my tin trunk. Apart from my clothes, it contained notebooks, diaries, photographs, scrapbooks, and other odds and ends that form a part of a writer's existence.

I did not live entirely alone. During cold or rainy weather, the boys from the tea shop, who normally slept on the pavement, crowded into the room. Apart from them, there were lizards on the walls and ceilings—friends these—and a large rat—definitely an enemy—who got in and out of the window and who sometimes carried away manuscripts and clothing.

June nights were the most uncomfortable. Mosquitoes emerged from all the ditches, gullies and ponds, to swarm over Pipalnagar. Bugs, finding it uncomfortable inside the woodwork of the cot, scrambled out at night and found their way under the sheet. The lizards wandered listlessly over the walls, impatient for the monsoon rains, when they would be able to feast off thousands of insects.

Everyone in Pipalnagar was waiting for the cool, quenching relief of the monsoon.

III

I woke every morning at five as soon as the first bus moved out of the shed, situated only twenty or thirty yards down the road. I dressed, went down to the tea shop for a glass of hot tea and some buttered toast, and then visited Deep Chand the barber, in his shop.

At eighteen, I shaved about three times a week. Sometimes I shaved myself. But often, when I felt lazy, Deep Chand shaved me, at the special concessional rate of two annas.

'Give my head a good massage, Deep Chand,' I said. 'My brain is not functioning these days. In my latest story there are three murders, but it is boring just the same.'

'You must write a good book,' said Deep Chand beginning the ritual of the head massage, his fingers squeezing my temples and tugging at my hair-roots. 'Then you can make some money and clear out of Pipalnagar. Delhi is the place to go! Why, I know a man who arrived in Delhi in 1947 with nothing but the clothes he wore and a few rupees. He began by selling thirsty travellers glasses of cold water at the railway station, then he opened a small tea shop; now he has two big restaurants and lives in a house as large as the prime minister's!'

Nobody intended to live in Pipalnagar forever. Delhi was the city most aspired to but as it was 200 miles away, few could afford to travel there.

Deep Chand would have shifted his trade to another town if he had had the capital. In Pipalnagar his main customers were small shopkeepers, factory workers and labourers from the railway station. 'Here I can charge only six annas for a haircut,' he lamented. 'In Delhi I could charge a rupee.'

IV

I was walking in the wheat fields beyond the railway tracks when I noticed a boy lying across the footpath, his head and shoulders hidden by wheat plants. I walked faster, and when I came near I saw that the boy's legs were twitching. He seemed to be having some kind of fit. The boy's face was white, his legs kept moving and his hands fluttered restlessly among the wheat stalks.

'What's the matter?' I said, kneeling down beside him but he was still unconscious.

I ran down the path to a Persian well, and dipping the end of my shirt in a shallow trough of water, soaked it well before returning to the boy. As I sponged his face the twitching ceased, and though he still breathed heavily, his face was calm and his hands still. He opened his eyes and stared at me, but he didn't really see me.

'You have bitten your tongue,' I said wiping a little blood from the corner of his mouth. 'Don't worry. I'll stay here with you until you are all right.'

The boy raised himself and, resting his chin on his knees he passed his arms around his drawn-up legs.

'I'm all right now,' he said.

'What happened?' I asked sitting, down beside him.

'Oh, it is nothing, it often happens. I don't know why. I cannot control it.'

'Have you been to a doctor?'

'Yes, when the fits first started, I went to the hospital. They gave me some pills that I had to take every day. But the pills made me so tired and sleepy that I couldn't work properly. So I stopped taking them. Now this happens once or twice a week. What does it matter? I'm all right when it's over and I do not feel anything when it happens.'

He got to his feet, dusting his clothes and smiling at me. He was a slim boy, long-limbed and bony. There was a little fluff on his cheeks and the promise of a moustache. He told me his name was Suraj, that he went to a night school in the city, and that he hoped to finish his high school exams in a few months' time. He was studying hard, he said, and if he passed he hoped to get a scholarship to a good college. If he failed, there was only the prospect of continuing in Pipalnagar.

I noticed a small tray of merchandise lying on the ground. It contained combs and buttons and little bottles of perfume. The tray was made to hang at Suraj's waist, supported by straps that went around his shoulders. All day he walked about Pipalnagar, sometimes covering ten or fifteen miles, selling odds and ends to people at their houses. He averaged about two rupees a day, which was enough for his food and other necessities; he managed to save about ten rupees a month for his school fees. He ate irregularly at little tea shops, at the stall near the bus stop, under the shady jamun and mango trees. When the jamun fruit was ripe, he would sit on a tree, sucking the sour fruit until his lips were stained purple. There was a small, nagging fear that he might get a fit while sitting on the tree and fall off, but the temptation to eat jamun was greater than his fear.

All this he told me while we walked through the fields towards the bazaar.

'Where do you live?' I asked. 'I'll walk home with you.'

'I don't live anywhere,' said Suraj. 'My home is not in Pipalnagar. Sometimes I sleep at the temple or at the railway station. In the summer months I sleep on the grass of the municipal park.'

'Well, wherever it is you stay, let me come with you.'

We walked together into the town, and parted near the bus stop. I returned to my room, and tried to do some writing while Suraj went into the bazaar to try selling his wares. We had agreed to meet each other again. I realized that Suraj was an epileptic, but there was nothing unusual about him being an orphan and a refugee. I liked his positive attitude to life. Most people in Pipalnagar were resigned to their circumstances, but he was ambitious. I also liked his gentleness, his quiet voice, and the smile that flickered across his face regardless of whether he was sad or happy.

V

The temperature had touched forty-three degrees Celsius, and the small streets of Pipalnagar were empty. To walk barefoot on the scorching pavements was possible only for labourers, whose feet had developed several hard layers of protective skin; and now even these hardy men lay stretched out in the shade provided by trees and buildings.

I hadn't written anything in two weeks, and though one or two small payments were due from a Delhi newspaper, I could think of no substantial amount that was likely to come my way in the near future. I decided that I would dash off a couple of articles that same night, and post them the following morning.

Having made this comforting decision, I lay down on the floor in preference to the cot. I liked the touch of things, the touch of a cool floor on a hot day; the touch of earth—soft, grassy grass was good, especially dew-drenched grass. Wet earth was soft, sensuous, as was splashing through puddles and streams.

I slept, and dreamt of a cool clear stream in a forest glade, where I bathed in gay abandon. A little further downstream was another bather. I hailed him, expecting to see Suraj but when the bather turned I found that it was my landlord's pot-bellied rent collector, holding an accounts ledger in his hands. This woke me up, and for the remainder of the day I worked feverishly at my articles.

Next morning, when I opened the door, I found Suraj asleep at the top of the steps. His tray lay at the bottom of the steps. He woke up as soon as I touched his shoulder.

'Have you been sleeping here all night?' I asked. 'Why didn't you come in?'

'It was very late,' said Suraj. 'I didn't want to disturb you.'

'Someone could have stolen your things while you were asleep.'

'Oh, I sleep quite lightly. Besides I have nothing of great value. But I came here to ask you a favour.'

'You need money?'

He laughed. 'Do all your friends mean money when they ask for favours? No, I want you to take your meal with me tonight.'

'But where? You have no place of your own and it would be too expensive in a restaurant.'

'In your room,' said Suraj. 'I shall bring the meat and vegetables and cook them here. Do you have a cooker?'

'I think so,' I said, scratching my head in some perplexity. 'I will have to look for it.'

Suraj brought a chicken for dinner—a luxury, one to be indulged in only two or three times a year. He had bought the bird for seven rupees, which was cheap. We spiced it and roasted it on a spit.

'I wish we could do this more often,' I said, as I dug my teeth into the soft flesh of a second chicken leg.

'We could do it at least once a month if we worked hard,' said Suraj.

'You know how to work. You work from morning to evening and then you work again.'

'But you are a writer. That is different. You have to wait for the right moment.'

I laughed. 'Moods and moments are for geniuses. No, it's really a matter of working hard, and I'm just plain lazy, to tell you the truth.'

'Perhaps you are writing the wrong things.'

'Perhaps, I wish I could do something else. Even if I repaired bicycle tyres, I'd make more money!'

'Then why don't you repair bicycle tyres?'

'Oh, I would rather be a bad writer than a good repairer of cycle tyres.' I brightened up, 'I could go into business, though. Do you know I once owned a vegetable stall?'

'Wonderful! When was that?'

'A couple of months ago. But it failed after two days.'

'Then you are not good at business. Let us think of something else.'

'I can tell fortunes with cards.'

'There are already too many fortune tellers in Pipalnagar.'

'Then we won't talk of fortunes. And you must sleep here tonight. It is better than sleeping on the roadside.'

VI

At noon when the shadows shifted and crossed the road, a band of children rushed down the empty street, shouting and waving their satchels. They had been at their desks from early morning, and now, despite the hot sun, they would have their fling while their elders slept on string charpoys beneath leafy neem trees.

On the soft sand near the riverbed, boys wrestled or played leapfrog. At alley corners, where tall buildings shaded narrow passages, the favourite game was gulli-danda. The gulli—a small piece of wood, about four inches long sharpened to a point at each end—is struck with the danda—a short, stout stick. A player is allowed three hits, and his score is the distance, in danda lengths, of his hits of the gulli. Boys who were experts at the game sent the gulli flying far down the road—sometimes into a shop or through a windowpane, which resulted in confusion, loud invective, and a dash for cover.

A game for both children and young men was kabaddi. This is a game that calls for good breath control and much agility. It is also known in different parts of India as hootoo-too, kho-kho and atya patya. Ramu, Deep Chand's younger brother, excelled at this game. He was the Pipalnagar kabaddi champion.

The game is played by two teams, consisting of eight or nine members each, who face each other across a dividing line. Each side in turn sends out one of its players into the opponent's area. This person has to keep on saying 'kabaddi, kabaddi' very fast and without taking a second breath. If he returns to his side after touching an opponent, that opponent is 'dead' and out of the game. If however, he is caught and cannot struggle back to his side while still holding his breath, he is 'dead'.

Ramu, who was also a good wrestler, knew all the kabaddi holds, and was particularly good at capturing opponents. He had vitality and confidence, rare things in Pipalnagar. He wanted to go into the army after finishing school, a happy choice I thought.

VII

Suraj did not know if his parents were dead or alive. He had literally lost them when he was six. His father had been a farmer, a dark unfathomable man who spoke little, thought perhaps even less and was vaguely aware he had a son—a weak boy given to introspection and dawdling at the riverbank when he should have been helping in the fields.

Suraj's mother had been a subdued, silent woman, frail and consumptive. Her husband seemed to expect that she would not live long, but Suraj did not know if she was living or dead. He had lost his parents at Amritsar railway station in the days of Partition, when trains coming across the border from Pakistan disgorged themselves of thousands of refugees or pulled into the station half-empty, drenched with blood and littered with corpses.

Suraj and his parents had been lucky to escape one of these massacres. Had they travelled on an earlier train (which they had tried desperately to catch), they might have been killed. Suraj was clinging to his mother's sari while she tried to keep up with her husband who was elbowing his way through the frightened bewildered throng of refugees. Suraj collided with a burly Sikh and lost his grip on the sari. The Sikh had a long curved sword at his waist, and Suraj stared up at him in awe and fascination—at the man's long hair, which had fallen loose, at his wild black beard, and at the bloodstains on his white shirt. The Sikh pushed him aside and when Suraj looked around for his mother, she was not to be seen. She was hidden from him by a mass of restless bodies, all pushing in different directions. He could hear her calling his name and he tried to force his way through the crowd in the direction of her voice, but he was carried on the other way.

At night, when the platform emptied, he was still searching for his mother. Eventually, the police came and took him away. They looked for his parents but without success, and finally they sent him to a home for orphans. Many children lost their parents at about the same time.

Suraj stayed at the orphanage for two years and when he was eight, and felt himself a man, he ran away. He worked for some time as a helper in a tea shop; but when he started having epileptic fits the shopkeepers asked him to leave, and the boy found himself on the streets, begging for a living. He begged for a year, moving from one town to the next and ended up finally in Pipalnagar. By then he was twelve and really too old to beg, but he had saved some money, and with it he bought a small stock of combs, buttons, cheap perfumes and bangles, and, converting himself into a mobile shop, went from door to door selling his wares.

Pipalnagar is a small town and there was no house which Suraj hadn't visited. Everyone knew him; some had offered him food and drink; and the children liked him because he often played on a small flute when he went on his rounds.

VIII

Suraj came to see me quite often and, when he stayed late, he slept in my room, curling up on the floor and sleeping fitfully. He would always leave early in the morning, before I could get him anything to eat.

'Should I go to Delhi, Suraj?' I asked him one evening.

'Why not? In Delhi, there are many ways of making money.'

'And spending it too. Why don't you come with me?'

'After my exams, perhaps. Not now.'

'Well, I can wait. I don't want to live alone in a big city.'

'In the meantime, write your book.'

'All right, I will try.'

We decided we could try to save a little money from Suraj's earnings and my own occasional payments from newspapers and magazines. Even if we were to give Delhi only a few days' trial, we would need money to live on. We managed to put away twenty rupees one week, but withdrew it the next when a friend, Pitamber, asked for a loan to repair his cycle rickshaw. He returned the money in three instalments but we could not save any of it. Pitamber and Deep Chand also had plans of going to Delhi. Pitamber wanted to own his own cycle rickshaw; Deep Chand dreamt of a swanky barber shop in the capital.

One day Suraj and I hired bicycles and rode out of Pipalnagar. It was a hot, sunny morning and we were perspiring after we had gone two miles, but a fresh wind sprang up suddenly, and we could smell the rain in the air though there were no clouds to be seen.

'Let us go where there are no people at all,' said Suraj. 'I am a little tired of people. I see too many of them all day.'

We got down from our cycles and, pushing them off the road, took a path through a paddy field and then one through a field of young maize, and in the distance we saw a tree, a crooked tree, growing beside a well. I do not even today know the name of that tree. I had never seen its kind before. It had a crooked trunk, crooked branches and it was clothed in thick, broad, crooked leaves, like the leaves on which food is served in bazaars.

In the trunk of the tree was a large hole and when I sat my cycle down with a crash, two green parrots flew out of the hole, and went dipping and swerving across the fields.

There was grass around the well, cropped short by grazing cattle, so we sat in the shade of the crooked tree and Suraj untied the red cloth in which we brought food. We ate our bread and vegetable curry, and meanwhile the parrots returned to the tree.

'Let us come here every week,' said Suraj, stretching himself out on the grass. It was a drowsy day, the air was humid and he soon fell asleep. I was aware of different sensations. I heard a cricket singing in the tree; the cooing of pigeons which lived in the walls of the old well; the soft breathing of Suraj; a rustling in the leaves of the tree; the distant drone of the bees. I smelt the grass and the old bricks around the well, and the promise of rain.

When I opened my eyes, I saw dark clouds on the horizon. Suraj was still sleeping with his arms thrown across his face to keep the glare out of his eyes. As I was thirsty, I went to the well and, putting my shoulders to it, turned the wheel very slowly, walking around the well four times, while cool clean water gushed out over the stones and along the channel to the fields. I drank from one of the trays, and the water tasted sweet; the deeper the wells, the sweeter the water. Suraj was sitting up now, looking at the sky.

'It's going to rain,' he said.

We pushed our cycles back to the main road and began riding homewards. We were a mile out of Pipalnagar when it began to rain. A lashing wind swept the rain across our faces, but we exulted in it and sang at the top of our voices until we reached the bus stop. Leaving the cycles at the hire shop, we ran up the rickety, swaying steps to my room.

In the evening, as the bazaar was lighting up, the rain stopped. We went to sleep quite early, but at midnight I was woken by the moon shining full in my face—a full moon, shedding its light all over Pipalnagar, peeping and prying into every home, washing the empty streets, silvering the corrugated tin roofs.

IX

The lizards hung listlessly on the walls and ceilings, waiting for the monsoon rains, which bring out all the insects from their cracks and crannies.

One day, clouds loomed up on the horizon, growing rapidly into enormous towers. A faint breeze sprang up, bringing with it the first of the monsoon raindrops. This was the moment everyone was waiting for. People ran out of their houses to take in the fresh breeze and the scent of those first few raindrops on the parched, dusty earth. Underground, in their cracks, the insects were moving. Termites and white ants, which had been sleeping through the hot season, emerged from their lairs.

And then, on the second or third night of the monsoon, came the great yearly flight of insects into the cool brief freedom of the night. Out of every crack, from under the roots of trees, huge winged ants emerged, at first fluttering about heavily, on the first and last flight of their lives. At night there was only one direction in which they could fly—towards the light; towards the electric bulbs and smoky kerosene lamps throughout Pipalnagar. The street lamp opposite the bus stop, beneath my room, attracted a massive quivering swarm of clumsy termites, which gave the impression of one thick, slowly revolving body.

This was the hour of the lizards. Now they had their reward for those days of patient waiting. Plying their sticky pink tongues, they devoured the insects as fast as they came. For hours, they crammed their stomachs, knowing that such a feast would not be theirs again for another year. How wasteful nature is, I thought. Through the whole hot season the insect world prepares for the flight out of the darkness into light and not one of them survives its freedom.

Suraj and I walked barefooted over the cool, wet pavements, across the railway lines and the riverbed, until we were not far from the crooked tree. Dotting the landscape were old abandoned brick kilns. When it rained heavily, the hollows made by the kilns filled up with water. Suraj and I found a small tank where we could bathe and swim. On a mound in the middle of the tank stood a ruined hut, formerly inhabited by a watchman at the kiln. We swam and then wrestled on the young green grass. Though I was heavier than Suraj and my chest as sound as a new drum, he had a lot of power in his long, wiry arms and legs, and he pinioned me about the waist with his bony knees.

And then suddenly, as I strained to press his back to the ground, I felt his body go tense. He stiffened, his thigh jerked against me and his legs began to twitch. I knew that a fit was coming on, but I was unable to get out of his grip. He held me more tightly as the fit took possession of him.

When I noticed his mouth working, I thrust the palm of my hand in, sideways to prevent him from biting his tongue. But so violent was the convulsion that his teeth bit into my flesh. I shouted with pain and tried to pull my hand away, but he was unconscious and his jaw was set. I closed my eyes and counted slowly up to seven and then I felt his muscles relax and I was able to take my hand away. It was bleeding a little but I bound it in a handkerchief before Suraj fully regained consciousness.

He didn't say much as we walked back to town. He looked depressed and weak, but I knew it wouldn't take long for him to recover his usual good spirits. He did not notice that I kept my hand out of sight and only after he had returned from classes that night did he notice the bandage and asked what happened.

X

'Do you want to make some money?' asked Pitamber, bursting into the room like a festive cracker.

'I do,' I said.

'What do we have to do for it?' asked Suraj, striking a cautious note.

'Oh nothing, carry a banner and walk in front of a procession.'

'Why?'

'Don't ask me. Some political stunt.'

'Which party?'

'I don't know. Who cares? All I know is that they are paying two rupees a day to anyone who'll carry a flag or banner.'

'We don't need two rupees that badly,' I said. 'And you can make more than that in a day with your rickshaw.'

'True, but they're paying me *five*. They're fixing a loudspeaker to my rickshaw, and one of the party's men will sit in it and make speeches as we go along. Come on, it will be fun.'

'No banners for us,' I said. 'But we may come along and watch.'

And we did watch, when, later that morning, the procession passed along our street. It was a ragged procession of about a hundred people, shouting slogans. Some of them were children, and some of them were men who did not know what it was all about, but all joined in the slogan-shouting.

We didn't know much about it, either. Because, though the man in Pitamber's rickshaw was loud and eloquent, his loudspeaker was defective, with the result that his words were punctuated with squeaks and an eerie whining sound. Pitamber looked up and saw us standing on the balcony and gave us a wave and a wide grin. We decided to follow the procession at a discreet distance. It was a protest march against something or other; we never did manage to find out the details. The destination was the municipal office, and by the time we got there the crowd had increased to two or three hundred people. Some rowdies had now joined in, and things began to get out of hand. The man in the rickshaw continued his speech; another man standing on a wall was making a speech; and someone from the municipal office was confronting the crowd and making a speech of his own.

A stone was thrown, then another. From a sprinkling of stones, it soon became a shower of stones; and then some police constables, who had been standing by watching the fun, were ordered into action. They ran at the crowd where it was thinnest, brandishing stout sticks.

We were caught in the stampede that followed. A stone—flung no doubt at a policeman—was badly aimed and struck me on the shoulder. Suraj pulled me down a side street. Looking back, we saw Pitamber's cycle rickshaw lying on its side in the middle of the road, but there was no sign of Pitamber.

Later, he turned up in my room, with a cut over his left eyebrow which was bleeding freely. Suraj washed the cut, and I poured iodine over it—Pitamber did not flinch—and covered it with sticking plaster. The cut was quite deep and should have had stitches, but Pitamber was superstitious about hospitals, saying he knew very few people to come out of them alive. He was of course thinking about the Pipalnagar hospital.

So he acquired a scar on his forehead. It went rather well with his demonic good looks.

XI

'Thank god for the monsoon,' said Suraj. 'We won't have any more demonstrations on the roads until the weather improves!'

And, until the rain stopped, Pipalnagar was fresh and clean and alive. The children ran naked out of their houses and romped through the streets. The gutters overflowed, and the road became a mountain stream, coursing merrily towards the bus stop.

At the bus stop there was confusion. Newly arrived passengers, surrounded on all sides by a sea of mud and rainwater, were met by scores of tongas and cycle rickshaws, each jostling the other trying to cater to the passengers. As a result, only half found conveyances, while the other half found themselves knee-deep in Pipalnagar mud.

Pipalnagar mud has a quality all its own—and it is not easily removed or forgotten. Only buffaloes love it because it is soft and squelchy. Two parts of it is thick sticky clay which seems to come alive at the slightest touch, clinging tenaciously to human flesh. Feet sink into it and have to be wrenched out. Fingers become webbed. Get it into your hair, and there is nothing you can do except go to Deep Chand and have your head shaved.

London has its fog, Paris its sewers, Pipalnagar its mud. Pitamber, of course, succeeded in getting as his passenger the most attractive girl to step off the bus, and showed her his skill and daring by taking her to her destination by the longest and roughest road.

The rain swirled over the trees and roofs of the town, and the parched earth soaked it up, giving out a fresh smell that came only once a year, the fragrance of quenched earth, that loveliest of all smells.

In my room I was battling against the elements, for the door would not close, and the rain swept into the room and soaked my cot. When finally I succeeded in closing the door, I discovered that the roof was leaking and the water was trickling down the walls, running through the dusty design I had made with my feet. I placed tins and mugs in strategic positions and, satisfied that everything was now under control, sat on the cot to watch the rooftops through my windows.

There was a loud banging on the door. It flew open, and there was Suraj, standing on the threshold, drenched. Coming in, he began to dry himself while I made desperate efforts to close the door again.

'Let's make some tea,' he said.

Glasses of hot, sweet milky tea on a rainy day…it was enough to make me feel fresh and full of optimism. We sat on the cot, enjoying the brew.

'One day, I'll write a book,' I said. 'Not just a thriller, but a real book, about real people. Perhaps about you and me and Pipalnagar. And then we'll be famous and our troubles will be over and new troubles will begin. I don't mind problems as long as they are new. While you're studying, I'll write my book. I'll start tonight. It is an auspicious time, the first night of the monsoon.

A tree must have fallen across the wires somewhere, because the lights would not come on. So I lit a small oil lamp, and while it spluttered in the steamy darkness, Suraj opened his book and, with one hand on the book, the other playing with his toe—this helped him to concentrate!—he began to study. I took the inkpot down from the shelf, and finding it empty, added a little rainwater to it from one of the mugs. I sat down beside Suraj and began to write, but the pen was no good and made blotches all over the paper. And, although I was full of writing just then, I didn't really know what I wanted to say.

So I went out and began pacing up and down the road. There I found Pitamber, a little drunk, very merry, and prancing about in the middle of the road.

'What are you dancing for?' I asked.

'I'm happy, so I'm dancing,' said Pitamber.

'And why are you happy?' I asked.

'Because I'm dancing,' he said.

The rain stopped and the neem trees gave out a strong, sweet smell.

XII

Flowers in Pipalnagar—did they exist? As a child I knew a garden in Lucknow where there were beds of phlox and petunias and another garden where only roses grew. In the fields around Pipalnagar was thorn apple—a yellow buttercup nestling among thorn leaves. But in the Pipalnagar bazaar, there were no flowers except one—marigold growing out of a crack on my balcony. I had removed the plaster from the base of the plant, and filled in a little earth which I watered every morning. The plant was healthy, and sometimes it produced a small orange marigold.

Sometimes Suraj plucked a flower and kept it in his tray, among the combs, buttons and scent bottles. Sometimes he gave the flower to passing child, once to a small boy who immediately tore it to shreds. Suraj was back on his rounds, as his exams were over.

Whenever he was tired of going from house to house, Suraj would sit beneath a shady banyan or pipal tree, put his tray aside, and take out his flute. The haunting notes travelled down the road in the afternoon stillness, drawing children to him. They would sit beside him and be very quiet when he played, because there was something melancholic and appealing about the tune. Suraj sometimes made flutes out of pieces of bamboo, but he never sold them. He would give them to the children he liked. He would sell almost anything, but not flutes.

Suraj sometimes played the flute at night, when he lay awake, unable to sleep; but even though I slept, I could hear the music in my dreams. Sometimes he took his flute with him to the crooked tree and played for the benefit of the birds. The parrots made harsh noises in response and flew away. Once, when Suraj was playing his flute to a small group of children, he had a fit. The flute fell from his hands. And he began to roll about in the dust on the roadside. The children became frightened and ran away, but they did not stay away for long. The next time they heard the flute, they came to listen as usual.

XIII

It was Lord Krishna's birthday, and the rain came down as heavily as it is said to have done on the day Krishna was born. Krishna is the best beloved of all the gods. Young mothers laugh or weep as they read or hear the pranks of his boyhood; young men pray to be as tall and as strong as Krishna was when he killed King Kamsa's elephant and wrestlers; young girls dream of a lover as daring as Krishna to carry them off in a war chariot; grown men envy the wisdom and statesmanship with which he managed the affairs of his kingdom.

The rain came so unexpectedly that it took everyone by surprise. In seconds, people were drenched, and within minutes, the streets were flooded. The temple tank overflowed, the railway lines disappeared, and the old wall near the bus stop shivered and silently fell—the sound of its collapse drowned in the downpour. A naked young man with a dancing bear cavorted in the middle of the vegetable market. Pitamber's rickshaw churned through the floodwater while he sang lustily as he worked.

Wading through knee-deep water down the road, I saw the roadside vendors salvaging whatever they could. Plastic toys, cabbages and utensils floated away and were seized by urchins. The water had risen to the level of the shop fronts and the floors were awash.

Deep Chand and Ramu, with the help of a customer, were using buckets to bail the water out of their shop. The rain stopped as suddenly as it had begun and the sun came out. The water began to find an outlet, flooding other low-lying areas, and a paper boat came sailing between my legs.

Next morning, the morning on which the result of Suraj's examinations was due, I rose early—the first time I ever got up before Suraj—and went down to the news agency. A small crowd of students had gathered at the bus stop, joking with each other and hiding their nervousness with a show of indifference. There were not many passengers on the first bus, and there was a mad grab for newspapers as the bundle landed with a thud on the pavement. Within half-an-hour, the newsboy had sold all his copies. It was the best day of the year for him.

I went through the columns relating to Pipalnagar, but I couldn't find Suraj's roll number on the list of successful candidates. I had the number on a slip of paper, and I looked at it again to make sure I had compared it correctly with the others; then I went through the newspaper once more. When I returned to the room, Suraj was sitting on the doorstep. I didn't have to tell him he had failed—he knew by the look on my face. I sat down beside him, and we said nothing for some time.

'Never mind,' Suraj said eventually. 'I will pass next year.'

I realized I was more depressed than he was and that he was trying to console me.

'If only you'd had more time,' I said.

'I have plenty of time now. Another year. And you will have time to finish your book, and then we can go away together. Another year of Pipalnagar won't be so bad. As long as I have your friendship almost everything can be tolerated.'

He stood up, the tray hanging from his shoulders. 'What would you like to buy?'

XIV

Another year of Pipalnagar! But it was not to be. A short time later, I received a letter from the editor of a newspaper, calling me to

Delhi for an interview. My friends insisted that I should go. Such an opportunity would not come again.

But I needed a shirt. The few I possessed were either frayed at the collar or torn at the shoulders. I hadn't been able to afford a new shirt for over a year, and I couldn't afford one now. Struggling writers weren't expected to dress well, but I felt in order to get the job I would need both a haircut and a clean shirt.

Where was I to go to get a shirt? Suraj generally wore an old red-striped T-shirt; he washed it every second evening, and by morning it was dry and ready to wear again; but it was tight even on him. He did not have another. Besides, I needed something white, something respectable!

I went to Deep Chand who had a collection of shirts. He was only too glad to lend me one. But they were all brightly coloured—pinks, purples and magentas... No editor was going to be impressed by a young writer in a pink shirt. They looked fine on Deep Chand, but he had no need to look respectable.

Finally, Pitamber came to my rescue. He didn't bother with shirts himself, except in winter, but he was able to borrow a clean white shirt from a guard at the jail, who'd got it from the relative of a convict in exchange for certain favours.

'This shirt will make you look respectable,' said Pitamber. 'To be respectable—what an adventure!'

XV

Freedom. The moment the bus was out of Pipalnagar, and the fields opened out on all sides, I knew that I was free, that I had always been free. Only my own weakness, hesitation, and the habits that had grown around me had held me back. All I had to do was sit in a bus and go somewhere.

I sat near the open window of the bus and let the cool breeze from the fields play against my face. Herons and snipe waded among the lotus roots in flat green ponds. Blue jays swooped around telegraph poles. Children jumped naked into the canals that wound through the fields. Because I was happy, it seemed to me that everyone else was happy—the driver, the conductor, the passengers, the farmers in the fields and those driving bullock-carts. When two women behind me started quarrelling over their seats. I helped to placate them. Then I took a small girl on my knee and pointed out camels, buffaloes, vultures and pariah dogs.

Six hours later, the bus crossed the bridge over the swollen Jamuna river, passed under the walls of the great Red Fort built by a Mughal emperor, and entered the old city of Delhi. I found it strange to be in a city again, after several years in Pipalnagar. It was a little frightening too. I felt like a stranger. No one was interested in me.

In Pipalnagar, people wanted to know each other, or at least to know about one another. In Delhi, no one cared who you were or where you came from, like big cities almost everywhere. It was prosperous but without a heart.

After a day and a night of loneliness, I found myself wishing that Suraj had accompanied me; wishing that I was back in Pipalnagar. But when the job was offered to me—at a starting salary of three hundred rupees per month, a princely sum compared to what I had been making on my own—I did not have the courage to refuse it. After accepting the job—which was to commence in a week's time—I spent the day wandering through the bazaars, down the wide shady roads of the capital, resting under the jamun trees, and thinking all the time what I would do in the months to come.

I slept at the railway waiting room and all night long I heard the shunting and whistling of engines which conjured up visions of places with sweet names like Kumbakonam, Krishnagiri, Polonnarurawa. I dreamt of palm-fringed beaches and inland lagoons; of the echoing chambers of deserted cities, red sandstone and white marble; of temples in the sun; and elephants crossing wide slow-moving rivers...

XVI

Pitamber was on the platform when the train steamed into the Pipalnagar station in the early hours of a damp September morning. I waved to him from the carriage window, and shouted that everything had gone well.

But everything was not well here. When I got off the train, Pitamber told me that Suraj had been ill—that he'd had a fit on a lonely stretch of road the previous afternoon and had lain in the sun for over an hour. Pitamber had found him, suffering from heatstroke, and brought him home. When I saw him, he was sitting up on the string bed drinking hot tea. He looked pale and weak, but his smile was reassuring.

'Don't worry,' he said. 'I will be all right.'

'He was bad last night,' said Pitamber. 'He had a fever and kept talking, as in a dream. But what he says is true—he is better this morning.'

'Thanks to Pitamber,' said Suraj. 'It is good to have friends.'

'Come with me to Delhi, Suraj,' I said. 'I have got a job now. You can live with me and attend a school regularly.'

'It is good for friends to help each other,' said Suraj, 'but only after I have passed my exam will I join you in Delhi. I made myself this promise. Poor Pipalnagar—nobody wants to stay here. Will you be sorry to leave?'

'Yes, I will be sorry. A part of me will still be here.'

XVII

Deep Chand was happy to know that I was leaving. 'I'll follow you soon,' he said. 'There is money to be made in Delhi, cutting hair. Girls are keeping it short these days.'

'But men are growing it long.'

'True. So I shall open a barbershop for ladies and a beauty salon for men! Ramu can attend to the ladies.'

Ramu winked at me in the mirror. He was still at the stage of teasing girls on their way to school or college.

The snip of Deep Chand's scissors made me sleepy, as I sat in his chair. His fingers beat a rhythmic tattoo on my scalp. It was my last haircut in Pipalnagar, and Deep Chand did not charge me for it. I promised to write as soon as I had settled down in Delhi.

The next day when Suraj was stronger, I said, 'Come, let us go for a walk and visit our crooked tree. Where is your flute, Suraj?'

'I don't know. Let us look for it.'

We searched the room and our belongings for the flute but could not find it.

'It must have been left on the roadside,' said Suraj. 'Never mind. I will make another.'

I could picture the flute lying in the dust on the roadside and somehow this made me sad. But Suraj was full of high spirits as we walked across the railway lines and through the fields.

'The rains are over,' he said, kicking off his chappals and lying down on the grass. 'You can smell the autumn in the air. Somehow, it makes me feel light-hearted. Yesterday I was sad, and tomorrow I might be sad again, but today I know that I am happy. I want to live on and on. One lifetime cannot satisfy my heart.'

'A day in a lifetime,' I said. 'I'll remember this day—the way the sun touches us, the way the grass bends, the smell of this leaf as I crush it…'

XVIII

At six every morning the first bus arrives, and the passengers alight, looking sleepy and dishevelled, and rather discouraged by their first sight of Pipalnagar. When they have gone their various ways, the bus is driven into the shed. Cows congregate at the dustbin and the pavement dwellers come to life, stretching their tired limbs on the hard stone steps. I carry the bucket up the steps to my room, and bathe for the last time on the open balcony. In the villages, the buffaloes are wallowing in green ponds while naked urchins sit astride them, scrubbing their backs, and a crow or water bird perches on their glistening necks. The parrots are busy in the crooked tree, and a slim green snake basks in the sun on our island near the brick-kiln. In the hills, the mists have lifted and the distant mountains are fringed with snow.

It is autumn, and the rains are over. The earth meets the sky in one broad bold sweep.

A land of thrusting hills. Terraced hills, wood-covered and windswept. Mountains where the gods speak gently to the lonely. Hills of green grass and grey rock, misty at dawn, hazy at noon, molten at sunset, where fierce fresh torrents rush to the valleys below. A quiet land of fields and ponds, shaded by ancient trees and ringed with palms, where sacred rivers are touched by temples, where temples are touched by southern seas.

This is the land I should write about. Pipalnagar should be forgotten. I should turn aside from it to sing instead of the splendours of exotic places.

But only yesterdays are truly splendid… And there are other singers, sweeter than I, to sing of tomorrow. I can only write of today, of Pipalnagar, where I have lived and loved.

THE LAST TIGER

On the left bank of the Ganga, where it emerges from the Himalayan foothills, there is a long stretch of heavy forest. There are villages on the fringe of the forest, inhabited by bamboo cutters and farmers, but there are few signs of commerce or religion. Hunters, however, have found it an ideal hunting ground over the last seventy years, and as a result the animals are not as numerous as they used to be. The trees, too, have been disappearing slowly; and, as the forest recedes, the animals lose their food and shelter and move on, further into the foothills. Slowly, they are being denied the right to live.

Only the elephants could cross the river. And two years ago, when a large area of forest was cleared to make way for a refugee resettlement camp, a herd of elephants—finding their favourite food, the green shoots of the bamboo, in short supply—waded across the river. They crashed through the suburbs of Haridwar, knocked down a factory wall, plucked away several tin roofs, held up a train, and left a trail of devastation in their wake until they reached a new forest, still untouched, where they settled down to a new life—but an unsettled, wary life. Because, they did not know when men would appear again, with tractors and bulldozers and dynamite.

There was a time when this forest provided food and shelter for some thirty or forty tigers; but men in search of trophies shot them all, and today there remains only one old tiger in the jungle. Many hunters have tried to get him. But he is a wise and crafty old tiger who knows the ways of men, and he has so far survived all attempts on his life.

This is his story. It is also the story of the jungle.

~

Although the tiger has passed the prime of his life, he has lost none of his majesty; his muscles ripple beneath the golden yellow of his coat, and he walks through the long grass with the confidence of one who knows that he is still king, even though his subjects are fewer. His great head pushes through the foliage, and it is only his tail, swinging high, that shows occasionally above the sea of grass.

He is heading for water, the only water in the forest (if you don't count the river, which is several miles away)—the water of a large jheel, which is almost a lake during the rainy season, but just a muddy marsh at this time of the year, in the late spring.

Here, at different times of the day and night, all the animals come to drink—the long-horned sambar deer, the delicate spotted chital, the swamp deer, the wolves and jackals, the wild boar, the panthers—and the tiger. Since the elephants have gone, the water is usually clear except when buffaloes from the nearest village come to wallow, and then it is very muddy. These buffaloes, though they are not wild, are not afraid of the panther or even of the tiger. They know the panther is afraid of their long horns and they know the tiger prefers the flesh of the deer.

Today, there are several sambar at the water's edge, but they do not stay long. The tiger is coming with the breeze, and there is no mistaking its strong feline odour. The deer hold their heads high for a few moments, their nostrils twitching, and then scatter into the forest, disappearing behind screens of leaf and bamboo.

When the tiger arrives, there is no other animal near the water. But the birds are still there. The egrets continue to wade in the shallows, and a kingfisher darts low over the water, dives suddenly, a flash of blue and gold, and makes off with a slim silver fish, which glistens in the sun like a polished gem. A long brown snake glides in amongst the water lilies and disappears beneath a fallen tree which lies rotting in the shallows.

The tiger waits in the shelter of a rock, his ears pricked up for the least unfamiliar sound; for he knows that it is often at this place that men lie up for him with guns; for they covet his beauty—they covet his stripes, and the gold of his body, and his fine teeth and his whiskers and his noble head. They would like to hang his pelt on a wall, and stick glass eyes in his head, and boast of their conquest over the king of the jungle.

The old tiger has been hunted before, and he does not usually show himself in the open during the day, but of late he has heard no guns, and if there were hunters around, you would have heard their guns (for a man with a gun cannot resist letting it off, even if it is only at a rabbit—or at another man). And, besides, the tiger is thirsty.

He is also feeling quite hot. It is March, and the shimmering dust-haze of summer has come early this year. Tigers—unlike other cats—are fond of water, and on a hot day will wallow for hours.

He walks into the water, in amongst the water lilies, and drinks slowly. He is seldom in a hurry when he eats or drinks. Other animals might bolt their food, but they are only other animals. A tiger has his dignity to preserve!

He raises his head and listens. One paw remains suspended in the air. A strange sound has come to him on the breeze, and he is wary of strange sounds. So he moves swiftly through the grass that borders the jheel, and climbs a hillock until he reaches his favourite rock. This rock is big enough to hide him and to give him shade. Anyone looking up from the jheel might think it strange that the rock has a round bump on the top. The bump is the tiger's head. He keeps it very still.

The sound he has heard is only the sound of a flute, sounding thin and reedy in the forest. It belongs to a boy, a slim brown boy who rides a buffalo. The boy blows vigorously on the flute, while another, slightly smaller boy, riding another buffalo, brings up the rear of the herd.

There are about eight buffaloes in the herd, and they belong to the families of Ramu and Shyam, the two Gujjar boys who are friends. The Gujjars are a caste who possess herds of buffaloes and earn their livelihood from the sale of milk and butter. The boys are about twelve years old, but they cannot tell you how many months past twelve, because in their village nobody thinks birthdays are important. They are almost the same age as the tiger, but he is old and experienced while they are still cubs.

The tiger has often seen them at the tank, and he is not worried. He knows the village people will bring him no harm as long as he leaves their buffaloes alone. Once, when he was younger and full of bravado, he had killed a buffalo—not because he was hungry but because he was young and wanted to test his strength—and after that the villagers had hunted him for days, with spears, bows and arrows, and an old muzzle-loader. Now he left the buffaloes alone, even though the deer in the forest were not as numerous as before.

The boys know that a tiger lives in the jungle, for they have often heard him roar, but they do not know that today he is so near to them.

The tiger gazes down from his rock, and the sight of eight fat black buffaloes does make him give a low, throaty moan. But the boys are there, and besides—a buffalo is not easy to kill.

He decides to move on and find a cool shady place in the heart of the jungle, where he can rest during the warm afternoon and be free of the flies and mosquitoes that swarm around in the vicinity of the tank. At night he will hunt.

With a lazy, half-humorous roar—'A—oonh!'—he gets up from his haunches and saunters off into the jungle.

Even the gentlest of a tiger's roars can be heard half a mile away, and the boys, who are barely fifty yards off, look up immediately.

'There he goes!' calls Ramu, taking the flute from his lips and pointing with it towards the hillock. He is not afraid, for he knows that an un-hunted and uninjured tiger is not aggressive. 'Did you see him?'

'I saw his tail, just before he disappeared. He's a big tiger!'

'Do not call him tiger. Call him Uncle, or Maharaj.'

'Oh, why?'

'Don't you know that it's unlucky to call a tiger a tiger? My father always told me so. But if you meet a tiger, and call him Uncle, he will leave you alone.'

'I'll try and remember that,' says Shyam.

The buffaloes are now well into the water, and some of them are lying down in the mud. Buffaloes love soft, wet mud and will wallow in it for hours. The more mud the better. Ramu, to avoid being dragged down into the mud with his buffalo, slips off its back and plunges into the water. Using an easy breaststroke, he swims across to a small islet covered with reeds and water lilies. Shyam is close behind him.

They lie down on their hard, flat stomachs, on a patch of grass, and allow the warm sun to beat down on their bare brown bodies. Ramu is the more knowledgeable boy, because he has been to Haridwar several times with his father. Shyam has never been out of the village.

Shyam says, 'The pool is not so deep this year.'

'We have had no rain since January,' says Ramu. 'If we do not get rain soon, the tank may dry up altogether.'

'And then what will we do?'

'We? There is a well in the village. But even that may dry up. My father told me that it failed once, just about the time I was born, and everyone had to walk ten miles to the river for water.'

'And what about the animals?'

'Some will stay here and die. Others will go to the river.

But there are too many people near the river now—not only temples, but houses and factories—and the animals stay away. And the trees have been cut, so that between the jungle and the river there is no place to hide. Animals are afraid of the open—they are afraid of men with guns.'

'Even at night?'

'At night men come in jeeps, with searchlights. They kill the deer for meat, and sell the skins of tigers and panthers.'

'I didn't know a tiger's skin was worth anything.'

'It is worth more than our skins,' says Ramu knowingly. 'It will fetch six hundred rupees. Who would pay that much for our skins?'

'Our fathers would.'

'True—if they had the money.'

'If my father sold his fields, he would get more than six hundred rupees.'

'True—but if he sold his fields, none of you would have anything to eat. A man needs land as much as a tiger needs a jungle.'

'True,' says Shyam. 'And that reminds me—my mother asked me to take some roots home.'

'I will help you.'

They wade into the jheel until the water is up to their waists, and begin pulling up water lilies by the root. The flower is beautiful but the villagers value the root more. When it is cooked, it makes a delicious and nourishing dish. The plant multiplies rapidly and is always in good supply. In the year when famine hit the village, it was only the root of the water lily that saved many from starvation.

When Shyam and Ramu have finished gathering roots, they emerge from the water and pass the time in wrestling with each other, slipping about in the soft mud which soon covers them from head to toe.

To get rid of the mud, they dive into the water again and swim across to their buffaloes. Then, digging their heels into the thick hides of the buffaloes, the boys race them across the jheel, shouting and hollering so much that all the birds fly away in disgust, and the monkeys set up a shrill chattering of their own in the dhak trees.

In March, the twisted, leafless flame of the forest or dhak trees are ablaze with flaming scarlet and orange flowers.

It is evening, and the twilight is fading fast, when the buffalo herd finally wends its way homewards, to be greeted outside the village by the barking of dogs, the gurgle of hookah pipes, and the homely smell of cowdung smoke.

∽

The tiger makes a kill that night. He approaches with the wind against him, and the unsuspecting spotted deer does not see him until it is too late. A blow on the deer's haunches from the tiger's paw brings it down, and then the great beast fastens onto the struggling deer's throat. It is all over in a few minutes. The tiger is too quick and strong, and the deer does not struggle for long.

The deer's life is over, but he has not lived in fear of death. It is only man's imagination and fear of the hereafter that makes him afraid of meeting death. In the jungle, sudden death appears at intervals. Wild creatures do not have to think about it, and so the sudden passing of one of their number due to the arrival of some flesh-eating animal is only a fleeting incident soon forgotten by the survivors.

The tiger feasts well, growling with pleasure as he eats, and then leaves the carcass in the jungle for the vultures and jackals. The old tiger never returns to the same deer's carcass, even if there is still some flesh on it. In the past, when he has done that, he has often found a man sitting in a tree over the kill, waiting for him with a rifle.

His belly full, the tiger comes to the edge of the forest, looks out across the wasteland out over the deep, singing river, at the twinkling lights of Haridwar on the opposite bank, and raises his head and roars his defiance at the world.

He is a lonesome bachelor. It is five or six years since he had a mate. She was shot by trophy-hunters, and the cubs, two of them, were trapped by men who trade in wild animals: one went to a circus, where it had to learn undignified tricks and respond to the flick of a whip, the other, more fortunate, went first to a zoo in Delhi and was later transferred to a zoo in America.

Sometimes, when the old tiger is very lonely, he gives a great roar, which can be heard throughout the forest. The villagers think he is roaring in anger, but the animals know that he is really roaring out of loneliness. When the sound of his roar has died away, he pauses, standing still, waiting for an answering roar, but it never comes. It is taken up instead by the shrill scream of a barbet high up in a sal tree.

It is dawn now, dew-fresh and cool, and the jungle dwellers are on the move. The black, beady little eyes of a jungle rat were fixed on a small brown hen who was returning cautiously to her nest. He had a large family to feed, and he knew that in the hen's nest was a clutch of delicious fawn-coloured eggs. He waited patiently for nearly an hour before he had the satisfaction of seeing the hen leave her nest and go off in search of food.

As soon as she had gone, the rat lost no time in making his

raid. Slipping quietly out of his hole, he slithered along among the leaves, but, clever as he was, he did not realize that his own movements were being watched.

A pair of grey mongooses were scouting about in the dry grass. They, too, were hungry, and eggs usually figured large on their menu. Now, lying still on an outcrop of rock, they watched the rat sneaking along, occasionally sniffing at the air, and finally vanishing behind a boulder. When he reappeared, he was struggling to roll an egg uphill towards his hole.

The rat was in difficulties, pushing the egg sometimes with his paws, sometimes with his nose. The ground was rough, and the egg wouldn't go straight. Deciding that he must have help, he scuttled off to call his spouse. Even now the mongoose did not descend on that tantalizing egg. He waited until the rat returned with his wife, and then watched as the male rat took the egg firmly between his forepaws and rolled over on to his back. The female rat then grabbed her mate's tail and began to drag him along.

Totally absorbed in their struggle with the egg, the rats did not hear the approach of the mongooses. When these two large furry visitors suddenly bobbed up from behind a stone, the rats squealed with fright, abandoned the egg, and fled for their lives.

The mongooses wasted no time in breaking open the egg and making a meal of it. But just as, a few minutes ago, the rat had not noticed their approach, so now they did not notice the village boy, carrying a small bright axe and a net bag in his hands, creeping along.

Ramu too was searching for eggs, and when he saw the mongooses busy with one, he stood still to watch them, his eyes roving in search of the nest. He was hoping the mongooses would lead him to the nest, but, when they had finished their meal, the breeze took them in another direction, and Ramu had to do his own searching. He failed to find the nest, and moved further into the forest. The rat's hopes were just reviving when, to his disgust, the mother hen returned.

Ramu now made his way to a mahua tree.

The flowers of the mahua tree can be eaten by animals as well as men. Bears are particularly fond of them and will eat large quantities of its flowers which gradually start fermenting in their stomachs with the result that the animals get quite drunk. Ramu had often seen a couple of bears stumbling home to their cave, bumping into each other or into the trunks of trees—they are short-sighted to begin with, and when drunk can hardly see at all—but their sense of smell and hearing are so good that they finally find their way home.

Ramu decided he would gather some mahua flowers, and climbed swiftly into the tree, which is leafless when it blossoms. He began breaking the white flowers and throwing them to the ground. He had been in the tree for about five minutes when he heard the whining grumble of a bear, and presently a young sloth bear ambled into the clearing beneath the tree.

He was a small bear, little more than a cub, and Ramu was not frightened, but, because he thought the mother might be in the vicinity, he decided to take no chances, and sat very still, waiting to see what the bear would do. He hoped it wouldn't choose the same mahua tree for a meal.

At first the young bear put his nose to the ground and sniffed his way along until he came to a large white anthill. Here he began huffing and puffing, blowing rapidly in and out of his nostrils, so that the dust from the anthill flew in all directions. But he was a disappointed bear, because the anthill had been deserted long ago. And so, grumbling, he made his way across to a wild plum—a tall tree, the wild plum—and shinning rapidly up the smooth trunk, was soon perched in its topmost branches. It was only then that he saw Ramu.

The bear at once scrambled several feet higher up the tree, and laid himself out flat on a branch. It wasn't a very thick branch and left a large expanse of bear showing on either side of it. The bear tucked his head away behind another branch, and, so long as he could not see Ramu, seemed quite satisfied that he was well hidden, though he couldn't help grumbling with anxiety, for a bear, like most animals, is afraid of man—until he discovers that man is afraid of him.

Bears, however, are also very curious—and curiosity has often led them into trouble. Slowly, inch by inch, the young bear's black snout appeared over the edge of the branch, but, immediately, the eyes came into view and met Ramu's. He drew back with a jerk and the head was once more hidden. The bear did this two or three times, and Ramu, highly amused, waited until it wasn't looking, then moved some way down the tree. When the bear looked up again and saw that the boy was missing, he was so pleased with himself that he stretched right across to the next branch, to get at a plum. Ramu chose this moment to burst into loud laughter. The startled bear tumbled out of the tree, dropped through the branches for a distance of some fifteen feet, and landed with a thud in a heap of dry leaves.

And then several things happened almost at the same time.

The mother bear came charging into the clearing. Spotting Ramu in the tree, she reared up on her hind legs, grunting fiercely. It was Ramu's turn to be startled. There are few animals as dangerous as a rampaging mother bear, and the boy knew that one blow from her clawed forepaws could rip his skull open.

But before the bear could approach the tree, there was a tremendous roar, and the tiger bounded into the clearing. He had been asleep in the bushes not far away—he liked a good sleep after a heavy meal—and the noise in the clearing had woken him.

He was in a very bad temper, and his loud 'A—oonh!' made his displeasure quite clear. The bears turned and ran from the clearing, the youngster squealing with fright.

The tiger then came into the centre of the clearing, looked up at the trembling boy, and roared again.

Ramu nearly fell out of the tree.

'Good day to you, Uncle,' he stammered, showing his teeth in a nervous grin.

Perhaps this was too much for the tiger. With a low growl, he turned his back on the mahua tree and padded off into the jungle, his tail twitching in disgust.

∽

That night, when Ramu told his parents and grandfather about the tiger and how it had saved him from a female bear, a number of stories were told about tigers, some of whom had been gentlemen, others rogues. Sooner or later the conversation came round to man-eaters, and Grandfather told two stories, which he swore were true, though the others only half believed him.

The first story concerned the belief that a man-eating tiger is guided towards his next victim by the spirit of a human being previously killed and eaten by the tiger. Grandfather said that he actually knew three hunters who sat up in a machan over a human kill, and when the tiger came, the corpse sat up and pointed with his right hand at the men in the tree. The tiger then went away. But the hunters knew he would return, and one man was brave enough to get down from the tree and tie the right arm of the corpse to the body. Later, when the tiger returned, the corpse sat up and pointed out the men with his left hand. The enraged tiger sprang into the tree and killed his enemies in the machan.

'And then there was a bania,' said Grandfather, beginning another story, 'who lived in a village in the jungle. He wanted to visit a neighbouring village to collect some money that was owed him, but as the road lay through heavy forest, in which lived a terrible man-eating tiger, he did not know what to do. Finally, he went to a sadhu who gave him two powders. By eating the first powder, he could turn into a huge tiger, capable of dealing with any other tiger in the jungle, and by eating the second he could become a bania again.

'Armed with his two powders, and accompanied by his pretty young wife, the bania set out on his journey. They had not gone far into the forest when they came upon the man-eater sitting in the middle of the road. Before swallowing the first powder, the bania told his wife to stay where she was, so that when he returned after killing the tiger, she could at once give him the second powder and enable him to resume his old shape.

'Well, the bania's plan worked, but only up to a point. He swallowed the first powder and immediately became a magnificent tiger. With a great roar, he bounded towards the man-eater, and after a brief, furious fight, killed his opponent. Then, with his jaws still dripping blood, he returned to his wife.

'The poor girl was terrified and spilt the second powder on the ground. The bania was so angry that he pounced on his wife and killed and ate her. And afterwards this terrible tiger was so enraged at not being able to become a human again that he killed and ate hundreds of people all over the country.'

'The only people he spared,' said Grandfather, with a twinkle in his eye, 'were those who owed him money. A bania never gives up a loan as lost, and the tiger still hoped that one day he might become a human again and be able to collect his dues.'

Next morning, when Ramu came back from the well which was used to irrigate his father's fields, he found a crowd of curious children surrounding a jeep and three strangers with guns. Each of the strangers had a gun, and they were accompanied by two bearers and a vast amount of provisions.

They had heard that there was a tiger in the area, and they wanted to shoot it.

One of the hunters, who looked even stranger than the others, had come all the way to India for tiger, and he had vowed that he would not leave the country without a tiger's skin in his baggage. One of his companions had said that he could buy a tiger's skin in Delhi, but the hunter did not like the idea and said he'd have nothing to do with a tiger that he hadn't shot.

These men had money to spend, and, as most of the villagers needed money badly, they were only too willing to construct a machan for the hunters. The platform, big enough to take the three men, was put up in the branches of a tall toon, or mahogany tree.

It was the only night the hunters used the machan. At the end of March, though the days are warm, the nights are still cold. The hunters had neglected to bring blankets, and by midnight their teeth were chattering. Ramu, having tied up a goat for them at the foot of the tree, made as if to go home but instead circled the area, hanging up bits and pieces of old clothing on small trees and bushes. He thought he owed that much to the tiger. He knew the wily old king of the jungle would keep well away from the goat if he thought there were humans in the vicinity. And where there are men's clothes, there will be men.

As soon as it was dark, the goat began bleating, loud enough for any self-respecting tiger to hear it, but perhaps the ruse was too obvious, or perhaps the clothes Ramu had hung out were warning enough, because the tiger did not come near the toon tree. In any case, the men in the tree soon gave themselves away.

The cold was really too much for them. A flask of brandy was produced, and passed round, and it was not long before there was more purpose to finishing the brandy than to finishing off a tiger. Silent at first, the men soon began talking in whispers, and to jungle creatures a human whisper is as telling as a trumpet call. Soon the men were quite merry, talking in loud voices. And when the first morning light crept over the forest, and Ramu and his friends came by to see if the goat still lived, they found the hunters fast asleep in the machan.

The shikaris looked surly and embarrassed when they trudged back to the village.

'No game left in these parts,' said one.

'The wrong time of the year for tiger,' said another.

'I don't know what the country's coming to,' said the third.

And complaining about the weather, the quality of cartridges, the quality of rum, and the perversity of tigers, they drove away in disgust.

It was not until the onset of summer that an event occurred which altered the hunting habits of the tiger and brought him into conflict with the villagers.

~

There had been no rain for almost two months, and the grass had become a dry yellow. Some refugee settlers, living in an area where the forest had been cleared, were careless in putting out a fire. The tiger sniffed at the acrid smell of smoke in the air, and, wandering to the edge of the jungle, saw in the distance the dancing lights of a forest fire. As night came on, the flames grew more vivid, the smell stronger. The tiger turned and made for the jheel, where he knew he would be safe, provided he swam across to the little island in the centre.

Next morning he was on the island, which was untouched by the fire. But his surroundings had changed. The slopes of the hills were black with burnt grass, and most of the tall bamboo had disappeared. The deer and the wild pig, finding that their natural cover had gone, fled further east.

The tiger prowled throughout the smoking forest but he found no game. Once he came across the body of a burnt rabbit, but he could not eat it. He drank at the jheel and settled down in a shady spot to sleep the day away. Perhaps, by evening, some of the animals would return. If not, he too would have to look for new hunting grounds—or new game.

The tiger had not eaten for five days and he was so hungry that he had been forced to scratch about in the grass and leaves for worms and beetles. This was a sad comedown for the king of the jungle. But even now he hesitated to leave the area, for he had a deep suspicion and fear of the forests further south and east—forests that were fast being swallowed up by human habitation. He could have gone north, into the hills, but they did not provide him with the long grass he needed. A panther could manage quite well in the hills, but not a tiger who loved the natural privacy of heavy jungle. In the hills, he would have to hide all the time.

At break of day, the tiger came to the jheel. The water was now shallow and muddy, and a green scum had spread over the top. But the water was still drinkable, and the tiger had quenched his thirst.

He lay down across his favourite rock, hoping for a deer, but none approached. He was about to get up and go away when he heard the warning chatter of a lone langur. Some animal was definitely approaching.

The tiger at once dropped flat on the ground, his tawny skin merging with the dry grass. A heavy animal was moving through the bushes, and the tiger waited patiently until a buffalo emerged and came to the water. The buffalo was alone.

He was a big male buffalo, and his long curved horns lay right back across his shoulders. He moved leisurely towards the water, completely unaware of the tiger's presence.

The tiger hesitated before making his charge. It was a long

time—many years—since he had killed a buffalo, and he knew the villagers would not like it. But hunger helped him to overcome his caution. There was no morning breeze, everything was still, and the smell of the tiger did not carry to the buffalo. The monkey still chattered in a nearby tree, but his warning went unheeded.

Moving at a crouch, the tiger skirted the edge of the jheel and approached the buffalo from the rear. The water birds, who were used to the presence of both animals, did not raise an alarm.

Getting closer, the tiger glanced around to see if there were men, or other buffaloes, in the vicinity. Then, satisfied that he was alone, he crept forward. The buffalo was drinking, standing in shallow water at the edge of the tank, when the tiger charged from the side and bit deep into the animal's thigh.

The buffalo turned to fight, but the tendons of his right hind leg had been snapped, and he could only stagger forward a few paces. But he was not afraid. He bellowed, and lowered his horns at the tiger, but the great cat was too fast and, circling the buffalo, bit into the other hind leg.

The buffalo crashed to the ground, both hind legs crippled, and then the tiger dashed in, using both tooth and claw, biting deep into the buffalo's throat until the blood gushed out from the jugular vein.

The buffalo gave one long last bellow before dying.

The tiger, having rested, now began to gorge himself, but, even though he had been starving for days, he could not finish the buffalo. At least one good meal still remained when, satisfied and feeling his strength return, he quenched his thirst at the jheel. Then he dragged the remains of the buffalo into the bushes and went off to find a place to sleep. He would return to the kill when he was hungry.

The villagers were upset when they discovered that a buffalo was missing, and next day, when Ramu and Shyam came running home to say that they had found the carcass near the jheel, half-eaten by the tiger, the men were disturbed and angry. They felt that the tiger had tricked and deceived them. And they knew that once he found he could kill buffaloes quite easily, he would make a habit of it.

Kundan Singh, Shyam's father, and the owner of the dead buffalo, said he would go after the tiger himself.

'It is all very well to talk about what you will do to the tiger,' said his wife, 'but you should never have let the buffalo go off on its own.'

'He had been out on his own before,' said Kundan. 'This is the first time the tiger has attacked one of our beasts. A shaitan—a devil—has entered the Maharaj.'

'He must have been very hungry,' said Shyam.

'Well, we are hungry too,' said Kundan. 'Our best buffalo—the only male in our herd—'

'The tiger will kill again,' said Ramu's father.

'If we let him,' said Kundan. 'Should we send for the shikaris?'

'No. They were not clever. The tiger will escape them easily. And, besides, there is no time. The tiger will return for another meal tonight. We must finish him off ourselves!'

'But how?'

Kundan Singh smiled secretively, played with the ends of his moustache for a few moments, and then, with great pride, produced from under his cot a double-barrelled gun of ancient vintage.

'My father bought it from an Englishman,' he said.

'How long ago was that?'

'At the time I was born.'

'And have you ever used it?' asked Ramu's father, who was not sure that the gun would work.

'Well, some years back, I let it off at some bandits. You remember the time when those dacoits raided our village? They chose the wrong village, and were severely beaten for their pains. As they left, I fired my gun off at them, and as a result they didn't stop running until they had crossed the Ganga!'

'Yes, but did you hit anyone?'

'I would have, if someone's goat hadn't got in the way at the last moment. But we had roast mutton that night! Don't worry, brother, I know how the thing works. It takes a fistful of powder and bullets the size of pigeon's eggs!'

Accompanied by Ramu's father and some others, Kundan set out for the jheel, where, without shifting the buffalo's carcass—for they knew the tiger would not come near them if it suspected a trap—they made another machan in a tall tree some thirty feet from the kill.

Later that evening—at the 'hour of cow-dust', Kundan Singh and Ramu's father settled down for the night on their crude tree platform.

Several hours passed, and nothing but a jackal was seen by the watchers. And then, just as the moon came up over the distant hills, Kundan and his companion were startled by a low 'A—oonh', followed by a suppressed, rumbling growl.

Kundan grasped his old gun, while his friend drew closer to him for comfort. There was complete silence for a minute or two—a time that was an agony of suspense for the watchers—and then there was the sound of a stealthy footfall on some dead leaves under the tree.

A moment later the tiger walked out into the moonlight and stood over his kill.

At first Kundan could do nothing. He was completely overawed by the size of this magnificent tiger. Ramu's father had to nudge him, and then Kundan quickly put the gun to his shoulder, aimed at the tiger's head, and pressed the trigger.

The gun went off with a flash and a tremendous roar, but the bullet only singed the tiger's shoulder.

The enraged animal rushed at the tree and tried to leap into its branches. Fortunately the machan had been built at a safe height, and the tiger, unable to reach it, roared twice, and then bounded off into the forest.

'What a tiger!' exclaimed Kundan, half in fear and half in admiration. 'I feel as though my liver has turned to water.'

'You missed him completely,' said Ramu's father. 'Your gun makes a big noise, but an arrow would have been more accurate.'

'I did not miss him,' said Kundan, feeling offended. 'You heard him roar, didn't you? He would not have been so angry if he had not been hit. If I have wounded him badly, he will die.'

'And if you have wounded him slightly, he may turn into a man-eater, and then where will we be?'

'I don't think he will come back,' said Kundan. 'He will leave these forests.'

They waited until the sun was up before coming down from the tree. They found a few drops of blood on the dry grass, but no trail led into the forest, and Ramu's father was convinced that the wound was only a slight one.

The bullet, missing the fatal spot behind the ear, had only grazed the back of the skull and cut a deep groove at its base.

It took a few days to heal, and during this time the tiger lay low and did not go near the jheel except when it was very dark and he was very thirsty. The villagers thought the tiger had gone away, and Ramu and Shyam—accompanied by some other youths, and always carrying sticks and axes—began bringing the buffaloes to the tank again during the day; but they were careful not to let any of them stray far from the herd, and they returned home while it was still daylight.

While the buffaloes wallowed in the muddy water, and the boys wrestled on their grassy islet, a tawny eagle circled high above them, looking for a meal—a sure sign that some of the animals were beginning to return to the forest. It was not long before his keen eyes detected a movement in the glade below.

What the eagle saw was a baby hare, a small fluffy thing, its long pink-tinted ears laid flat along its sides. Had it not been creeping along between two large stones, it would have escaped notice. The eagle waited to see if the mother was about, and even as he waited he realized that he was not the only one who coveted this juicy hare. From the bushes there had appeared a sinuous yellow creature, pressed low to the ground and moving rapidly towards the hare. It was a yellow jungle cat, hardly noticeable in the scorched grass. With great stealth and artistry the jungle cat stalked the baby hare.

He pounced. The hare's squeal was cut short by the cat's cruel claws, but it had been heard by the mother hare, who now bounded into the glade and without the slightest hesitation attacked the surprised cat.

There was nothing haphazard about the hare's attack. She flashed around behind the cat and jumped clean over it. As she landed, she kicked back, sending a stinging jet of dust shooting into the cat's face. She did this again and again.

The bewildered cat, crouching and snarling, picked up the kill and tried to run away with it. But the hare would not permit this. She continued her leaping and buffeting till eventually the cat, out of sheer frustration, dropped the kill and attacked the mother.

The cat sprang at the hare a score of times lashing out with its claws, but the mother hare was both clever and agile enough to keep just out of reach of those terrible claws, and drew the cat further and further away from her baby—for she did not as yet know that it was dead.

The tawny eagle saw his chance. Swift and true, he swooped.

For a brief moment, as his wings overspread the furry little hare and his talons sank deep into it, he caught a glimpse of the cat racing towards him and the mother hare fleeing into the bushes. And then, with a shrill 'kee-ee-ee' of triumph, he rose and whirled away with his dinner.

The boys had heard this shrill cry and looked up just in time to see the eagle flying over the jheel with the small hare held firmly in its talons.

'Poor hare,' said Shyam. 'Its life was short.'

'That's the law of the jungle,' said Ramu. 'The eagle has a family too, and must feed it.'

'I wonder if we are any better than animals,' said Shyam.

'Perhaps we are a little better,' said Ramu. 'Grandfather always says, "To be able to laugh and to be merciful are the only things that make man better than the beast".'

∽

The next day, while the boys were taking the herd home, one of the buffaloes lagged behind. Ramu did not know the animal was missing until he heard her agonized bellow. He glanced over his shoulder just in time to see the big striped tiger dragging the buffalo into a clump of young bamboo. At the same time the herd became aware of the danger, and the buffaloes snorted with fear as they hurried along the forest path. To urge them forward, and to warn his friends, Ramu cupped his hands to his mouth and gave vent to a yodelling call.

The buffaloes bellowed, the boys shouted, and the birds flew shrieking from the trees. It was almost a stampede by the time the herd emerged from the forest. The villagers heard the thunder of hoofs, and saw the herd coming home in dust and confusion, and knew that something was wrong. 'The tiger!' shouted Ramu. 'He is here! He has killed one of the buffaloes.'

'He is afraid of us no longer,' said Shyam.

'Did you see where he went?' asked Kundan Singh, hurrying up to them.

'I remember the place,' said Ramu. 'He dragged the buffalo in amongst the bamboo.'

'Then there is no time to lose,' said his father.

'Kundan, you take your gun and two men, and wait near the suspension bridge, where the Garur stream joins the Ganga. The jungle narrows there. We will beat the jungle from our side, and drive the tiger towards you. He will not escape us, unless he swims the river!'

'Good!' said Kundan, running into his house for his gun, with Shyam close at his heels. 'Was it one of our buffaloes again?' he asked.

'It was Ramu's buffalo this time,' said Shyam, 'A good milk buffalo.'

'Then Ramu's father will beat the jungle thoroughly. You boys had better come with me. It will not be safe for you to accompany the beaters.'

~

And so, Kundan Singh carrying his gun and accompanied by Ramu, Shyam and two men, headed for the river junction, while Ramu's father collected about twenty men from the village and, guided by one of the boys who had been with Ramu, made for the spot where the tiger had killed the buffalo.

The tiger was still eating when he heard the men coming. He had not expected to be disturbed so soon. With an angry 'Whoof!' he bounded into the bamboo thicket and watched the men through a screen of leaves and tall grass.

The men did not seem to take much notice of the dead buffalo, but gathered round their leader and held a consultation. Most of them carried hand drums which hung down to their waists by shoulder-straps. They also carried sticks, spears and axes.

After a hurried conversation, they turned to face the jungle and began beating their drums with the palms of their hands.

Some of the men banged empty kerosene tins. These made even more noise than the drums.

The tiger did not like the noise and retreated further into the jungle. But he was surprised to find that the men, instead of going away, came after him into the jungle, banging away on their drums and tins, and shouting at the top of their voices. They had separated now, and advanced singly or in pairs, but nowhere were they more than fifteen yards apart. The tiger could easily have broken through this slowly advancing semicircle of men—one swift blow from his paw would have felled the strongest of them—but his main aim was to get away from the noise. He hated and feared the noise made by men.

He was not a man-eater and he would not attack a man unless he was very angry or very frightened or very desperate; and he was none of these things as yet. He had eaten well, and he would like to rest in peace—but there would be no rest for any animal until the men had gone with their tremendous clatter and din.

For an hour Ramu's father and the others beat the jungle, calling, drumming and trampling the undergrowth. The tiger had no rest. Whenever he was able to put some distance between himself and the men, he would sink down in some shady spot to rest, but, within five or ten minutes, the trampling and drumming would sound nearer, and the tiger, with an angry snarl, would get up and pad silently north along the narrowing strip of jungle, towards the junction of the Garur stream and the Ganga. Ten years back, he would have had jungle on his right in which to hide; but the trees had been felled long ago, to make way for more humans, and now he could only move to the left, towards the river.

It was about noon when the tiger finally appeared in the open. He longed for the darkness and security of the night, for the sun was his enemy. Kundan and the boys had a clear view of him as he stalked slowly along, now in the open with the sun glinting on his glossy side, now in the shade, or passing through the shorter reeds. He was still out of range of Kundan's gun, but there was no fear of his getting out of the beat, as the 'stops' were all picked men from the village. He disappeared among some bushes but soon reappeared to retrace his steps, the beaters having done their work well. He was now only one hundred and fifty yards from the rocks where Kundan Singh waited, and he looked very big.

The beat had closed in, and his exit along the bank downstream was completely blocked; so the tiger turned into a belt of reeds, and Kundan Singh expected that his head would soon peer out of the cover a few yards away. The beaters were now making a great noise, shouting and beating their drums, but nothing moved, and Ramu, watching from a distance, wondered, 'Has he slipped through the beaters?' And hoped he had.

Tins clashed, drums beat, and some of the men poked into the reeds with their spears or long bamboos. Perhaps one of these thrusts found a mark, because at last the tiger was roused, and with an angry, desperate snarl he charged out of the reeds, splashing his way through an inlet of mud and water.

Kundan Singh fired, and his bullet struck the tiger on the thigh.

The mighty animal stumbled; but he was up in a minute, and, rushing through a gap in the narrowing line of beaters, he made straight for the only way across the river—the suspension bridge that passed over the Ganga here, providing a route into the high hills beyond.

'We'll get him now,' said Kundan, priming his gun again. 'He's right in the open!'

The suspension bridge swayed and trembled as the wounded tiger lurched across it. Kundan fired, and this time the bullet hit the tiger on the shoulder. The animal bounded forward, lost his footing on the unfamiliar, slippery planks of the swaying bridge, and went over the side, falling headlong into the strong, swirling waters of the river.

He rose to the surface once, but the current took him under and away, and only a thin streak of blood remained on the river's surface.

Kundan and the others hurried downstream to see if the dead tiger had been washed up on the river's banks; but though they searched the riverside for several miles, they did not find the tiger. The river had taken him to its bosom. He had not provided anyone with a trophy. His skin would not be spread on a couch, nor would his head be hung upon a wall. No claw of his would be hung as a charm around the neck of a child. No villager would use his fat as a cure for rheumatism.

∽

At first the villagers were glad because they felt their buffaloes were safe. Then the men began to feel that something had gone out of their lives, out of the life of the forest; they began to feel that the forest was no longer a forest. It had been shrinking year after year, but, as long as the tiger had been there and the villagers had heard it roar at night, they had known that they were still secure from the intruders and newcomers who came to fell the trees and eat up the land and let the floodwaters into the village. But, now that the tiger had gone, it was as though a protector had gone, leaving the forest open and vulnerable, easily destroyable. And, once the forest was destroyed, they too would be in danger…

There was another thing that had gone with the tiger, another thing that had been lost, a thing that was being lost everywhere—something called 'nobility'.

Ramu remembered something that his grandfather had once said, 'The tiger is the very soul of India, and when the last tiger has gone, so will the soul of the country.'

The boys lay flat on their stomachs on their little mud island and watched the monsoon clouds gathering overhead.

'The king of our forest is dead,' said Shyam. 'There are no more tigers.'

'There must be tigers,' said Ramu. 'How can there be an India without tigers?'

The river had carried the tiger many miles away from its home, from the forest it had always known, and brought it ashore on a strip of warm yellow sand, where it lay in the sun, quite still but breathing.

Vultures gathered and waited at a distance, some of them perching on the branches of nearby trees.

But the tiger was more drowned than hurt, and as the river water oozed out of his mouth, and the warm sun made new life throb through his body, he stirred and stretched, and his glazed eyes came into focus. Raising his head, he saw trees and tall grass.

Slowly he heaved himself off the ground and moved at a crouch to where the grass waved in the afternoon breeze. Would he be harried again, and shot at? There was no smell of Man. The tiger moved forward with greater confidence.

There was, however, another smell in the air—a smell that reached back to the time when he was young and fresh and full of vigour—a smell that he had almost forgotten but could never quite forget—the smell of a tigress!

He raised his head high, and new life surged through his tired limbs. He gave a full-throated roar and moved purposefully through the tall grass. And the roar came back to him, calling him, calling him forward—a roar that meant there would be more tigers in the land.

ANGRY RIVER

In the middle of the big river, the river that began in the mountains and ended in the sea, was a small island. The river swept round the island, sometimes clawing at its banks, but never going right over it. It was over twenty years since the river had flooded the island, and at that time no one had lived there. But for the last ten years a small hut had stood there, a mud-walled hut with a sloping thatched roof. The hut had been built into a huge rock, so only three of the walls were mud, and the fourth was rock.

Goats grazed on the short grass which grew on the island, and on the prickly leaves of thorn bushes. A few hens followed them about. There was a melon patch and a vegetable patch. In the middle of the island stood a peepul tree. It was the only tree there. Even during the Great Flood, when the island had been under water, the tree had stood firm.

It was an old tree. A seed had been carried to the island by a strong wind some fifty years back, had found shelter between two rocks, had taken root there, and had sprung up to give shade and shelter to a small family; and Indians love peepul trees, especially during the hot summer months when the heart-shaped leaves catch the least breath of air and flutter eagerly, fanning those who sit beneath.

A sacred tree, the peepul: the abode of spirits, good and bad.

'Don't yawn when you are sitting beneath the tree,' Grandmother used to warn Sita.

'And if you must yawn, always snap your fingers in front of your mouth. If you forget to do that, a spirit might jump down your throat!'

'And then what will happen?' asked Sita.

'It will probably ruin your digestion,' said Grandfather, who wasn't much of a believer in spirits.

The peepul had a beautiful leaf, and Grandmother likened it to the body of the mighty god Krishna—broad at the shoulders, then tapering down to a very slim waist.

It was an old tree, and an old man sat beneath it. He was mending a fishing net. He had fished in the river for ten years, and he was a good fisherman. He knew where to find the slim silver chilwa fish and the big beautiful mahseer and the long-moustached singhara; he knew where the river was deep and where it was shallow; he knew which baits to use—which fish liked worms and which liked gram. He had taught his son to fish, but his son had gone to work in a factory in a city, nearly a hundred miles away. He had no grandson; but he had a granddaughter, Sita, and she could do all the things a boy could do, and sometimes she could do them better. She had lost her mother when she was very small. Grandmother had taught her all the things a girl should know, and she could do these as well as most girls. But neither of her grandparents could read or write, and as a result Sita couldn't read or write either.

There was a school in one of the villages across the river, but Sita had never seen it. There was too much to do on the island.

While Grandfather mended his net, Sita was inside the hut, pressing her Grandmother's forehead, which was hot with fever. Grandmother had been ill for three days and could not eat. She had been ill before, but she had never been so bad. Grandfather had brought her some sweet oranges from the market in the nearest town, and she could suck the juice from the oranges, but she couldn't eat anything else.

She was younger than Grandfather, but because she was sick, she looked much older. She had never been very strong.

When Sita noticed that Grandmother had fallen asleep, she tiptoed out of the room on her bare feet and stood outside.

The sky was dark with monsoon clouds. It had rained all night, and in a few hours it would rain again. The monsoon rains had come early, at the end of June. Now it was the middle of July, and already the river was swollen. Its rushing sound seemed nearer and more menacing than usual.

Site went to her grandfather and sat down beside him beneath the peepul tree.

'When you are hungry, tell me,' she said, 'and I will make the bread.'

'Is your grandmother asleep?'

'She sleeps. But she will wake soon, for she has a deep pain.'

The old man stared out across the river, at the dark green of the forest, at the grey sky, and said, 'Tomorrow, if she is not better, I will take her to the hospital at Shahganj. There they will know how to make her well. You may be on your own for a few days—but you have been on your own before…'

Sita nodded gravely; she had been alone before, even during the rainy season. Now she wanted Grandmother to get well, and she knew that only Grandfather had the skill to take the small dugout boat across the river when the current was so strong. Someone would have to stay behind to look after their few possessions.

Sita was not afraid of being alone, but she did not like the look of the river. That morning, when she had gone down to fetch water, she had noticed that the level had risen. Those rocks which were normally spattered with the droppings of snipe and curlew and other water birds had suddenly disappeared.

They disappeared every year—but not so soon, surely?

'Grandfather, if the river rises, what will I do?'

'You will keep to the high ground.'

'And if the water reaches the high ground?'

'Then take the hens into the hut, and stay there.'

'And if the water comes into the hut?'

'Then climb into the peepul tree. It is a strong tree. It will not fall. And the water cannot rise higher than the tree!'

'And the goats, Grandfather?'

'I will be taking them with me, Sita. I may have to sell them to pay for good food and medicines for your grandmother. As for the hens, if it becomes necessary, put them on the roof. But do not worry too much'—and he patted Sita's head—'the water will not rise as high. I will be back soon, remember that.'

'And won't Grandmother come back?'

'Yes, of course, but they may keep her in the hospital for some time.'

~

Towards evening, it began to rain again—big pellets of rain, scarring the surface of the river. But it was warm rain, and Sita could move about in it. She was not afraid of getting wet, she rather liked it. In the previous month, when the first monsoon shower had arrived, washing the dusty leaves of the tree and bringing up the good smell of the earth, she had exulted in it, had run about shouting for joy. She was used to it now, and indeed a little tired of the rain, but she did not mind getting wet. It was steamy indoors, and her thin dress would soon dry in the heat from the kitchen fire.

She walked about barefooted, barelegged. She was very sure on her feet; her toes had grown accustomed to gripping all kinds of rocks, slippery or sharp. And though thin, she was surprisingly strong.

Black hair streaming across her face. Black eyes. Slim brown arms. A scar on her thigh—when she was small, visiting her mother's village, a hyena had entered the house where she was sleeping, fastened on to her leg and tried to drag her away, but her screams had roused the villagers and the hyena had run off.

She moved about in the pouring rain, chasing the hens into a shelter behind the hut. A harmless brown snake, flooded out of its hole, was moving across the open ground. Sita picked up a stick, scooped the snake up, and dropped it between a cluster of rocks. She had no quarrel with snakes. They kept down the rats and the frogs. She wondered how the rats had first come to the island—probably in someone's boat, or in a sack of grain. Now it was a job to keep their numbers down.

When Sita finally went indoors, she was hungry. She ate some dried peas and warmed up some goat's milk. Grandmother woke once and asked for water, and Grandfather held the brass tumbler to her lips.

~

It rained all night.

The roof was leaking, and a small puddle formed on the floor. They kept the kerosene lamp alight. They did not need the light, but somehow it made them feel safer.

The sound of the river had always been with them, although they were seldom aware of it; but that night they noticed a change in its sound. There was something like a moan, like a wind in the tops of tall trees and a swift hiss as the water swept round the rocks and carried away pebbles. And sometimes there was a rumble, as loose earth fell into the water.

Sita could not sleep.

She had a rag doll, made with Grandmother's help out of bits of old clothing. She kept it by her side every night. The doll was someone to talk to, when the nights were long and sleep elusive. Her grandparents were often ready to talk—and Grandmother, when she was well, was a good storyteller—but sometimes Sita wanted to have secrets, and though there were no special secrets in her life, she made up a few, because it was fun to have them. And if you have secrets, you must have a friend to share them with, a companion of one's own age. Since there were no other children on the island, Sita shared her secrets with the rag doll whose name was Mumta.

Grandfather and Grandmother were asleep, though the sound of Grandmother's laboured breathing was almost as persistent as the sound of the river.

'Mumta,' whispered Sita in the dark, starting one of her private conversations.

'Do you think Grandmother will get well again?'

Mumta always answered Sita's questions, even though the answers could only be heard by Sita.

'She is very old,' said Mumta.

'Do you think the river will reach the hut?' asked Sita.

'If it keeps raining like this, and the river keeps rising, it will reach the hut.'

'I am a little afraid of the river, Mumta. Aren't you afraid?'

'Don't be afraid. The river has always been good to us.'

'What will we do if it comes into the hut?'

'We will climb on to the roof.'

'And if it reaches the roof?'

'We will climb the peepul tree. The river has never gone higher than the peepul tree.'

As soon as the first light showed through the little skylight, Sita got up and went outside. It wasn't raining hard, it was drizzling, but it was the sort of drizzle that could continue for days, and it probably meant that heavy rain was falling in the hills where the river originated.

Sita went down to the water's edge. She couldn't find her favourite rock, the one on which she often sat dangling her feet in the water, watching the little chilwa fish swim by. It was still there, no doubt, but the river had gone over it.

She stood on the sand, and she could feel the water oozing and bubbling beneath her feet.

The river was no longer green and blue and flecked with white, but a muddy colour.

She went back to the hut. Grandfather was up now. He was getting his boat ready.

Sita milked a goat. Perhaps it was the last time she would milk it.

∽

The sun was just coming up when Grandfather pushed off in the boat. Grandmother lay in the prow. She was staring hard at Sita, trying to speak, but the words would not come. She raised her hand in a blessing.

Sita bent and touched her grandmother's feet, and then Grandfather pushed off. The little boat—with its two old people and three goats—riding swiftly on the river, moved slowly, very slowly, towards the opposite bank. The current was so swift now that Sita realized the boat would be carried about half a mile downstream before Grandfather could get it to dry land.

It bobbed about on the water, getting smaller and smaller, until it was just a speck on the broad river.

And suddenly Sita was alone.

There was a wind, whipping the raindrops against her face; and there was the water, rushing past the island; and there was the distant shore, blurred by rain; and there was the small hut; and there was the tree.

Sita got busy. The hens had to be fed. They weren't bothered about anything except food. Sita threw them handfuls of coarse grain and potato peelings and peanut shells.

Then she took the broom and swept out the hut, lit the charcoal burner, warmed some milk, and thought, 'Tomorrow there will be no milk...' She began peeling onions. Soon her eyes started smarting and, pausing for a few moments and glancing round the quiet room, she became aware again that she was alone. Grandfather's hookah stood by itself in one corner. It was a beautiful old hookah, which had belonged to Sita's great-grandfather. The bowl was made out of a coconut encased in silver. The long winding stem was at least four feet in length. It was their most valuable possession. Grandmother's sturdy shisham-wood walking stick stood in another corner.

Sita looked around for Mumta, found the doll beneath the cot, and placed her within sight and hearing.

Thunder rolled down from the hills. BOOM—BOOM—BOOM...

'The gods of the mountains are angry,' said Sita.

'Do you think they are angry with me?'

'Why should they be angry with you?' asked Mumta.

'They don't have to have a reason for being angry. They are angry with everything, and we are in the middle of everything. We are so small—do you think they know we are here?'

'Who knows what the gods think?'

'But I made you,' said Sita, 'and I know you are here.'

'And will you save me if the river rises?'

'Yes, of course. I won't go anywhere without you, Mumta.'

Sita couldn't stay indoors for long. She went out, taking Mumta with her, and stared out across the river, to the safe land on the other side. But was it safe there? The river looked much wider now. Yes, it had crept over its banks and spread far across the flat plain. Far away, people were driving their cattle through waterlogged, flooded fields, carrying their belongings in bundles on their heads or shoulders, leaving their homes, making for the high land. It wasn't safe anywhere.

She wondered what had happened to Grandfather and

Grandmother. If they had reached the shore safely, Grandfather would have to engage a bullock cart, or a pony-drawn carriage, to get Grandmother to the district town, five or six miles away, where there was a market, a court, a jail, a cinema and a hospital.

She wondered if she would ever see Grandmother again. She had done her best to look after the old lady, remembering the times when Grandmother had looked after her, had gently touched her fevered brow and had told her stories—stories about the gods: about the young Krishna, friend of birds and animals, so full of mischief, always causing confusion among the other gods; and Indra, who made the thunder and lightning; and Vishnu, the preserver of all good things, whose steed was a great white bird; and Ganesh, with the elephant's head; and Hanuman, the monkey god, who helped the young Prince Rama in his war with the King of Ceylon. Would Grandmother return to tell her more about them, or would she have to find out for herself?

The island looked much smaller now. In parts, the mud banks had dissolved quickly, sinking into the river. But in the middle of the island there was rocky ground, and the rocks would never crumble, they could only be submerged. In a space in the middle of the rocks grew the tree.

Sita climbed up the tree to get a better view. She had climbed the tree many times and it took her only a few seconds to reach the higher branches. She put her hand to her eyes to shield them from the rain, and gazed upstream.

There was water everywhere. The world had become one vast river. Even the trees on the forested side of the river looked as though they had grown from the water, like mangroves. The sky was banked with massive, moisture-laden clouds. Thunder rolled down from the hills and the river seemed to take it up with a hollow booming sound.

Something was floating down with the current, something big and bloated. It was closer now, and Sita could make out the bulky object—a drowned buffalo, being carried rapidly downstream.

So the water had already inundated the villages further upstream. Or perhaps the buffalo had been grazing too close to the rising river.

Sita's worst fears were confirmed when, a little later, she saw planks of wood, small trees and bushes, and then a wooden bedstead, floating past the island.

How long would it take for the river to reach her own small hut?

As she climbed down from the tree, it began to rain more heavily. She ran indoors, shooing the hens before her. They flew into the hut and huddled under Grandmother's cot. Sita thought it would be best to keep them together now. And having them with her took away some of the loneliness.

There were three hens and a cock bird. The river did not bother them. They were interested only in food, and Sita kept them happy by throwing them a handful of onion skins.

She would have liked to close the door and shut out the swish of the rain and the boom of the river, but then she would have no way of knowing how fast the water rose.

She took Mumta in her arms, and began praying for the rain to stop and the river to fall. She prayed to the god Indra, and, just in case he was busy elsewhere, she prayed to other gods too. She prayed for the safety of her grandparents and for her own safety. She put herself last but only with great difficulty.

She would have to make herself a meal. So she chopped up some onions, fried them, then added turmeric and red chilli powder and stirred until she had everything sizzling; then she added a tumbler of water, some salt, and a cup of one of the cheaper lentils. She covered the pot and allowed the mixture to simmer. Doing this took Sita about ten minutes. It would take at least half an hour for the dish to be ready.

When she looked outside, she saw pools of water amongst the rocks and near the tree. She couldn't tell if it was rain water or overflow from the river.

She had an idea.

A big tin trunk stood in a corner of the room. It had belonged to Sita's mother. There was nothing in it except a cotton-filled quilt, for use during the cold weather. She would stuff the trunk with everything useful or valuable, and weigh it down so that it wouldn't be carried away— just in case the river came over the island...

Grandfather's hookah went into the trunk. Grandmother's walking stick went in too. So did a number of small tins containing the spices used in cooking—nutmeg, caraway seed, cinnamon, coriander and pepper—a bigger tin of flour and a tin of raw sugar. Even if Sita had to spend several hours in the tree, there would be something to eat when she came down again.

A clean white cotton shirt of Grandfather's, and Grandmother's only spare sari also went into the trunk. Never mind if they got stained with yellow curry powder! Never mind if they got to smell of salted fish, some of that went in too.

Sita was so busy packing the trunk that she paid no attention to the lick of cold water at her heels. She locked the trunk, placed the key high on the rock wall, and turned to give her attention to the lentils. It was only then that she discovered that she was walking about on a watery floor.

She stood still, horrified by what she saw. The water was oozing over the threshold, pushing its way into the room.

Sita was filled with panic. She forgot about her meal and everything else. Darting out of the hut, she ran splashing through ankle-deep water towards the safety of the peepul tree. If the tree hadn't been there, such a well-known landmark, she might have floundered into deep water, into the river.

She climbed swiftly into the strong arms of the tree, made herself secure on a familiar branch, and thrust the wet hair away from her eyes.

∽

She was glad she had hurried. The hut was now surrounded by water. Only the higher parts of the island could still be seen—a few rocks, the big rock on which the hut was built, a hillock on which some thorny bilberry bushes grew.

The hens hadn't bothered to leave the hut. They were probably perched on the cot now.

Would the river rise still higher? Sita had never seen it like this before. It swirled around her, stretching in all directions.

More drowned cattle came floating down. The most unusual

things went by on the water—an aluminium kettle, a cane chair, a tin of tooth powder, an empty cigarette packet, a wooden slipper, a plastic doll…

A doll!

With a sinking feeling, Sita remembered Mumta.

Poor Mumta! She had been left behind in the hut. Sita, in her hurry, had forgotten her only companion.

Well, thought Sita, if I can be careless with someone I've made, how can I expect the gods to notice me, alone in the middle of the river?

The waters were higher now, the island fast disappearing.

Something came floating out of the hut.

It was an empty kerosene tin, with one of the hens perched on top. The tin came bobbing along on the water, not far from the tree, and was then caught by the current and swept into the river. The hen still managed to keep its perch.

A little later, the water must have reached the cot because the remaining hens flew up to the rock ledge and sat huddled there in the small recess.

The water was rising rapidly now, and all that remained of the island was the big rock that supported the hut, the top of the hut itself and the peepul tree.

It was a tall tree with many branches and it seemed unlikely that the water could ever go right over it. But how long would Sita have to remain there? She climbed a little higher, and as she did so, a jet-black jungle crow settled in the upper branches, and Sita saw that there was a nest in them—a crow's nest, an untidy platform of twigs wedged in the fork of a branch.

In the nest were four blue-green, speckled eggs. The crow sat on them and cawed disconsolately. But though the crow was miserable, its presence brought some cheer to Sita. At least she was not alone. Better to have a crow for company than no one at all.

Other things came floating out of the hut—a large pumpkin; a red turban belonging to Grandfather, unwinding in the water like a long snake; and then—Mumta! The doll, being filled with straw and wood shavings, moved quite swiftly on the water and passed close to the peepul tree. Sita saw it and wanted to call out, to urge her friend to make for the tree, but she knew that Mumta could not swim—the doll could only float, travel with the river, and perhaps be washed ashore many miles downstream.

The tree shook in the wind and the rain. The crow cawed and flew up, circled the tree a few times and returned to the nest. Sita clung to her branch.

The tree trembled throughout its tall frame. To Sita it felt like an earthquake tremor; she felt the shudder of the tree in her own bones.

The river swirled all around her now. It was almost up to the roof of the hut. Soon the mud walls would crumble and vanish. Except for the big rock and some trees far, far away, there was only water to be seen.

For a moment or two Sita glimpsed a boat with several people in it moving sluggishly away from the ruins of a flooded village, and she thought she saw someone pointing towards her, but the river swept them on and the boat was lost to view.

The river was very angry; it was like a wild beast, a dragon on the rampage, thundering down from the hills and sweeping across the plain, bringing with it dead animals, uprooted trees, household goods and huge fish choked to death by the swirling mud.

The tall old peepul tree groaned. Its long, winding roots clung tenaciously to the earth from which the tree had sprung many, many years ago. But the earth was softening; the stones were being washed away. The roots of the tree were rapidly losing their hold.

The crow must have known that something was wrong, because it kept flying up and circling the tree, reluctant to settle in it and reluctant to fly away. As long as the nest was there, the crow would remain, flapping about and cawing in alarm.

Sita's wet cotton dress clung to her thin body. The rain ran down from her long black hair. It poured from every leaf of the tree. The crow, too, was drenched and groggy.

The tree groaned and moved again. It had seen many monsoons. Once before, it had stood firm while the river had swirled around its massive trunk. But it had been young then. Now, old in years and tired of standing still, the tree was ready to join the river.

With a flurry of its beautiful leaves, and a surge of mud from below, the tree left its place in the earth, and, tilting, moved slowly forward, turning a little from side to side, dragging its roots along the ground. To Sita, it seemed as though the river was rising to meet the sky.

Then the tree moved into the main current of the river, and went a little faster, swinging Sita from side to side. Her feet were in the water but she clung tenaciously to her branch.

∽

The branches swayed, but Sita did not lose her grip. The water was very close now. Sita was frightened. She could not see the extent of the flood or the width of the river. She could only see the immediate danger—the water surrounding the tree.

The crow kept flying around the tree. The bird was in a terrible rage. The nest was still in the branches, but not for long… The tree lurched and twisted slightly to one side, and the nest fell into the water. Sita saw the eggs go one by one.

The crow swooped low over the water, but there was nothing it could do. In a few moments, the nest had disappeared.

The bird followed the tree for about fifty yards, as though hoping that something still remained in the tree. Then, flapping its wings, it rose high into the air and flew across the river until it was out of sight.

Sita was alone once more. But there was no time for feeling lonely. Everything was in motion—up and down and sideways and forwards. 'Any moment,' thought Sita, 'the tree will turn right over and I'll be in the water!'

She saw a turtle swimming past—a great river turtle, the kind that feeds on decaying flesh. Sita turned her face away. In the distance she saw a flooded village and people in flat-bottomed boats but they were very far away.

Because of its great size, the tree did not move very swiftly on the river. Sometimes, when it passed into shallow water, it stopped, its roots catching in the rocks; but not for long—the river's momentum soon swept it on.

At one place, where there was a bend in the river, the tree struck a sandbank and was still.

Sita felt very tired. Her arms were aching and she was no longer upright. With the tree almost on its side, she had to cling tightly to her branch to avoid falling off.

The grey weeping sky was like a great shifting dome. She knew she could not remain much longer in that position. It might be better to try swimming to some distant rooftop or tree. Then she heard someone calling.

Craning her neck to look upriver, she was able to make out a small boat coming directly towards her.

The boat approached the tree. There was a boy in the boat who held on to one of the branches to steady himself, giving his free hand to Sita. She grasped it, and slipped into the boat beside him. The boy placed his bare foot against the tree trunk and pushed away. The little boat moved swiftly down the river. The big tree was left far behind. Sita would never see it again.

~

She lay stretched out in the boat, too frightened to talk. The boy looked at her, but he did not say anything, he did not even smile. He lay on his two small oars, stroking smoothly, rhythmically, trying to keep from going into the middle of the river. He wasn't strong enough to get the boat right out of the swift current, but he kept trying.

A small boat on a big river—a river that had no boundaries but which reached across the plains in all directions. The boat moved swiftly on the wild waters, and Sita's home was left far behind.

The boy wore only a loincloth. A sheathed knife was knotted into his waistband. He was a slim, wiry boy, with a hard flat belly; he had high cheekbones, strong white teeth. He was a little darker than Sita.

'You live on the island,' he said at last, resting on his oars and allowing the boat to drift a little, for he had reached a broader, more placid stretch of the river.

'I have seen you sometimes. But where are the others?'

'My grandmother was sick,' said Sita, 'so Grandfather took her to the hospital in Shahganj.'

'When did they leave?'

'Early this morning.'

Only that morning—and yet it seemed to Sita as though it had been many mornings ago.

'Where have you come from?' she asked. She had never seen the boy before.

'I come from…' he hesitated, '…near the foothills. I was in my boat, trying to get across the river with the news that one of the villages was badly flooded, but the current was too strong. I was swept down past your island. We cannot fight the river, we must go wherever it takes us.'

'You must be tired. Give me the oars.'

'No. There is not much to do now, except keep the boat steady.'

He brought in one oar, and with his free hand he felt under the seat where there was a small basket. He produced two mangoes, and gave one to Sita.

They bit deep into the ripe fleshy mangoes, using their teeth to tear the skin away. The sweet juice trickled down their chins. The flavour of the fruit was heavenly—truly this was the nectar of the gods!

Sita hadn't tasted a mango for over a year. For a few moments she forgot about the flood—all that mattered was the mango!

The boat drifted, but not so swiftly now, for as they went further away across the plains, the river lost much of its tremendous force.

'My name is Krishan,' said the boy. 'My father has many cows and buffaloes, but several have been lost in the flood.'

'I suppose you go to school,' said Sita.

'Yes, I am supposed to go to school. There is one not far from our village. Do you have to go to school?'

'No—there is too much work at home.'

It was no use wishing she was at home—home wouldn't be there any more—but she wished, at that moment, that she had another mango.

Towards evening, the river changed colour. The sun, low in the sky, emerged from behind the clouds, and the river changed slowly from grey to gold, from gold to a deep orange, and then, as the sun went down, all these colours were drowned in the river, and the river took on the colour of the night.

The moon was almost at the full and Sita could see across the river, to where the trees grew on its banks.

'I will try to reach the trees,' said the boy, Krishan.

'We do not want to spend the night on the water, do we?'

And so he pulled for the trees. After ten minutes of strenuous rowing, he reached a turn in the river and was able to escape the pull of the main current. Soon they were in a forest, rowing between tall evergreens.

∽

They moved slowly now, paddling between the trees, and the moon lighted their way, making a crooked silver path over the water.

'We will tie the boat to one of these trees,' said Krishan.

'Then we can rest. Tomorrow we will have to find our way out of the forest.'

He produced a length of rope from the bottom of the boat, tied one end to the boat's stern and threw the other end over a stout branch which hung only a few feet above the water. The boat came to rest against the trunk of the tree.

It was a tall, sturdy toon tree—the Indian mahogany—and it was quite safe, for there was no rush of water here; besides, the trees grew close together, making the earth firm and unyielding.

But the denizens of the forest were on the move.

The animals had been flooded out of their holes, caves and lairs, and were looking for shelter and dry ground.

Sita and Krishan had barely finished tying the boat to the tree when they saw a huge python gliding over the water towards them. Sita was afraid that it might try to get into the boat; but it went past them, its head above water, its great awesome length trailing behind, until it was lost in the shadows.

Krishan had more mangoes in the basket, and he and Sita sucked hungrily on them while they sat in the boat.

A big sambar stag came thrashing through the water. He did not have to swim; he was so tall that his head and shoulders remained well above the water. His antlers were big and beautiful.

'There will be other animals,' said Sita. 'Should we climb into the tree?'

'We are quite safe in the boat,' said Krishan.

'The animals are interested only in reaching dry land. They will not even hunt each other. Tonight, the deer are safe from the panther and the tiger. So lie down and sleep, and I will keep watch.'

Sita stretched herself out in the boat and closed her eyes, and the sound of the water lapping against the sides of the boat soon lulled her to sleep. She woke once, when a strange bird called overhead. She raised herself on one elbow, but Krishan was awake, sitting in the prow, and he smiled reassuringly at her.

He looked blue in the moonlight, the colour of the young god Krishna, and for a few moments Sita was confused and wondered if the boy was indeed Krishna; but when she thought about it, she decided that it wasn't possible. He was just a village boy and she had seen hundreds like him—well, not exactly like him; he was different, in a way she couldn't explain to herself...

And when she slept again, she dreamt that the boy and Krishna were one, and that she was sitting beside him on a great white bird which flew over mountains, over the snow peaks of the Himalayas, into the cloudland of the gods. There was a great rumbling sound, as though the gods were angry about the whole thing, and she woke up to this terrible sound and looked about her, and there in the moonlit glade, up to his belly in water, stood a young elephant, his trunk raised as he trumpeted his predicament to the forest—for he was a young elephant, and he was lost, and he was looking for his mother.

He trumpeted again, and then lowered his head and listened. And presently, from far away, came the shrill trumpeting of another elephant. It must have been the young one's mother, because he gave several excited trumpet calls, and then went stamping and churning through the flood water towards a gap in the trees. The boat rocked in the waves made by his passing.

'It's all right now,' said Krishan. 'You can go to sleep again.'

'I don't think I will sleep now,' said Sita.

'Then I will play my flute for you,' said the boy, 'and the time will pass more quickly.'

From the bottom of the boat he took a flute, and putting it to his lips, he began to play. The sweetest music that Sita had ever heard came pouring from the little flute, and it seemed to fill the forest with its beautiful sound. And the music carried her away again, into the land of dreams, and they were riding on the bird once more, Sita and the blue god, and they were passing through clouds and mist, until suddenly the sun shot out through the clouds. And at the same moment, Sita opened her eyes and saw the sun streaming through the branches of the toon tree, its bright green leaves making a dark pattern against the blinding blue of the sky.

Sita sat up with a start, rocking the boat. There were hardly any clouds left. The trees were drenched with sunshine.

The boy Krishan was fast asleep at the bottom of the boat. His flute lay in the palm of his half-opened hand. The sun came slanting across his bare brown legs. A leaf had fallen on his upturned face, but it had not woken him, it lay on his cheek as though it had grown there.

Sita did not move again. She did not want to wake the boy. It didn't look as though the water had gone down, but it hadn't risen, and that meant the flood had spent itself.

The warmth of the sun, as it crept up Krishan's body, woke him at last. He yawned, stretched his limbs, and sat up beside Sita.

'I'm hungry,' he said with a smile.

'So am I,' said Sita.

'The last mangoes,' he said, and emptied the basket of its last two mangoes.

After they had finished the fruit, they sucked the big seeds until they were quite dry. The discarded seeds floated well on the water. Sita had always preferred them to paper boats.

'We had better move on,' said Krishan.

He rowed the boat through the trees, and then for about an hour they were passing through the flooded forest, under the dripping branches of rain-washed trees.

Sometimes they had to use the oars to push away vines and creepers. Sometimes drowned bushes hampered them. But they were out of the forest before noon.

Now the water was not very deep and they were gliding over flooded fields. In the distance they saw a village. It was on high ground. In the old days, people had built their villages on hilltops, which gave them a better defence against bandits and invading armies.

This was an old village, and though its inhabitants had long ago exchanged their swords for pruning forks, the hill on which it stood now protected it from the flood.

The people of the village—long-limbed, sturdy Jats—were generous, and gave the stranded children food and shelter. Sita was anxious to find her grandparents, and an old farmer who had business in Shahganj offered to take her there. She was hoping that Krishan would accompany her, but he said he would wait in the village, where he knew others would soon be arriving, his own people among them.

'You will be all right now,' said Krishan.

'Your grandfather will be anxious for you, so it is best that you go to him as soon as you can. And in two or three days, the water will go down and you will be able to return to the island.'

'Perhaps the island has gone forever,' said Sita.

As she climbed into the farmer's bullock cart, Krishan handed her his flute.

'Please keep it for me,' he said. 'I will come for it one day.'

And when he saw her hesitate, he added, his eyes twinkling, 'It is a good flute!'

∽

It was slow going in the bullock cart. The road was awash, the wheels got stuck in the mud, and the farmer, his grown son and Sita had to keep getting down to heave and push in order to free the big wooden wheels.

They were still in a foot or two of water. The bullocks were bespattered with mud, and Sita's legs were caked with it.

They were a day and a night in the bullock cart before they reached Shahganj; by that time, Sita, walking down the narrow bazaar of the busy market town, was hardly recognizable.

Grandfather did not recognize her. He was walking stiffly down the road, looking straight ahead of him, and would have walked right past the dusty, dishevelled girl if she had not charged straight at his thin, shaky legs and clasped him around the waist.

'Sita!' he cried, when he had recovered his wind and his balance. 'But how are you here? How did you get off the island? I was so worried—it has been very bad these last two days…'

'Is Grandmother all right?' asked Sita.

But even as she spoke, she knew that Grandmother was no longer with them. The dazed look in the old man's eyes told her as much. She wanted to cry, not for Grandmother, who could suffer no more, but for Grandfather, who looked so helpless and bewildered; she did not want him to be unhappy. She forced back her tears, took his gnarled and trembling hand, and led him down the crowded street. And she knew, then, that it would be on her shoulder that Grandfather would have to lean in the years to come.

They returned to the island after a few days, when the river was no longer in spate. There was more rain, but the worst was over. Grandfather still had two of the goats; it had not been necessary to sell more than one.

He could hardly believe his eyes when he saw that the tree had disappeared from the island—the tree that had seemed as permanent as the island, as much a part of his life as the river itself. He marvelled at Sita's escape.

'It was the tree that saved you,' he said.

'And the boy,' said Sita.

Yes, and the boy.

She thought about the boy, and wondered if she would ever see him again. But she did not think too much, because there was so much to do.

For three nights they slept under a crude shelter made out of jute bags. During the day she helped Grandfather rebuild the mud hut. Once again, they used the big rock as a support.

The trunk which Sita had packed so carefully had not been swept off the island, but the water had got into it, and the food and clothing had been spoilt. But Grandfather's hookah had been saved, and, in the evenings, after their work was done and they had eaten the light meal which Sita prepared, he would smoke with a little of his old contentment, and tell Sita about other floods and storms which he had experienced as a boy.

Sita planted a mango seed in the same spot where the peepul tree had stood. It would be many years before it grew into a big tree, but Sita liked to imagine sitting in its branches one day, picking the mangoes straight from the tree, and feasting on them all day. Grandfather was more particular about making a vegetable garden and putting down peas, carrots, gram and mustard.

One day, when most of the hard work had been done and the new hut was almost ready, Sita took the flute which had been given to her by the boy, and walked down to the water's edge and tried to play it.

But all she could produce were a few broken notes, and even the goats paid no attention to her music.

Sometimes Sita thought she saw a boat coming down the river and she would run to meet it; but usually there was no boat, or if there was, it belonged to a stranger or to another fisherman. And so she stopped looking out for boats. Sometimes she thought she heard the music of a flute, but it seemed very distant and she could never tell where the music came from.

Slowly, the rains came to an end. The flood waters had receded, and in the villages people were beginning to till the land again and sow crops for the winter months. There were cattle fairs and wrestling matches. The days were warm and sultry. The water in the river was no longer muddy, and one evening Grandfather brought home a huge mahseer fish and Sita made it into a delicious curry.

Grandfather sat outside the hut, smoking his hookah. Sita was at the far end of the island, spreading clothes on the rocks to dry.

One of the goats had followed her. It was the friendlier of the two, and often followed Sita about the island. She had made it a necklace of coloured beads.

She sat down on a smooth rock, and, as she did so, she noticed a small bright object in the sand near her feet. She stooped and picked it up. It was a little wooden toy—a coloured peacock—that must have come down on the river and been swept ashore on the island. Some of the paint had rubbed off, but for Sita, who had no toys, it was a great find. Perhaps it would speak to her, as Mumta had spoken to her.

As she held the toy peacock in the palm of her hand, she thought she heard the flute music again, but she did not look up. She had heard it before, and she was sure that it was all in her mind. But this time the music sounded nearer, much nearer. There was a soft footfall in the sand. And, looking up, she saw the boy, Krishan, standing over her.

'I thought you would never come,' said Sita.

'I had to wait until the rains were over. Now that I am free, I will come more often. Did you keep my flute?'

'Yes, but I cannot play it properly. Sometimes it plays by itself, I think, but it will not play for me!'

'I will teach you to play it,' said Krishan.

He sat down beside her, and they cooled their feet in the water, which was clear now, reflecting the blue of the sky. You could see the sand and the pebbles of the riverbed.

'Sometimes the river is angry, and sometimes it is kind,' said Sita.

'We are part of the river,' said the boy.

'We cannot live without it.'

It was a good river, deep and strong, beginning in the mountains and ending in the sea. Along its banks, for hundreds of miles, lived millions of people, and Sita was only one small girl among them, and no one had ever heard of her, no one knew her—except for the old man, the boy and the river.

THE BLUE UMBRELLA

I

'Neelu! Neelu!' cried Binya.

She scrambled barefoot over the rocks, ran over the short summer grass, up and over the brow of the hill, all the time calling 'Neelu, Neelu!' Neelu—Blue—was the name of the blue-grey cow. The other cow, which was white, was called Gori, meaning Fair One. They were fond of wandering off on their own, down to the stream or into the pine forest, and sometimes they came back by themselves and sometimes they stayed away—almost deliberately, it seemed to Binya.

If the cows didn't come home at the right time, Binya would be sent to fetch them. Sometimes her brother, Bijju, went with her, but these days he was busy preparing for his exams and didn't have time to help with the cows.

Binya liked being on her own, and sometimes she allowed the cows to lead her into some distant valley, and then they would all be late coming home. The cows preferred having Binya with them, because she let them wander. Bijju pulled them by their tails if they went too far.

Binya belonged to the mountains, to this part of the Himalayas known as Garhwal. Dark forests and lonely hilltops held no terrors for her. It was only when she was in the market town, jostled by the crowds in the bazaar, that she felt rather nervous and lost. The town, five miles from the village, was also a pleasure resort for tourists from all over India.

Binya was probably ten. She may have been nine or even eleven, she couldn't be sure because no one in the village kept birthdays; but her mother told her she'd been born during a winter when the snow had come up to the windows, and that was just over ten years ago, wasn't it? Two years later, her father had died, but his passing had made no difference to their way of life. They had three tiny terraced fields on the side of the mountain, and they grew potatoes, onions, ginger, beans, mustard and maize: not enough to sell in the town, but enough to live on.

Like most mountain girls, Binya was quite sturdy, fair of skin, with pink cheeks and dark eyes and her black hair tied in a pigtail. She wore pretty glass bangles on her wrists, and a necklace of glass beads. From the necklace hung a leopard's claw. It was a lucky charm, and Binya always wore it. Bijju had one, too, only his was attached to a string.

Binya's full name was Binyadevi, and Bijju's real name was Vijay, but everyone called them Binya and Bijju. Binya was two years younger than her brother.

She had stopped calling for Neelu; she had heard the cowbells tinkling, and knew the cows hadn't gone far. Singing to herself, she walked over fallen pine needles into the forest glade on the spur of the hill. She heard voices, laughter, the clatter of plates and cups, and stepping through the trees, she came upon a party of picnickers.

They were holidaymakers from the plains. The women were dressed in bright saris, the men wore light summer shirts, and the children had pretty new clothes. Binya, standing in the shadows between the trees, went unnoticed; for some time she watched the picnickers, admiring their clothes, listening to their unfamiliar accents, and gazing rather hungrily at the sight of all their food. And then her gaze came to rest on a bright blue umbrella, a frilly thing for women, which lay open on the grass beside its owner.

Now Binya had seen umbrellas before, and her mother had a big black umbrella which nobody used anymore because the field rats had eaten holes in it, but this was the first time Binya had seen such a small, dainty, colourful umbrella and she fell in love with it. The umbrella was like a flower, a great blue flower that had sprung up on the dry brown hillside.

She moved forward a few paces so that she could see the umbrella better. As she came out of the shadows into the sunlight, the picnickers saw her.

'Hello, look who's here!' exclaimed the older of the two women. 'A little village girl!'

'Isn't she pretty?' remarked the other. 'But how torn and dirty her clothes are!' It did not seem to bother them that Binya could hear and understand everything they said about her.

'They're very poor in the hills,' said one of the men.

'Then let's give her something to eat.' And the older woman beckoned to Binya to come closer.

Hesitantly, nervously, Binya approached the group.

Normally she would have turned and fled, but the attraction was the pretty blue umbrella. It had cast a spell over her, drawing her forward almost against her will.

'What's that on her neck?' asked the younger woman.

'A necklace of sorts.'

'It's a pendant—see, there's a claw hanging from it!'

'It's a tiger's claw,' said the man beside her. (He had never seen a tiger's claw.) 'A lucky charm. These people wear them to keep away evil spirits.' He looked to Binya for confirmation, but Binya said nothing.

'Oh, I want one too!' said the woman, who was obviously his wife.

'You can't get them in shops.'

'Buy hers, then. Give her two or three rupees, she's sure to need the money.'

The man, looking slightly embarrassed but anxious to please his young wife, produced a two-rupee note and offered it to Binya, indicating that he wanted the pendant in exchange. Binya put her hand to the necklace, half afraid that the excited woman would snatch it away from her. Solemnly she shook her head.

The man then showed her a five-rupee note, but again Binya shook her head.

'How silly she is!' exclaimed the young woman.

'It may not be hers to sell,' said the man. 'But I'll try again. How much do you want—what can we give you?' And he waved his hand towards the picnic things scattered about on the grass.

Without any hesitation Binya pointed to the umbrella.

'My umbrella!' exclaimed the young woman. 'She wants my

umbrella. What cheek!'

'Well, you want her pendant, don't you?'

'That's different.'

'Is it?'

The man and his wife were beginning to quarrel with each other.

'I'll ask her to go away,' said the older woman.

'We're making such fools of ourselves.'

'But I want the pendant!' cried the other, petulantly.

And then, on an impulse, she picked up the umbrella and held it out to Binya.

'Here, take the umbrella!'

Binya removed her necklace and held it out to the young woman, who immediately placed it around her own neck. Then Binya took the umbrella and held it up. It did not look so small in her hands; in fact, it was just the right size.

She had forgotten about the picnickers, who were busy examining the pendant. She turned the blue umbrella this way and that, looked through the bright blue silk at the pulsating sun, and then, still keeping it open, turned and disappeared into the forest glade.

II

Binya seldom closed the blue umbrella. Even when she had it in the house, she left it lying open in a corner of the room. Sometimes Bijju snapped it shut, complaining that it got in the way. She would open it again a little later. It wasn't beautiful when it was closed.

Whenever Binya went out—whether it was to graze the cows, or fetch water from the spring, or carry milk to the little tea shop on the Tehri road—she took the umbrella with her. That patch of skyblue silk could always be seen on the hillside.

Old Ram Bharosa (Ram the Trustworthy) kept the tea shop on the Tehri road. It was a dusty, un-metalled road. Once a day, the Tehri bus stopped near his shop and passengers got down to sip hot tea or drink a glass of curd. He kept a few bottles of Coca-Cola too, but as there was no ice, the bottles got hot in the sun and so were seldom opened. He also kept sweets and toffees, and when Binya or Bijju had a few coins to spare, they would spend them at the shop. It was only a mile from the village.

Ram Bharosa was astonished to see Binya's blue umbrella.

'What have you there, Binya?' he asked.

Binya gave the umbrella a twirl and smiled at Ram Bharosa. She was always ready with her smile, and would willingly have lent it to anyone who was feeling unhappy.

'That's a lady's umbrella,' said Ram Bharosa. 'That's only for memsahibs. Where did you get it?'

'Someone gave it to me—for my necklace.'

'You exchanged it for your lucky claw!'

Binya nodded.

'But what do you need it for? The sun isn't hot enough, and it isn't meant for the rain. It's just a pretty thing for rich ladies to play with!'

Binya nodded and smiled again. Ram Bharosa was quite right; it was just a beautiful plaything. And that was exactly why she had fallen in love with it.

'I have an idea,' said the shopkeeper. 'It's no use to you, that umbrella. Why not sell it to me? I'll give you five rupees for it.'

'It's worth fifteen,' said Binya.

'Well, then, I'll give you ten.'

Binya laughed and shook her head.

'Twelve rupees?' said Ram Bharosa, but without much hope.

Binya placed a five-paise coin on the counter.

'I came for a toffee,' she said.

Ram Bharosa pulled at his drooping whiskers, gave Binya a wry look, and placed a toffee in the palm of her hand. He watched Binya as she walked away along the dusty road. The blue umbrella held him fascinated, and he stared after it until it was out of sight.

The villagers used this road to go to the market town. Some used the bus, a few rode on mules and most people walked. Today, everyone on the road turned their heads to stare at the girl with the bright blue umbrella.

Binya sat down in the shade of a pine tree. The umbrella, still open, lay beside her. She cradled her head in her arms, and presently she dozed off. It was that kind of day, sleepily warm and summery.

And while she slept, a wind sprang up.

It came quietly, swishing gently through the trees, humming softly. Then it was joined by other random gusts, bustling over the tops of the mountains. The trees shook their heads and came to life. The wind fanned Binya's cheeks. The umbrella stirred on the grass.

The wind grew stronger, picking up dead leaves and sending them spinning and swirling through the air. It got into the umbrella and began to drag it over the grass. Suddenly it lifted the umbrella and carried it about six feet from the sleeping girl. The sound woke Binya.

She was on her feet immediately, and then she was leaping down the steep slope. But just as she was within reach of the umbrella, the wind picked it up again and carried it further downhill.

Binya set off in pursuit. The wind was in a wicked, playful mood. It would leave the umbrella alone for a few moments but as soon as Binya came near, it would pick up the umbrella again and send it bouncing, floating, dancing away from her.

The hill grew steeper. Binya knew that after twenty yards it would fall away in a precipice. She ran faster. And the wind ran with her, ahead of her, and the blue umbrella stayed up with the wind.

A fresh gust picked it up and carried it to the very edge of the cliff. There it balanced for a few seconds, before toppling over, out of sight.

Binya ran to the edge of the cliff. Going down on her hands and knees, she peered down the cliff face. About a hundred feet below, a small stream rushed between great boulders. Hardly anything grew on the cliff face—just a few stunted bushes, and, halfway down, a wild cherry tree growing crookedly out of the rocks and hanging across the chasm. The umbrella had stuck in the cherry tree.

Binya didn't hesitate. She may have been timid with strangers, but she was at home on a hillside. She stuck her bare leg over the edge of the cliff and began climbing down. She kept her face to the hillside, feeling her way with her feet, only changing her handhold when she knew her feet were secure. Sometimes she held on to the thorny bilberry bushes, but she did not trust the other plants, which came away very easily.

Loose stones rattled down the cliff. Once on their way, the stones did not stop until they reached the bottom of the hill; and they took other stones with them, so that there was soon a cascade of stones, and Binya had to be very careful not to start a landslide.

As agile as a mountain goat, she did not take more than five minutes to reach the crooked cherry tree. But the most difficult task remained—she had to crawl along the trunk of the tree, which stood out at right angles from the cliff. Only by doing this could she reach the trapped umbrella.

Binya felt no fear when climbing trees. She was proud of the fact that she could climb them as well as Bijju. Gripping the rough cherry bark with her toes, and using her knees as leverage, she crawled along the trunk of the projecting tree until she was almost within reach of the umbrella. She noticed with dismay that the blue cloth was torn in a couple of places.

She looked down, and it was only then that she felt afraid. She was right over the chasm, balanced precariously about eighty feet above the boulder-strewn stream. Looking down, she felt quite dizzy. Her hands shook, and the tree shook too. If she slipped now, there was only one direction in which she could fall—down, down, into the depths of that dark and shadowy ravine.

There was only one thing to do; concentrate on the patch of blue just a couple of feet away from her. She did not look down or up, but straight ahead, and willing herself forward, she managed to reach the umbrella.

She could not crawl back with it in her hands. So, after dislodging it from the forked branch in which it had stuck, she let it fall, still open, into the ravine below.

Cushioned by the wind, the umbrella floated serenely downwards, landing in a thicket of nettles.

Binya crawled back along the trunk of the cherry tree. Twenty minutes later, she emerged from the nettle clump, her precious umbrella held aloft. She had nettle stings all over her legs, but she was hardly aware of the smarting. She was as immune to nettles as Bijju was to bees.

III

About four years previously, Bijju had knocked a hive out of an oak tree, and had been badly stung on the face and legs. It had been a painful experience. But now, if a bee stung him, he felt nothing at all: he had been immunized for life!

He was on his way home from school. It was two o'clock and he hadn't eaten since six in the morning. Fortunately, the kingora bushes—the bilberries—were in fruit, and already Bijju's lips were stained purple with the juice of the wild, sour fruit.

He didn't have any money to spend at Ram Bharosa's shop, but he stopped there anyway to look at the sweets in their glass jars.

'And what will you have today?' asked Ram Bharosa.

'No money,' said Bijju.

'You can pay me later.'

Bijju shook his head. Some of his friends had taken sweets on credit, and at the end of the month they had found they'd eaten more sweets than they could possibly pay for! As a result, they'd had to hand over to Ram Bharosa some of their most treasured possessions—such as a curved knife for cutting grass, or a small hand-axe, or a jar for pickles, or a pair of earrings—and these had become the shopkeeper's possessions and were kept by him or sold in his shop.

Ram Bharosa had set his heart on having Binya's blue umbrella, and so naturally he was anxious to give credit to either of the children, but so far neither had fallen into the trap.

Bijju moved on, his mouth full of Kingora berries. Halfway home, he saw Binya with the cows. It was late evening, and the sun had gone down, but Binya still had the umbrella open. The two small rents had been stitched up by her mother.

Bijju gave his sister a handful of berries. She handed him the umbrella while she ate the berries.

'You can have the umbrella until we get home,' she said. It was her way of rewarding Bijju for bringing her the wild fruit.

Calling 'Neelu! Gori!' Binya and Bijju set out for home, followed at some distance by the cows.

It was dark before they reached the village, but Bijju still had the umbrella open.

Most of the people in the village were a little envious of Binya's blue umbrella. No one else had ever possessed one like it. The schoolmaster's wife thought it was quite wrong for a poor cultivator's daughter to have such a fine umbrella while she, a second-class BA, had to make do with an ordinary black one. Her husband offered to have their old umbrella dyed blue; she gave him a scornful look, and loved him a little less than before. The pujari, who looked after the temple, announced that he would buy a multi-coloured umbrella the next time he was in the town. A few days later he returned looking annoyed and grumbling that they weren't available except in Delhi. Most people consoled themselves by saying that Binya's pretty umbrella wouldn't keep out the rain, if it rained heavily; that it would shrivel in the sun, if the sun was fierce; that it would collapse in a wind, if the wind was strong; that it would attract lightning, if lightning fell near it; and that it would prove unlucky, if there was any ill luck going about. Secretly, everyone admired it.

Unlike the adults, the children didn't have to pretend. They were full of praise for the umbrella. It was so light, so pretty, so bright a blue! And it was just the right size for Binya. They knew that if they said nice things about the umbrella, Binya would smile and give it to them to hold for a little while—just a very little while!

Soon it was the time of the monsoon. Big black clouds kept piling up, and thunder rolled over the hills.

Binya sat on the hillside all afternoon, waiting for the rain. As soon as the first big drop of rain came down, she raised the umbrella over her head. More drops, big ones, came pattering down. She could see them through the umbrella silk, as they broke against the cloth.

And then there was a cloudburst, and it was like standing under a waterfall. The umbrella wasn't really a rain umbrella, but it held up bravely. Only Binya's feet got wet. Rods of rain fell around her in a curtain of shivered glass.

Everywhere on the hillside people were scurrying for shelter.

Some made for a charcoal burner's hut, others for a mule-shed, or Ram Bharosa's shop. Binya was the only one who didn't run. This was what she'd been waiting for—rain on her umbrella—and she wasn't in a hurry to go home. She didn't mind getting her feet wet. The cows didn't mind getting wet either.

Presently she found Bijju sheltering in a cave. He would have enjoyed getting wet, but he had his schoolbooks with him and he couldn't afford to let them get spoilt. When he saw Binya, he came out of the cave and shared the umbrella. He was a head taller than his sister, so he had to hold the umbrella for her, while she held his books.

The cows had been left far behind.

'Neelu, Neelu!' called Binya.

'Gori!' called Bijju.

When their mother saw them sauntering home through the driving rain, she called out: 'Binya! Bijju! Hurry up, and bring the cows in! What are you doing out there in the rain?'

'Just testing the umbrella,' said Bijju.

IV

The rains set in, and the sun only made brief appearances. The hills turned a lush green. Ferns sprang up on walls and tree trunks. Giant lilies reared up like leopards from the tall grass. A white mist coiled and uncoiled as it floated up from the valley. It was a beautiful season, except for the leeches.

Every day, Binya came home with a couple of leeches fastened to the flesh of her bare legs. They fell off by themselves just as soon as they'd had their thimbleful of blood, but you didn't know they were on you until they fell off, and then, later, the skin became very sore and itchy. Some of the older people still believed that to be bled by leeches was a remedy for various ailments. Whenever Ram Bharosa had a headache, he applied a leech to his throbbing temple.

Three days of incessant rain had flooded out a number of small animals who lived in holes in the ground. Binya's mother suddenly found the roof full of field rats. She had to drive them out; they ate too much of her stored-up wheat flour and rice. Bijju liked lifting up large rocks to disturb the scorpions who were sleeping beneath. And snakes came out to bask in the sun.

Binya had just crossed the small stream at the bottom of the hill when she saw something gliding out of the bushes and coming towards her. It was a long black snake. A clatter of loose stones frightened it. Seeing the girl in its way, it rose up, hissing, prepared to strike. The forked tongue darted out, the venomous head lunged at Binya.

Binya's umbrella was open as usual. She thrust it forward, between herself and the snake, and the snake's hard snout thudded twice against the strong silk of the umbrella. The reptile then turned and slithered away over the wet rocks, disappearing into a clump of ferns.

Binya forgot about the cows and ran all the way home to tell her mother how she had been saved by the umbrella. Bijju had to put away his books and go out to fetch the cows. He carried a stout stick, in case he met with any snakes.

∽

First the summer sun, and now the endless rain, meant that the umbrella was beginning to fade a little. From a bright blue it had changed to a light blue. But it was still a pretty thing, and tougher than it looked, and Ram Bharosa still desired it. He did not want to sell it; he wanted to own it. He was probably the richest man in the area—so why shouldn't he have a blue umbrella? Not a day passed without his getting a glimpse of Binya and the umbrella; and the more he saw the umbrella, the more he wanted it.

The schools closed during the monsoon, but this didn't mean that Bijju could sit at home doing nothing. Neelu and Gori were providing more milk than was required at home, so Binya's mother was able to sell a kilo of milk every day: half a kilo to the schoolmaster, and half a kilo (at reduced rate) to the temple pujari. Bijju had to deliver the milk every morning.

Ram Bharosa had asked Bijju to work in his shop during the holidays, but Bijju didn't have time—he had to help his mother with the ploughing and the transplanting of the rice seedlings. So Ram Bharosa employed a boy from the next village, a boy called Rajaram. He did all the washing-up, and ran various errands. He went to the same school as Bijju, but the two boys were not friends.

One day, as Binya passed the shop, twirling her blue umbrella, Rajaram noticed that his employer gave a deep sigh and began muttering to himself.

'What's the matter, Babuji?' asked the boy.

'Oh, nothing,' said Ram Bharosa. 'It's just a sickness that has come upon me. And it's all due to that girl Binya and her wretched umbrella.'

'Why, what has she done to you?'

'Refused to sell me her umbrella! There's pride for you. And I offered her ten rupees.'

'Perhaps, if you gave her twelve...'

'But it isn't new any longer. It isn't worth eight rupees now. All the same, I'd like to have it.'

'You wouldn't make a profit on it,' said Rajaram.

'It's not the profit I'm after, wretch! It's the thing itself. It's the beauty of it!'

'And what would you do with it, Babuji? You don't visit anyone—you're seldom out of your shop. Of what use would it be to you?'

'Of what use is a poppy in a cornfield? Of what use is a rainbow? Of what use are you, numbskull? Wretch! I, too, have a soul. I want the umbrella, because—because I want its beauty to be mine!'

Rajaram put the kettle on to boil, began dusting the counter, all the time muttering: 'I'm as useful as an umbrella,' and then, after a short period of intense thought, said: 'What will you give me, Babuji, if I get the umbrella for you?'

'What do you mean?' asked the old man.

'You know what I mean. What will you give me?'

'You mean to steal it, don't you, you wretch? What a delightful child you are! I'm glad you're not my son or my enemy. But look, everyone will know it has been stolen, and then how will I be able to show off with it?'

'You will have to gaze upon it in secret,' said Rajaram with a chuckle. 'Or take it into Tehri, and have it coloured red! That's your problem. But tell me, Babuji, do you want it badly enough to pay me three rupees for stealing it without being seen?'

Ram Bharosa gave the boy a long, sad look. 'You're a sharp boy,' he said. 'You'll come to a bad end. I'll give you two rupees.'

'Three,' said the boy.

'Two,' said the old man.

'You don't really want it, I can see that,' said the boy.

'Wretch!' said the old man. 'Evil one! Darkener of my doorstep! Fetch me the umbrella, and I'll give you three rupees.'

V

Binya was in the forest glade where she had first seen the umbrella. No one came there for picnics during the monsoon. The grass was always wet and the pine needles were slippery underfoot. The tall trees shut out the light, and poisonous-looking mushrooms, orange and purple, sprang up everywhere. But it was a good place for porcupines, who seemed to like the mushrooms, and Binya was searching for porcupine quills.

The hill people didn't think much of porcupine quills, but far away in southern India, the quills were valued as charms and sold at a rupee each. So Ram Bharosa paid a tenth of a rupee for each quill brought to him, and he in turn sold the quills at a profit to a trader from the plains.

Binya had already found five quills, and she knew there'd be more in the long grass. For once, she'd put her umbrella down. She had to put it aside if she was to search the ground thoroughly.

It was Rajaram's chance.

He'd been following Binya for some time, concealing himself behind trees and rocks, creeping closer whenever she became absorbed in her search. He was anxious that she should not see him and be able to recognize him later.

He waited until Binya had wandered some distance from the umbrella. Then, running forward at a crouch, he seized the open umbrella and dashed off with it.

But Rajaram had very big feet. Binya heard his heavy footsteps and turned just in time to see him as he disappeared between the trees. She cried out, dropped the porcupine quills, and gave chase.

Binya was swift and sure-footed, but Rajaram had a long stride.

All the same, he made the mistake of running downhill. A long-legged person is much faster going uphill than down. Binya reached the edge of the forest glade in time to see the thief scrambling down the path to the stream. He had closed the umbrella so that it would not hinder his flight.

Binya was beginning to gain on the boy. He kept to the path, while she simply slid and leapt down the steep hillside. Near the bottom of the hill the path began to straighten out, and it was here that the long-legged boy began to forge ahead again.

Bijju was coming home from another direction. He had a bundle of sticks which he'd collected for the kitchen fire. As he reached the path, he saw Binya rushing down the hill as though all the mountain spirits in Garhwal were after her.

'What's wrong?' he called. 'Why are you running?'

Binya paused only to point at the fleeing Rajaram.

'My umbrella!' she cried. 'He has stolen it!'

Bijju dropped his bundle of sticks, and ran after his sister. When he reached her side, he said, 'I'll soon catch him!' and went sprinting away over the lush green grass. He was fresh, and he was soon well ahead of Binya and gaining on the thief.

Rajaram was crossing the shallow stream when Bijju caught up with him. Rajaram was the taller boy, but Bijju was much stronger. He flung himself at the thief, caught him by the legs, and brought him down in the water. Rajaram got to his feet and tried to drag himself away, but Bijju still had him by a leg. Rajaram overbalanced and came down with a great splash. He had let the umbrella fall. It began to float away on the current. Just then Binya arrived, flushed and breathless, and went dashing into the stream after the umbrella.

Meanwhile, a tremendous fight was taking place. Locked in fierce combat, the two boys swayed together on a rock, tumbled on to the sand, rolled over and over the pebbled bank until they were again thrashing about in the shallows of the stream. The magpies, bulbuls and other birds were disturbed, and flew away with cries of alarm.

Covered with mud, gasping and spluttering, the boys groped for each other in the water. After five minutes of frenzied struggle, Bijju emerged victorious.

Rajaram lay flat on his back on the sand, exhausted, while Bijju sat astride him, pinning him down with his arms and legs.

'Let me get up!' gasped Rajaram. 'Let me go—I don't want your useless umbrella!'

'Then why did you take it?' demanded Bijju. 'Come on—tell me why!'

'It was that skinflint Ram Bharosa,' said Rajaram. 'He told me to get it for him. He said if I didn't fetch it, I'd lose my job.'

VI

By early October, the rains were coming to an end. The leeches disappeared. The ferns turned yellow, and the sunlight on the green hills was mellow and golden, like the limes on the small tree in front of Binya's home. Bijju's days were happy ones as he came home from school, munching on roasted corn. Binya's umbrella had turned a pale milky blue, and was patched in several places, but it was still the prettiest umbrella in the village, and she still carried it with her wherever she went.

The cold, cruel winter wasn't far off, but somehow October seems longer than other months, because it is a kind month: the grass is good to be upon, the breeze is warm and gentle and pine-scented. That October, everyone seemed contented— everyone, that is, except Ram Bharosa.

The old man had by now given up all hope of ever possessing Binya's umbrella. He wished he had never set eyes on it. Because of the umbrella, he had suffered the tortures of greed, the despair of loneliness. Because of the umbrella, people had stopped coming to his shop!

Ever since it had become known that Ram Bharosa had tried to have the umbrella stolen, the village people had turned against him. They stopped trusting the old man, instead of buying their soap and tea and matches from his shop, they preferred to walk an extra mile to the shops near the Tehri bus stand. Who would have dealings with a man who had sold his soul for an umbrella? The children taunted him, twisted his name around. From 'Ram the Trustworthy' he became 'Trusty Umbrella Thief '.

The old man sat alone in his empty shop, listening to the eternal hissing of his kettle and wondering if anyone would ever again step in for a glass of tea. Ram Bharosa had lost his own appetite, and ate and drank very little. There was no money coming in. He had his savings in a bank in Tehri, but it was a terrible thing to have to dip into them! To save money, he had dismissed the blundering Rajaram. So he was left without any company. The roof leaked and the wind got in through the corrugated tin sheets, but Ram Bharosa didn't care.

Bijju and Binya passed his shop almost every day. Bijju went by with a loud but tuneless whistle. He was one of the world's whistlers; cares rested lightly on his shoulders. But, strangely enough, Binya crept quietly past the shop, looking the other way, almost as though she was in some way responsible for the misery of Ram Bharosa.

She kept reasoning with herself, telling herself that the umbrella was her very own, and that she couldn't help it if others were jealous of it. But had she loved the umbrella too much? Had it mattered more to her than people mattered? She couldn't help feeling that, in a small way, she was the cause of the sad look on Ram Bharosa's face ('His face is a yard long,' said Bijju) and the ruinous condition of his shop. It was all due to his own greed, no doubt, but she didn't want him to feel too bad about what he'd done, because it made her feel bad about herself; and so she closed the umbrella whenever she came near the shop, opening it again only when she was out of sight.

One day towards the end of October, when she had ten paise in her pocket, she entered the shop and asked the old man for a toffee.

She was Ram Bharosa's first customer in almost two weeks. He looked suspiciously at the girl. Had she come to taunt him, to flaunt the umbrella in his face? She had placed her coin on the counter. Perhaps it was a bad coin. Ram Bharosa picked it up and bit it; he held it up to the light; he rang it on the ground. It was a good coin. He gave Binya the toffee.

Binya had already left the shop when Ram Bharosa saw the closed umbrella lying on his counter. There it was, the blue umbrella he had always wanted, within his grasp at last! He had only to hide it at the back of his shop, and no one would know that he had it, no one could prove that Binya had left it behind.

He stretched out his trembling, bony hand, and took the umbrella by the handle. He pressed it open. He stood beneath it, in the dark shadows of his shop, where no sun or rain could ever touch it.

'But I'm never in the sun or in the rain,' he said aloud. 'Of what use is an umbrella to me?'

And he hurried outside and ran after Binya.

'Binya, Binya!' he shouted. 'Binya, you've left your umbrella behind!'

He wasn't used to running, but he caught up with her, held out the umbrella, saying, 'You forgot it—the umbrella!'

In that moment it belonged to both of them.

But Binya didn't take the umbrella. She shook her head and said, 'You keep it. I don't need it anymore.'

'But it's such a pretty umbrella!' protested Ram Bharosa. 'It's the best umbrella in the village.'

'I know,' said Binya. 'But an umbrella isn't everything.'

And she left the old man holding the umbrella, and went tripping down the road, and there was nothing between her and the bright blue sky.

VII

Well, now that Ram Bharosa has the blue umbrella—a gift from Binya, as he tells everyone—he is sometimes persuaded to go out into the sun or the rain, and as a result he looks much healthier. Sometimes he uses the umbrella to chase away pigs or goats. It is always left open outside the shop, and anyone who wants to borrow it may do so; and so in a way it has become everyone's umbrella. It is faded and patchy, but it is still the best umbrella in the village.

People are visiting Ram Bharosa's shop again. Whenever Bijju or Binya stop for a cup of tea, he gives them a little extra milk or sugar. They like their tea sweet and milky.

A few nights ago, a bear visited Ram Bharosa's shop. There had been snow on the higher ranges of the Himalayas, and the bear had been finding it difficult to obtain food; so it had come lower down, to see what it could pick up near the village. That night it scrambled on to the tin roof of Ram Bharosa's shop, and made off with a huge pumpkin which had been ripening on the roof. But in climbing off the roof, the bear had lost a claw.

Next morning Ram Bharosa found the claw just outside the door of his shop. He picked it up and put it in his pocket. A bear's claw was a lucky find.

A day later, when he went into the market town, he took the claw with him, and left it with a silversmith, giving the craftsman certain instructions. The silversmith made a locket for the claw, then he gave it a thin silver chain. When Ram Bharosa came again, he paid the silversmith ten rupees for his work.

The days were growing shorter, and Binya had to be home a little earlier every evening. There was a hungry leopard at large, and she couldn't leave the cows out after dark.

She was hurrying past Ram Bharosa's shop when the old man called out to her.

'Binya, spare a minute! I want to show you something.'

Binya stepped into the shop.

'What do you think of it?' asked Ram Bharosa, showing her the silver pendant with the claw.

'It's so beautiful,' said Binya, just touching the claw and the silver chain.

'It's a bear's claw,' said Ram Bharosa. 'That's even luckier than a leopard's claw. Would you like to have it?'

'I have no money,' said Binya.

'That doesn't matter. You gave me the umbrella, I give you the claw! Come, let's see what it looks like on you.'

He placed the pendant on Binya, and indeed it looked very beautiful on her.

Ram Bharosa says he will never forget the smile she gave him when she left the shop.

She was halfway home when she realized she had left the cows behind.

'Neelu, Neelu!' she called. 'Oh, Gori!'

There was a faint tinkle of bells as the cows came slowly down the mountain path.

In the distance she could hear her mother and Bijju calling for her.

She began to sing. They heard her singing, and knew she was safe and near.

She walked home through the darkening glade, singing of the stars, and the trees stood still and listened to her, and the mountains were glad.

NIGHT OF THE LEOPARD

I

In the entire village, he was the first to get up. Even the dog, a big hill mastiff called Sheroo, was asleep in a corner of the dark room, curled up near the cold embers of the previous night's fire. Bisnu's tousled head emerged from his blanket. He rubbed the sleep from his eyes and sat up on his haunches. Then, gathering his wits, he crawled in the direction of the loud ticking that came from the battered little clock which occupied the second most honoured place in a niche in the wall. The most honoured place belonged to a picture of Ganesha, the god of learning, who had an elephant's head and a fat boy's body. Bringing his face close to the clock, Bisnu could just make out the hands. It was five o'clock. He had half an hour in which to get ready and leave.

He got up, in vest and underpants, and moved quietly towards the door. The soft tread of his bare feet woke Sheroo, and the big black dog rose silently and padded behind the boy. The door opened and closed, and then the boy and the dog were outside in the early dawn. The month was June, and the nights were warm, even in the Himalayan valleys; but there was fresh dew on the grass. Bisnu felt the dew beneath his feet. He took a deep breath and began walking down to the stream.

The sound of the stream filled the small valley. At that early hour of the morning, it was the only sound; but Bisnu was hardly conscious of it. It was a sound he lived with and took for granted. It was only when he had crossed the hill, on his way to the town—and the sound of the stream grew distant—that he really began to notice it. And it was only when the stream was too far away to be heard that he really missed its sound.

He slipped out of his underclothes, gazed for a few moments at the goose pimples rising on his flesh, and then dashed into the shallow stream. As he went further in, the cold mountain water reached his loins and navel, and he gasped with shock and pleasure. He drifted slowly with the current, swam across to a small inlet which formed a fairly deep pool, and plunged into the water. Sheroo hated cold water at this early hour. Had the sun been up, he would not have hesitated to join Bisnu. Now he contented himself with sitting on a smooth rock and gazing placidly at the slim brown boy splashing about in the clear water, in the widening light of dawn.

Bisnu did not stay long in the water. There wasn't time. When he returned to the house, he found his mother up, making tea and chapattis. His sister, Puja, was still asleep. She was a little older than Bisnu, a pretty girl with large black eyes, good teeth and strong arms and legs. During the day, she helped her mother in the house and in the fields. She did not go to the school with Bisnu. But when he came home in the evenings, he would try teaching her some of the things he had learnt. Their father was dead. Bisnu, at twelve, considered himself the head of the family.

He ate two chapattis, after spreading butter-oil on them. He drank a glass of hot sweet tea. His mother gave two thick chapattis to Sheroo, and the dog wolfed them down in a few minutes. Then she wrapped two chapattis and a gourd curry in some big green leaves, and handed these to Bisnu. This was his lunch packet. His mother and Puja would take their meal afterwards.

When Bisnu was dressed, he stood with folded hands before the picture of Ganesha. Ganesha is the god who blesses all beginnings. The author who begins to write a new book, the banker who opens a new ledger, the traveller who starts on a journey, all invoke the kindly help of Ganesha. And as Bisnu made a journey every day, he never left without the goodwill of the elephant-headed god.

How, one might ask, did Ganesha get his elephant's head? When born, he was a beautiful child. Parvati, his mother, was so proud of him that she went about showing him to everyone.

Unfortunately she made the mistake of showing the child to that envious planet, Saturn, who promptly burnt off poor Ganesha's head. Parvati in despair went to Brahma, the Creator, for a new head for her son. He had no head to give her, but advised her to search for some man or animal caught in a sinful or wrong act. Parvati wandered about until she came upon an elephant sleeping with its head the wrong way, that is, to the south. She promptly removed the elephant's head and planted it on Ganesha's shoulders, where it took root.

Bisnu knew this story. He had heard it from his mother. Wearing a white shirt and black shorts, and a pair of worn white keds, he was ready for his long walk to school, five miles up the mountain.

His sister woke up just as he was about to leave. She pushed the hair away from her face and gave Bisnu one of her rare smiles.

'I hope you have not forgotten,' she said.

'Forgotten?' said Bisnu, pretending innocence. 'Is there anything I am supposed to remember?'

'Don't tease me. You promised to buy me a pair of bangles, remember? I hope you won't spend the money on sweets, as you did last time.'

'Oh, yes, your bangles,' said Bisnu.

'Girls have nothing better to do than waste money on trinkets. Now, don't lose your temper! I'll get them for you. Red and gold are the colours you want?'

'Yes, Brother,' said Puja gently, pleased that Bisnu had remembered the colours.

'And for your dinner tonight we'll make you something special. Won't we, Mother?'

'Yes. But hurry up and dress. There is some ploughing to be done today. The rains will soon be here, if the gods are kind.'

'The monsoon will be late this year,' said Bisnu.

'Mr Nautiyal, our teacher, told us so. He said it had nothing to do with the gods.'

'Be off, you are getting late,' said Puja, before Bisnu could begin an argument with his mother. She was diligently winding the old clock. It was quite light in the room. The sun would be up any minute.

Bisnu shouldered his school bag, kissed his mother, pinched his sister's cheeks and left the house. He started climbing the steep path up the mountainside. Sheroo bounded ahead; for he, too, always went with Bisnu to school.

Five miles to school. Every day, except Sunday, Bisnu walked five miles to school; and in the evening, he walked home again. There was no school in his own small village of Manjari, for the village consisted of only five families. The nearest school was at Kemptee, a small township on the bus route through the district of Garhwal. A number of boys walked to school, from distances of two or three miles; their villages were not quite as remote as Manjari. But Bisnu's village lay right at the bottom of the mountain, a drop of over two thousand feet from Kemptee. There was no proper road between the village and the town.

In Kemptee there was a school, a small mission hospital, a post office and several shops. In Manjari village there were none of these amenities. If you were sick, you stayed at home until you got well; if you were very sick, you walked or were carried to the hospital, up the five-mile path. If you wanted to buy something, you went without it; but if you wanted it very badly, you could walk the five miles to Kemptee.

Manjari was known as the Five-Mile Village.

Twice a week, if there were any letters, a postman came to the village. Bisnu usually passed the postman on his way to and from school.

There were other boys in Manjari village, but Bisnu was the only one who went to school. His mother would not have fussed if he had stayed at home and worked in the fields. That was what the other boys did; all except lazy Chittru, who preferred fishing in the stream or helping himself to the fruit off other people's trees. But Bisnu went to school. He went because he wanted to. No one could force him to go; and no one could stop him from going. He had set his heart on receiving a good schooling. He wanted to read and write as well as anyone in the big world, the world that seemed to begin only where the mountains ended. He felt cut off from the world in his small valley. He would rather live at the top of a mountain than at the bottom of one. That was why he liked climbing to Kemptee, it took him to the top of the mountain; and from its ridge he could look down on his own valley to the north, and on the wide endless plains stretching towards the south.

The plainsman looks to the hills for the needs of his spirit but the hill man looks to the plains for a living. Leaving the village and the fields below him, Bisnu climbed steadily up the bare hillside, now dry and brown. By the time the sun was up, he had entered the welcome shade of an oak and rhododendron forest. Sheroo went bounding ahead, chasing squirrels and barking at langurs.

A colony of langurs lived in the oak forest. They fed on oak leaves, acorns and other green things, and usually remained in the trees, coming down to the ground only to play or bask in the sun. They were beautiful, supple-limbed animals, with black faces and silver-grey coats and long, sensitive tails. They leapt from tree to tree with great agility. The young ones wrestled on the grass like boys.

A dignified community, the langurs did not have the cheekiness or dishonest habits of the red monkeys of the plains; they did not approach dogs or humans. But they had grown used to Bisnu's comings and goings, and did not fear him. Some of the older ones would watch him quietly, a little puzzled. They did not go near the town, because the Kemptee boys threw stones at them. And anyway, the oak forest gave them all the food they required. Emerging from the trees, Bisnu crossed a small brook. Here he stopped to drink the fresh clean water of a spring. The brook tumbled down the mountain and joined the river a little below Bisnu's village. Coming from another direction was a second path, and at the junction of the two paths Sarru was waiting for him. Sarru came from a small village about three miles from Bisnu's and closer to the town. He had two large milk cans slung over his shoulders. Every morning he carried this milk to town, selling one can to the school and the other to Mrs Taylor, the lady doctor at the small mission hospital. He was a little older than Bisnu but not as well-built.

They hailed each other, and Sarru fell into step beside Bisnu. They often met at this spot, keeping each other company for the remaining two miles to Kemptee.

'There was a panther in our village last night,' said Sarru.

This information interested but did not excite Bisnu. Panthers were common enough in the hills and did not usually present a problem except during the winter months, when their natural prey was scarce. Then, occasionally, a panther would take to haunting the outskirts of a village, seizing a careless dog or a stray goat.

'Did you lose any animals?' asked Bisnu.

'No. It tried to get into the cowshed but the dogs set up an alarm. We drove it off.'

'It must be the same one which came around last winter. We lost a calf and two dogs in our village.'

'Wasn't that the one the shikaris wounded? I hope it hasn't become a cattle lifter.'

'It could be the same. It has a bullet in its leg. These hunters are the people who cause all the trouble. They think it's easy to shoot a panther. It would be better if they missed altogether, but they usually wound it.'

'And then the panther's too slow to catch the barking deer, and starts on our own animals.'

'We're lucky it didn't become a man-eater. Do you remember the man-eater six years ago? I was very small then. My father told me all about it. Ten people were killed in our valley alone. What happened to it?'

'I don't know. Some say it poisoned itself when it ate the headman of another village.'

Bisnu laughed. 'No one liked that old villain. He must have been a man-eater himself in some previous existence!' They linked arms and scrambled up the stony path. Sheroo began barking and ran ahead. Someone was coming down the path. It was Mela Ram, the postman.

II

'Any letters for us?' asked Bisnu and Sarru together. They never received any letters but that did not stop them from asking. It was one way of finding out who had received letters.

'You're welcome to all of them,' said Mela Ram, 'if you'll carry my bag for me.'

'Not today,' said Sarru. 'We're busy today. Is there a letter from

Corporal Ghanshyam for his family?'

'Yes, there is a postcard for his people. He is posted on the Ladakh border now and finds it very cold there.'

Postcards, unlike sealed letters, were considered public property and were read by everyone. The senders knew that too, and so Corporal Ghanshyam Singh was careful to mention that he expected a promotion very soon. He wanted everyone in his village to know it.

Mela Ram, complaining of sore feet, continued on his way, and the boys carried on up the path. It was eight o'clock when they reached Kemptee. Dr Taylor's outpatients were just beginning to trickle in at the hospital gate. The doctor was trying to prop up a rose creeper which had blown down during the night. She liked attending to her plants in the mornings, before starting on her patients. She found this helped her in her work. There was a lot in common between ailing plants and ailing people.

Dr Taylor was fifty, white-haired but fresh in the face and full of vitality. She had been in India for twenty years, and ten of these had been spent working in the hill regions.

She saw Bisnu coming down the road. She knew about the boy and his long walk to school and admired him for his keenness and sense of purpose. She wished there were more like him.

Bisnu greeted her shyly. Sheroo barked and put his paws up on the gate.

'Yes, there's a bone for you,' said Dr Taylor. She often put aside bones for the big black dog, for she knew that Bisnu's people could not afford to give the dog a regular diet of meat—though he did well enough on milk and chapattis.

She threw the bone over the gate and Sheroo caught it before it fell. The school bell began ringing and Bisnu broke into a run.

Sheroo loped along behind the boy.

When Bisnu entered the school gate, Sheroo sat down on the grass of the compound. He would remain there until the lunch break. He knew of various ways of amusing himself during school hours and had friends among the bazaar dogs. But just then he didn't want company. He had his bone to get on with.

Mr Nautiyal, Bisnu's teacher, was in a bad mood. He was a

keen rose grower and only that morning, on getting up and looking out of his bedroom window, he had been horrified to see a herd of goats in his garden. He had chased them down the road with a stick but the damage had already been done. His prize roses had all been consumed.

Mr Nautiyal had been so upset that he had gone without his breakfast. He had also cut himself whilst shaving. Thus, his mood had gone from bad to worse. Several times during the day, he brought down his ruler on the knuckles of any boy who irritated him. Bisnu was one of his best pupils. But even Bisnu irritated him by asking too many questions about a new sum which Mr Nautiyal didn't feel like explaining.

That was the kind of day it was for Mr Nautiyal. Most schoolteachers know similar days.

'Poor Mr Nautiyal,' thought Bisnu. 'I wonder why he's so upset. It must be because of his pay. He doesn't get much money. But he's a good teacher. I hope he doesn't take another job.'

But after Mr Nautiyal had eaten his lunch, his mood improved (as it always did after a meal), and the rest of the day passed serenely. Armed with a bundle of homework, Bisnu came out from the school compound at four o'clock, and was immediately joined by Sheroo. He proceeded down the road in the company of several of his classfellows. But he did not linger long in the bazaar. There were five miles to walk, and he did not like to get home too late. Usually, he reached his house just as it was beginning to get dark.

Sarru had gone home long ago, and Bisnu had to make the return journey on his own. It was a good opportunity to memorize the words of an English poem he had been asked to learn. Bisnu had reached the little brook when he remembered the bangles he had promised to buy for his sister.

'Oh, I've forgotten them again,' he said aloud. 'Now I'll catch it—and she's probably made something special for my dinner!'

Sheroo, to whom these words were addressed, paid no attention but bounded off into the oak forest. Bisnu looked around for the monkeys but they were nowhere to be seen.

'Strange,' he thought, 'I wonder why they have disappeared.'

He was startled by a sudden sharp cry, followed by a fierce yelp. He knew at once that Sheroo was in trouble. The noise came from the bushes down the khud, into which the dog had rushed but a few seconds previously.

Bisnu jumped off the path and ran down the slope towards the bushes. There was no dog and not a sound. He whistled and called, but there was no response. Then he saw something lying on the dry grass. He picked it up. It was a portion of a dog's collar, stained with blood. It was Sheroo's collar and Sheroo's blood.

Bisnu did not search further. He knew, without a doubt, that Sheroo had been seized by a panther. No other animal could have attacked so silently and swiftly and carried off a big dog without a struggle. Sheroo was dead—must have been dead within seconds of being caught and flung into the air. Bisnu knew the danger that lay in wait for him if he followed the blood trail through the trees. The panther would attack anyone who interfered with its meal.

With tears starting in his eyes, Bisnu carried on down the path to the village. His fingers still clutched the little bit of blood-stained collar that was all that was left to him of his dog.

III

Bisnu was not a very sentimental boy, but he sorrowed for his dog who had been his companion on many a hike into the hills and forests. He did not sleep that night, but turned restlessly from side to side moaning softly. After some time he felt Puja's hand on his head. She began stroking his brow. He took her hand in his own and the clasp of her rough, warm familiar hand gave him a feeling of comfort and security.

Next morning, when he went down to the stream to bathe, he missed the presence of his dog. He did not stay long in the water. It wasn't as much fun when there was no Sheroo to watch him.

When Bisnu's mother gave him his food, she told him to be careful and hurry home that evening. A panther, even if it is only a cowardly lifter of sheep or dogs, is not to be trifled with. And this particular panther had shown some daring by seizing the dog even before it was dark.

Still, there was no question of staying away from school. If Bisnu remained at home every time a panther put in an appearance, he might just as well stop going to school altogether.

He set off even earlier than usual and reached the meeting of the paths long before Sarru. He did not wait for his friend, because he did not feel like talking about the loss of his dog. It was not the day for the postman, and so Bisnu reached Kemptee without meeting anyone on the way. He tried creeping past the hospital gate unnoticed, but Dr Taylor saw him and the first thing she said was: 'Where's Sheroo? I've got something for him.'

When Dr Taylor saw the boy's face, she knew at once that something was wrong.

'What is it, Bisnu?' she asked. She looked quickly up and down the road. 'Is it Sheroo?'

He nodded gravely.

'A panther took him,' he said.

'In the village?'

'No, while we were walking home through the forest. I did not see anything—but I heard.'

Dr Taylor knew that there was nothing she could say that would console him, and she tried to conceal the bone which she had brought out for the dog, but Bisnu noticed her hiding it behind her back and the tears welled up in his eyes. He turned away and began running down the road.

His schoolfellows noticed Sheroo's absence and questioned Bisnu. He had to tell them everything. They were full of sympathy, but they were also quite thrilled at what had happened and kept pestering Bisnu for all the details. There was a lot of noise in the classroom, and Mr Nautiyal had to call for order. When he learnt what had happened, he patted Bisnu on the head and told him that he need not attend school for the rest of the day. But Bisnu did not want to go home. After school, he got into a fight with one of the boys, and that helped him forget.

IV

The panther that plunged the village into an atmosphere of gloom and terror may not have been the same panther that took Sheroo. There was no way of knowing, and it would have made no difference, because the panther that came by night and struck at the people of Manjari was that most feared of wild creatures, a man-eater.

Nine-year-old Sanjay, son of Kalam Singh, was the first child to be attacked by the panther.

Kalam Singh's house was the last in the village and nearest the stream. Like the other houses, it was quite small, just a room above and a stable below, with steps leading up from outside the house. He lived there with his wife, two sons (Sanjay was the youngest) and little daughter Basanti who had just turned three.

Sanjay had brought his father's cows home after grazing them on the hillside in the company of other children. He had also brought home an edible wild plant, which his mother cooked into a tasty dish for their evening meal. They had their food at dusk, sitting on the floor of their single room, and soon after settled down for the night. Sanjay curled up in his favourite spot, with his head near the door, where he got a little fresh air. As the nights were warm, the door was usually left a little ajar. Sanjay's mother piled ash on the embers of the fire and the family was soon asleep.

No one heard the stealthy padding of a panther approaching the door, pushing it wider open. But suddenly there were sounds of a frantic struggle, and Sanjay's stifled cries were mixed with the grunts of the panther. Kalam Singh leapt to his feet with a shout. The panther had dragged Sanjay out of the door and was pulling him down the steps, when Kalam Singh started battering at the animal with a large stone. The rest of the family screamed in terror, rousing the entire village. A number of men came to Kalam Singh's assistance, and the panther was driven off. But Sanjay lay unconscious.

Someone brought a lantern and the boy's mother screamed when she saw her small son with his head lying in a pool of blood. It looked as if the side of his head had been eaten off by the panther. But he was still alive, and as Kalam Singh plastered ash on the boy's head to stop the bleeding, he found that though the scalp had been torn off one side of the head, the bare bone was smooth and unbroken.

'He won't live through the night,' said a neighbour. 'We'll have to carry him down to the river in the morning.'

The dead were always cremated on the banks of a small river which flowed past Manjari village.

Suddenly the panther, still prowling about the village, called out in rage and frustration, and the villagers rushed to their homes in panic and barricaded themselves in for the night.

Sanjay's mother sat by the boy for the rest of the night, weeping and watching. Towards dawn he started to moan and show signs of coming round. At this sign of returning consciousness, Kalam Singh rose determinedly and looked around for his stick.

He told his elder son to remain behind with the mother and daughter, as he was going to take Sanjay to Dr Taylor at the hospital.

'See, he is moaning and in pain,' said Kalam Singh. 'That means he has a chance to live if he can be treated at once.'

With a stout stick in his hand, and Sanjay on his back, Kalam Singh set off on the two miles of hard mountain track to the hospital at Kemptee. His son, a blood-stained cloth around his head, was moaning but still unconscious. When at last Kalam Singh climbed up through the last fields below the hospital, he asked for the doctor and stammered out an account of what had happened.

It was a terrible injury, as Dr Taylor discovered. The bone over almost one-third of the head was bare and the scalp was torn all round. As the father told his story, the doctor cleaned and dressed the wound, and then gave Sanjay a shot of penicillin to prevent sepsis. Later, Kalam Singh carried the boy home again.

V

After this, the panther went away for some time. But the people of Manjari could not be sure of its whereabouts. They kept to their houses after dark and shut their doors. Bisnu had to stop going to school, because there was no one to accompany him and it was dangerous to go alone. This worried him, because his final exam was only a few weeks off and he would be missing important classwork. When he wasn't in the fields, helping with the sowing of rice and maize, he would be sitting in the shade of a chestnut tree, going through his well-thumbed second-hand school books. He had no other reading, except for a copy of the Ramayana and a Hindi translation of *Alice in Wonderland*. These were well-preserved, read only in fits and starts, and usually kept locked in his mother's old tin trunk.

Sanjay had nightmares for several nights and woke up screaming. But with the resilience of youth, he quickly recovered. At the end of the week he was able to walk to the hospital, though his father always accompanied him. Even a desperate panther will hesitate to attack a party of two. Sanjay, with his thin little face and huge bandaged head, looked a pathetic figure, but he was getting better and the wound looked healthy.

Bisnu often went to see him, and the two boys spent long hours together near the stream. Sometimes Chittru would join them, and they would try catching fish with a home-made net. They were often successful in taking home one or two mountain trout. Sometimes, Bisnu and Chittru wrestled in the shallow water or on the grassy banks of the stream. Chittru was a chubby boy with a broad chest, strong legs and thighs, and when he used his weight he got Bisnu under him. But Bisnu was hard and wiry and had very strong wrists and fingers. When he had Chittru in a vice, the bigger boy would cry out and give up the struggle. Sanjay could not join in these games.

He had never been a very strong boy and he needed plenty of rest if his wounds were to heal well.

The panther had not been seen for over a week, and the people of Manjari were beginning to hope that it might have moved on over the mountain or further down the valley.

'I think I can start going to school again,' said Bisnu. 'The panther has gone away.'

'Don't be too sure,' said Puja. 'The moon is full these days and perhaps it is only being cautious.'

'Wait a few days,' said their mother. 'It is better to wait. Perhaps you could go the day after tomorrow when Sanjay goes to the hospital with his father. Then you will not be alone.'

And so, two days later, Bisnu went up to Kemptee with Sanjay and Kalam Singh. Sanjay's wound had almost healed over. Little islets of flesh had grown over the bone. Dr Taylor told him that he need come to see her only once a fortnight, instead of every third day.

Bisnu went to his school, and was given a warm welcome by his friends and by Mr Nautiyal.

'You'll have to work hard,' said his teacher. 'You have to catch up with the others. If you like, I can give you some extra time after classes.'

'Thank you, sir, but it will make me late,' said Bisnu. 'I must get home before it is dark, otherwise my mother will worry. I think the panther has gone but nothing is certain.'

'Well, you mustn't take risks. Do your best, Bisnu. Work hard and you'll soon catch up with your lessons.'

Sanjay and Kalam Singh were waiting for him outside the school. Together they took the path down to Manjari, passing the postman on the way. Mela Ram said he had heard that the panther was in another district and that there was nothing to fear. He was on his rounds again.

Nothing happened on the way. The langurs were back in their favourite part of the forest. Bisnu got home just as the kerosene lamp was being lit. Puja met him at the door with a winsome smile.

'Did you get the bangles?' she asked.

But Bisnu had forgotten again.

VI

There had been a thunderstorm and some rain—a short, sharp shower which gave the villagers hope that the monsoon would arrive on time. It brought out the thunder lilies—pink, crocus-like flowers which sprang up on the hillsides immediately after a summer shower.

Bisnu, on his way home from school, was caught in the rain. He knew the shower would not last, so he took shelter in a small cave and, to pass the time, began doing sums, scratching figures in the damp earth with the end of a stick.

When the rain stopped, he came out from the cave and continued down the path. He wasn't in a hurry. The rain had made everything smell fresh and good. The scent from fallen pine needles rose from wet earth. The leaves of the oak trees had been washed clean and a light breeze turned them about, showing their silver undersides. The birds, refreshed and high-spirited, set up a terrific noise. The worst offenders were the yellow-bottomed bulbuls who squabbled and fought in the blackberry bushes. A barbet, high up in the branches of a deodar, set up its querulous, plaintive call. And a flock of bright green parrots came swooping down the hill to settle on a wild plum tree and feast on the unripe fruit. The langurs, too, had been revived by the rain. They leapt friskily from tree to tree greeting Bisnu with little grunts.

He was almost out of the oak forest when he heard a faint bleating. Presently, a little goat came stumbling up the path towards him. The kid was far from home and must have strayed from the rest of the herd. But it was not yet conscious of being lost. It came to Bisnu with a hop, skip and a jump and started nuzzling against his legs like a cat.

'I wonder who you belong to,' mused Bisnu, stroking the little creature. 'You'd better come home with me until someone claims you.'

He didn't have to take the kid in his arms. It was used to humans and followed close at his heels. Now that darkness was coming on, Bisnu walked a little faster.

He had not gone very far when he heard the sawing grunt of a panther.

The sound came from the hill to the right, and Bisnu judged the distance to be anything from a hundred to two hundred yards. He hesitated on the path, wondering what to do. Then he picked the kid up in his arms and hurried on in the direction of home and safety.

The panther called again, much closer now. If it was an ordinary panther, it would go away on finding that the kid was with Bisnu. If it was the man-eater, it would not hesitate to attack the boy, for no man-eater fears a human. There was no time to lose and there did not seem much point in running. Bisnu looked up and down the hillside. The forest was far behind him and there were only a few trees in his vicinity. He chose a spruce.

The branches of the Himalayan spruce are very brittle and snap easily beneath a heavy weight. They were strong enough to support Bisnu's light frame. It was unlikely they would take the weight of a full-grown panther. At least that was what Bisnu hoped.

Holding the kid with one arm, Bisnu gripped a low branch and swung himself up into the tree. He was a good climber. Slowly, but confidently he climbed halfway up the tree, until he was about twelve feet above the ground. He couldn't go any higher without risking a fall.

He had barely settled himself in the crook of a branch when the panther came into the open, running into the clearing at a brisk trot. This was no stealthy approach, no wary stalking of its prey. It was the man-eater, all right. Bisnu felt a cold shiver run down his spine. He felt a little sick.

The panther stood in the clearing with a slight thrusting forward of the head. This gave it the appearance of gazing intently and rather short-sightedly at some invisible object in the clearing. But there is nothing short-sighted about a panther's vision. Its sight and hearing are acute.

Bisnu remained motionless in the tree and sent up a prayer to all the gods he could think of. But the kid began bleating. The panther looked up and gave its deep-throated, rasping grunt—a fearsome sound, calculated to strike terror in any tree-borne animal. Many a monkey, petrified by a panther's roar, has fallen from its perch to make a meal for Mr Spots. The man-eater was trying the same technique on Bisnu. But though the boy was trembling with fright, he clung firmly to the base of the spruce tree.

The panther did not make any attempt to leap into the tree. Perhaps, it knew instinctively that this was not the type of tree that it could climb. Instead, it described a semicircle round the tree, keeping its face turned towards Bisnu. Then it disappeared into the bushes.

The man-eater was cunning. It hoped to put the boy off his guard, perhaps entice him down from the tree. For, a few seconds later, with a half-pitched growl, it rushed back into the clearing and then stopped, staring up at the boy in some surprise. The panther was getting frustrated. It snarled, and putting its forefeet up against the tree trunk began scratching at the bark in the manner of an ordinary domestic cat. The tree shook at each thud of the beast's paw.

Bisnu began shouting for help.

The moon had not yet come up. Down in Manjari village, Bisnu's mother and sister stood in their lighted doorway, gazing anxiously up the pathway. Every now and then, Puja would turn to take a look at the small clock.

Sanjay's father appeared in a field below. He had a kerosene lantern in his hand.

'Sister, isn't your boy home as yet?' he asked.

'No, he hasn't arrived. We are very worried. He should have been home an hour ago. Do you think the panther will be about tonight? There's going to be a moon.'

'True, but it won't be dark for another hour. I will fetch the other menfolk, and we will go up the mountain for your boy. There may have been a landslide during the rain. Perhaps the path has been washed away.'

'Thank you, brother. But arm yourselves, just in case the panther is about.'

'I will take my spear,' said Kalam Singh. 'I have sworn to spear that devil when I find him. There is some evil spirit dwelling in the beast and it must be destroyed!'

'I am coming with you,' said Puja.

'No, you cannot go,' said her mother. 'It's bad enough that Bisnu is in danger. You stay at home with me. This is work for men.'

'I shall be safe with them,' insisted Puja. 'I am going, Mother!'

And she jumped down the embankment into the field and followed Sanjay's father through the village.

Ten minutes later, two men armed with axes had joined Kalam Singh in the courtyard of his house, and the small party moved silently and swiftly up the mountain path. Puja walked in the middle of the group, holding the lantern. As soon as the village lights were hidden by a shoulder of the hill, the men began to shout—both to frighten the panther, if it was about, and to give themselves courage.

Bisnu's mother closed the front door and turned to the image of Ganesha, the god for comfort and help.

Bisnu's calls were carried on the wind, and Puja and the men heard him while they were still half a mile away. Their own shouts increased in volume and, hearing their voices, Bisnu felt strength return to his shaking limbs. Emboldened by the approach of his own people, he began shouting insults at the snarling panther, then throwing twigs and small branches at the enraged animal. The kid added its bleats to the boy's shouts, the birds took up the chorus. The langurs squealed and grunted, the searchers shouted themselves hoarse, and the panther howled with rage. The forest had never before been so noisy.

As the search party drew near, they could hear the panther's savage snarls, and hurried, fearing that perhaps Bisnu had been seized. Puja began to run.

'Don't rush ahead, girl,' said Kalam Singh. 'Stay between us.'

The panther, now aware of the approaching humans, stood still in the middle of the clearing, head thrust forward in a familiar stance. There seemed too many men for one panther. When the animal saw the light of the lantern dancing between the trees, it turned, snarled defiance and hate, and without another look at the boy in the tree, disappeared into the bushes. It was not yet ready for a showdown.

VII

Nobody turned up to claim the little goat, so Bisnu kept it. A goat was a poor substitute for a dog, but, like Mary's lamb, it followed Bisnu wherever he went, and the boy couldn't help being touched by its devotion. He took it down to the stream, where it would skip about in the shallows and nibble the sweet grass that grew on the banks.

As for the panther, frustrated in its attempt on Bisnu's life, it did not wait long before attacking another human.

It was Chittru who came running down the path one afternoon, bubbling excitedly about the panther and the postman.

Chittru, deeming it safe to gather ripe bilberries in the daytime, had walked about half a mile up the path from the village, when he had stumbled across Mela Ram's mailbag lying on the ground. Of the postman himself there was no sign. But a trail of blood led through the bushes.

Once again, a party of men headed by Kalam Singh and accompanied by Bisnu and Chittru, went out to look for the postman. But though they found Mela Ram's bloodstained clothes, they could not find his body. The panther had made no mistake this time.

It was to be several weeks before Manjari had a new postman.

A few days after Mela Ram's disappearance, an old woman was sleeping with her head near the open door of her house. She had been advised to sleep inside with the door closed, but the nights were hot and anyway the old woman was a little deaf, and in the middle of the night, an hour before moonrise, the panther seized her by the throat. Her strangled cry woke her grown-up son, and all the men in the village woke up at his shouts and came running.

The panther dragged the old woman out of the house and down the steps, but left her when the men approached with their axes and spears, and made off into the bushes. The old woman was still alive, and the men made a rough stretcher of bamboo and vines and started carrying her up the path. But they had not gone far when she began to cough, and because of her terrible throat wounds, her lungs collapsed and she died.

It was the 'dark of the month'—the week of the new moon when nights are darkest.

Bisnu, closing the front door and lighting the kerosene lantern, said, 'I wonder where that panther is tonight!'

The panther was busy in another village: Sarru's village.

A woman and her daughter had been out in the evening bedding the cattle down in the stable. The girl had gone into the house and the woman was following. As she bent down to go in at the low door, the panther sprang from the bushes. Fortunately, one of its paws hit the doorpost and broke the force of the attack, or the woman would have been killed. When she cried out, the men came round shouting and the panther slunk off. The woman had deep scratches on her back and was badly shocked.

The next day, a small party of villagers presented themselves in front of the magistrate's office at Kemptee and demanded that something be done about the panther. But the magistrate was away on tour, and there was no one else in Kemptee who had a gun. Mr

Nautiyal met the villagers and promised to write to a well-known shikari, but said that it would be at least a fortnight before the shikari would be able to come.

Bisnu was fretting because he could not go to school. Most boys would be only too happy to miss school, but when you are living in a remote village in the mountains and having an education is the only way of seeing the world, you look forward to going to school, even if it is five miles from home. Bisnu's exams were only two weeks off, and he didn't want to remain in the same class while the others were promoted. Besides, he knew he could pass even though he had missed a number of lessons. But he had to sit for the exams. He couldn't miss them.

'Cheer up, Bhaiya,' said Puja, as they sat drinking glasses of hot tea after their evening meal. 'The panther may go away once the rains break.'

'Even the rains are late this year,' said Bisnu. 'It's so hot and dry. Can't we open the door?'

'And be dragged down the steps by the panther?' said his mother. 'It isn't safe to have the window open, let alone the door.'

And she went to the small window—through which a cat would have found difficulty in passing—and bolted it firmly.

With a sigh of resignation, Bisnu threw off all his clothes except his underwear and stretched himself out on the earthen floor.

'We will be rid of the beast soon,' said his mother. 'I know it in my heart. Our prayers will be heard, and you shall go to school and pass your exams.'

To cheer up her children, she told them a humorous story which had been handed down to her by her grandmother. It was all about a tiger, a panther and a bear, the three of whom were made to feel very foolish by a thief hiding in the hollow trunk of a banyan tree. Bisnu was sleepy and did not listen very attentively. He dropped off to sleep before the story was finished.

When he woke, it was dark and his mother and sister were asleep on the cot. He wondered what it was that had woken him. He could hear his sister's easy breathing and the steady ticking of the clock. Far away an owl hooted—an unlucky sign, his mother would have said; but she was asleep and Bisnu was not superstitious.

And then he heard something scratching at the door, and the hair on his head felt tight and prickly. It was like a cat scratching, only louder. The door creaked a little whenever it felt the impact of the paw—a heavy paw, as Bisnu could tell from the dull sound it made.

'It's the panther,' he muttered under his breath, sitting up on the hard floor.

The door, he felt, was strong enough to resist the panther's weight. And if he set up an alarm, he could rouse the village. But the middle of the night was no time for the bravest of men to tackle a panther.

In a corner of the room stood a long bamboo stick with a sharp knife tied to one end, which Bisnu sometimes used for spearing fish. Crawling on all fours across the room, he grasped the home-made spear, and then scrambling on to a cupboard, he drew level with the skylight window. He could get his head and shoulders through the window.

'What are you doing up there?' said Puja, who had woken up at the sound of Bisnu shuffling about the room.

'Be quiet,' said Bisnu. 'You'll wake Mother.'

Their mother was awake by now. 'Come down from there, Bisnu. I can hear a noise outside.'

'Don't worry,' said Bisnu, who found himself looking down on the wriggling animal which was trying to get its paw in under the door. With his mother and Puja awake, there was no time to lose.

He had got the spear through the window, and though he could not manoeuvre it so as to strike the panther's head, he brought the sharp end down with considerable force on the animal's rump.

With a roar of pain and rage the man-eater leapt down from the steps and disappeared into the darkness. It did not pause to see what had struck it. Certain that no human could have come upon it in that fashion, it ran fearfully to its lair, howling until the pain subsided.

VIII

A panther is an enigma. There are occasions when it proves itself to be the most cunning animal under the sun, and yet the very next day it will walk into an obvious trap that no self-respecting jackal would ever go near. One day a panther will prove itself to be a complete coward and run like a hare from a couple of dogs, and the very next it will dash in amongst half a dozen men sitting round a camp fire and inflict terrible injuries on them.

It is not often that a panther is taken by surprise, as its power of sight and hearing are very acute. It is a master at the art of camouflage, and its spotted coat is admirably suited for the purpose. It does not need heavy jungle to hide in. A couple of bushes and the light and shade from surrounding trees are enough to make it almost invisible.

Because the Manjari panther had been fooled by Bisnu, it did not mean that it was a stupid panther. It simply meant that it had been a little careless. And Bisnu and Puja, growing in confidence since their midnight encounter with the animal, became a little careless themselves.

Puja was hoeing the last field above the house and Bisnu, at the other end of the same field, was chopping up several branches of green oak, prior to leaving the wood to dry in the loft. It was late afternoon and the descending sun glinted in patches on the small river. It was a time of day when only the most desperate and daring of man-eaters would be likely to show itself.

Pausing for a moment to wipe the sweat from his brow, Bisnu glanced up at the hillside, and his eye caught sight of a rock on the brow of the hill which seemed unfamiliar to him. Just as he was about to look elsewhere, the round rock began to grow and then alter its shape, and Bisnu watching in fascination was at last able to make out the head and forequarters of the panther. It looked enormous from the angle at which he saw it, and for a moment he thought it was a tiger. But Bisnu knew instinctively that it was the man-eater.

Slowly, the wary beast pulled itself to its feet and began to walk round the side of the great rock. For a second it disappeared and Bisnu wondered if it had gone away. Then it reappeared and the boy was all excitement again. Very slowly and silently the panther walked across the face of the rock until it was in direct line with the corner of the field where Puja was working.

With a thrill of horror Bisnu realized that the panther was stalking his sister. He shook himself free from the spell which had woven itself round him and shouting hoarsely ran forward.

'Run, Puja, run!' he called. 'It's on the hill above you!'

Puja turned to see what Bisnu was shouting about. She saw him gesticulate to the hill behind her, looked up just in time to see the panther crouching for his spring.

With great presence of mind, she leapt down the banking of the field and tumbled into an irrigation ditch.

The springing panther missed its prey, lost its foothold on the slippery shale banking and somersaulted into the ditch a few feet away from Puja. Before the animal could recover from its surprise, Bisnu was dashing down the slope, swinging his axe and shouting, 'Maro, maro!'

Two men came running across the field. They, too, were armed with axes. Together with Bisnu they made a half-circle around the snarling animal, which turned at bay and plunged at them in order to get away. Puja wriggled along the ditch on her stomach. The men aimed their axes at the panther's head, and Bisnu had the satisfaction of getting in a well-aimed blow between the eyes. The animal then charged straight at one of the men, knocked him over and tried to get at his throat. Just then Sanjay's father arrived with his long spear. He plunged the end of the spear into the panther's neck.

The panther left its victim and ran into the bushes, dragging the spear through the grass and leaving a trail of blood on the ground.

The men followed cautiously—all except the man who had been wounded and who lay on the ground, while Puja and the other womenfolk rushed up to help him.

The panther had made for the bed of the stream and Bisnu, Sanjay's father and their companion were able to follow it quite easily. The water was red where the panther had crossed the stream, and the rocks were stained with blood. After they had gone downstream for about a furlong, they found the panther lying still on its side at the edge of the water. It was mortally wounded, but it continued to wave its tail like an angry cat. Then, even the tail lay still.

'It is dead,' said Bisnu. 'It will not trouble us again in this body.'

'Let us be certain,' said Sanjay's father, and he bent down and pulled the panther's tail.

There was no response.

'It is dead,' said Kalam Singh. 'No panther would suffer such an insult were it alive!'

They cut down a long piece of thick bamboo and tied the panther to it by its feet. Then, with their enemy hanging upside down from the bamboo pole, they started back for the village.

'There will be a feast at my house tonight,' said Kalam Singh. 'Everyone in the village must come. And tomorrow we will visit all the villages in the valley and show them the dead panther, so that they may move about again without fear.'

'We can sell the skin in Kemptee,' said their companion. 'It will fetch a good price.'

'But the claws we will give to Bisnu,' said Kalam Singh, putting his arm around the boy's shoulders. 'He has done a man's work today. He deserves the claws.'

A panther's or tiger's claws are considered to be lucky charms.

'I will take only three claws,' said Bisnu. 'One each for my mother and sister, and one for myself. You may give the others to Sanjay and Chittru and the smaller children.'

As the sun set, a big fire was lit in the middle of the village of Manjari and the people gathered round it, singing and laughing. Kalam Singh killed his fattest goat and there was meat for everyone.

IX

Bisnu was on his way home. He had just handed in his first paper, arithmetic, which he had found quite easy. Tomorrow it would be algebra, and when he got home he would have to practice square roots and cube roots and fractional coefficients.

Mr Nautiyal and the entire class had been happy that he had been able to sit for the exams. He was also a hero to them for his part in killing the panther. The story had spread through the villages with the rapidity of a forest fire, a fire which was now raging in

Kemptee town.

When he walked past the hospital, he was whistling cheerfully. Dr Taylor waved to him from the veranda steps.

'How is Sanjay now?' she asked.

'He is well,' said Bisnu.

'And your mother and sister?'

'They are well,' said Bisnu.

'Are you going to get yourself a new dog?'

'I am thinking about it,' said Bisnu. 'At present I have a baby goat—I am teaching it to swim!'

He started down the path to the valley. Dark clouds had gathered and there was a rumble of thunder. A storm was imminent.

'Wait for me!' shouted Sarru, running down the path behind Bisnu, his milk pails clanging against each other. He fell into step beside Bisnu.

'Well, I hope we don't have any more man-eaters for some time,' he said. 'I've lost a lot of money by not being able to take milk up to Kemptee.'

'We should be safe as long as a shikari doesn't wound another panther. There was an old bullet wound in the man-eater's thigh. That's why it couldn't hunt in the forest. The deer were too fast for it.'

'Is there a new postman yet?'

'He starts tomorrow. A cousin of Mela Ram's.'

When they reached the parting of their ways, it had begun to rain a little.

'I must hurry,' said Sarru. It's going to get heavier any minute.'

'I feel like getting wet,' said Bisnu. 'This time it's the monsoon, I'm sure.'

Bisnu entered the forest on his own, and at the same time the rain came down in heavy opaque sheets. The trees shook in the wind and the langurs chattered with excitement.

It was still pouring when Bisnu emerged from the forest, drenched to the skin. But the rain stopped suddenly, just as the village of Manjari came into view. The sun appeared through a rift in the clouds. The leaves and the grass gave out a sweet, fresh smell.

Bisnu could see his mother and sister in the field transplanting the rice seedlings. The menfolk were driving the yoked oxen through the thin mud of the fields, while the children hung on to the oxen's tails, standing on the plain wooden harrows, and with weird cries and shouts sending the animals almost at a gallop along the narrow terraces.

Bisnu felt the urge to be with them, working in the fields. He ran down the path, his feet falling softly on the wet earth. Puja saw him coming and waved at him. She met him at the edge of the field.

'How did you find your paper today?' she asked.

'Oh, it was easy.' Bisnu slipped his hand into hers and together they walked across the field. Puja felt something smooth and hard against her fingers, and before she could see what Bisnu was doing, he had slipped a pair of bangles on her wrist.

'I remembered,' he said with a sense of achievement.

Puja looked at the bangles and blurted out: 'But they are blue, Bhai, and I wanted red and gold bangles!' And then, when she saw him looking crestfallen, she hurried on: 'But they are very pretty and you did remember… Actually, they are just as nice as red and gold bangles! Come into the house when you are ready. I have made something special for you.'

'I am coming,' said Bisnu, turning towards the house. 'You don't know how hungry a man gets, walking five miles to reach home!'

TALES OF FOSTERGANJ

FOSTER OF FOSTERGANJ

Straddling a spur of the Mussoorie range, as it dips into the Doon valley, Fosterganj came into existence some two hundred years ago and was almost immediately forgotten. And today it is not very different from what it was in 1961, when I lived there briefly.

A quiet corner, where I could live like a recluse and write my stories—that was what I was looking for. And in Fosterganj I thought I'd found my retreat: a cluster of modest cottages, a straggling little bazaar, a post office, a crumbling castle (supposedly haunted), a mountain stream at the bottom of the hill, a winding footpath that took you either uphill or down. What more could one ask for? It reminded me a little of an English village, and indeed that was what it had once been; a tiny settlement on the outskirts of the larger hill station. But the British had long since gone, and the residents were now a fairly mixed lot, as we shall see.

I forget what took me to Fosterganj in the first place. Destiny, perhaps; although I'm not sure why destiny would have bothered to guide an itinerant writer to an obscure hamlet in the hills. Chance would be a better word. For chance plays a great part in all our lives. And it was just by chance that I found myself in the Fosterganj bazaar one fine morning early in May. The oaks and maples were in new leaf; geraniums flourished on sunny balconies; a boy delivering milk whistled a catchy Dev Anand song; a mule train clattered down the street. The chill of winter had gone and there was warmth in the sunshine that played upon old walls.

I sat in a teashop, tested my teeth on an old bun, and washed it down with milky tea. The bun had been around for some time, but so had I, so we were quits. At the age of forty I could digest almost anything.

The teashop owner, Melaram, was a friendly sort, as are most teashop owners. He told me that not many tourists made their way down to Fosterganj. The only attraction was the waterfall, and you had to be fairly fit in order to scramble down the steep and narrow path that led to the ravine where a little stream came tumbling over the rocks. I would visit it one day, I told him.

'Then you should stay here a day or two,' said Melaram.

'Explore the stream. Walk down to Rajpur. You'll need a good walking stick. Look, I have several in my shop. Cherry wood, walnut wood, oak.' He saw me wavering. 'You'll also need one to climb the next hill—it's called Pari Tibba.' I was charmed by the name—Fairy Hill.

I hadn't planned on doing much walking that day—the walk down to Fosterganj from Mussoorie had already taken almost an hour—but I liked the look of a sturdy cherry-wood walking stick, and I bought one for two rupees. Those were the days of simple living. You don't see two-rupee notes any more. You don't see walking sticks either. Hardly anyone walks.

I strolled down the small bazaar, without having to worry about passing cars and lorries or a crush of people. Two or three schoolchildren were sauntering home, burdened by their school bags bursting with homework. A cow and a couple of stray dogs examined the contents of an overflowing dustbin. A policeman sitting on a stool outside a tiny police outpost yawned, stretched, stood up, looked up and down the street in anticipation of crimes to come, scratched himself in the anal region and sank back upon his stool.

A man in a crumpled shirt and threadbare trousers came up to me, looked me over with his watery grey eyes, and said,

'Sir, would you like to buy some gladioli bulbs?' He held up a basket full of bulbs which might have been onions. His chin was covered with a grey stubble, some of his teeth were missing, the remaining ones yellow with neglect.

'No, thanks,' I said. 'I live in a tiny flat in Delhi. No room for flowers.'

'A world without flowers,' he shook his head. 'That's what it's coming to.'

'And where do you plant your bulbs?'

'I grow gladioli, sir, and sell the bulbs to good people like you. My name's Foster. I own the lands all the way down to the waterfall.'

For a landowner he did not look very prosperous. But his name intrigued me. 'Isn't this area called Fosterganj?' I asked.

'That's right. My grandfather was the first to settle here. He was a grandson of Bonnie Prince Charlie who fought the British at Bannockburn. I'm the last Foster of Fosterganj. Are you sure you won't buy my daffodil bulbs?'

'I thought you said they were gladioli.'

'Some gladioli, some daffodils.'

They looked like onions to me, but to make him happy I parted with two rupees (which seemed the going rate in Fosterganj) and relieved him of his basket of bulbs. Foster shuffled off, looking a bit like Chaplin's tramp but not half as dapper. He clearly needed the two rupees. Which made me feel less foolish about spending money that I should have held on to. Writers were poor in those days. Though I didn't feel poor.

Back at the teashop I asked Melaram if Foster really owned a lot of land.

'He has a broken-down cottage and the right-of-way. He charges people who pass through his property. Spends all the money on booze. No one owns the hillside, it's government land. Reserved forest. But everyone builds on it.'

Just as well, I thought, as I returned to town with my basket of onions. Who wanted another noisy hill station? One Mall Road was more than enough. Back in my hotel room, I was about to throw the bulbs away, but on second thoughts decided to keep them. After all, even an onion makes a handsome plant.

BATHROOM WITH A VIEW

Next morning I found myself trudging down from Mussoorie to Fosterganj again. I didn't quite know why I was attracted to the place—but it was quaint, isolated, a forgotten corner of an otherwise changing hill town; and I had always been attracted to forgotten corners.

There was no hotel or guesthouse in the area, which in itself was a blessing; but I needed somewhere to stay, if I was going to spend some time there.

Melaram directed me to the local bakery. Hassan, the baker, had a room above his shop that had lain vacant since he built it a few years ago. An affable man, Hassan was the proud father of a dozen children; I say dozen at random, because I never did get to ascertain the exact number as they were never in one place at the same time. They did not live in the room above the bakery, which was much too small, but in a rambling old building below the bazaar, which housed a number of large families—the baker's, the tailor's, the postman's, among others.

I was shown the room. It was scantily furnished, the bed taking up almost half the space. A small table and chair stood near the window. Windows are important. I find it impossible to live in a room without a window. This one provided a view of the street and the buildings on the other side. Nothing very inspiring, but at least it wouldn't be dull.

A narrow bathroom was attached to the room. Hassan was very proud of it, because he had recently installed a flush tank and western-style potty. I complimented him on the potty and said it looked very comfortable. But what really took my fancy was the bathroom window. It hadn't been opened for some time, and the glass panes were caked with dirt. But when finally we got it open, the view was remarkable. Below the window was a sheer drop of two or three hundred feet. Ahead, an open vista, a wide valley, and then the mountains striding away towards the horizon. I don't think any hotel in town had such a splendid view. I could see myself sitting for hours on that potty, enraptured, enchanted, having the valley and the mountains all to myself. Almost certain constipation of course, but I would take that risk.

'Forty rupees a month,' said Hassan, and I gave him two months' rent on the spot.

'I'll move in next week,' I said. 'First I have to bring my books from Delhi.'

On my way back to the town I took a short cut through

the forest. A swarm of yellow butterflies drifted across the path. A woodpecker pecked industriously on the bark of a tree, searching for young cicadas. Overhead, wild duck flew north, on their way across Central Asia, all travelling without passports. Birds and butterflies recognize no borders.

I hadn't been this way before, and I was soon lost. Two village boys returning from town with their milk cans gave me the wrong directions. I was put on the right path by a girl who was guiding a cow home. There was something about her fresh face and bright smile that I found tremendously appealing. She was less than beautiful but more than pretty, if you know what I mean. A face to remember.

A little later I found myself in an open clearing, with a large pool in the middle. Its still waters looked very deep. At one end there were steps, apparently for bathers. But the water did not look very inviting. It was a sunless place, several old oaks shutting out the light. Fallen off leaves floated on the surface. No birds sang. It was a strange, haunted sort of place. I hurried on.

LATE FOR A FUNERAL

When I said that Fosterganj appeared to be the sort of sleepy hollow where nothing ever happened, it only served to show that appearances can be deceptive. When I returned that summer, carrying books and writing materials, I found the little hamlet in a state of turmoil.

There was a rabies scare.

On my earlier visit I had noticed the presence of a number of stray dogs. The jackal population must have been fairly large too. And jackals are carriers of the rabies virus.

I had barely alighted from the town's only Ambassador taxi when I had to jump in again. Down the road came some ten to fifteen dogs, of no particular breed but running with the urgency of greyhounds, ears flattened, tails between their legs, teeth bared in terror, for close behind them came the dog-catchers, three or four men carrying staves and what appeared to be huge butterfly nets. Even as I gaped in astonishment one of the dogs took a tumble and, howling with fright, was scooped up and dumped in a metal cage on wheels which stood at the side of the road.

The dog chase swept past me, one young man staying behind to secure the trapped canine. Some people have faces that bear an uncanny resemblance to the features of different animals. This particular youth had something of the wolf in his countenance. The dog obviously thought so too, for it whimpered and cowered in a corner of its rusty cage. I am not a great dog-lover but I felt sorry for this frightened creature and put my hand through the bars to try and pat it. Immediately it bared its teeth and lunged at my hand. I withdrew it in a hurry.

The young man laughed at my discomfiture.

'Mad dog,' he said. 'All the dogs are going mad. Biting people. Running all over the place and biting people. We have to round them up.'

'And then what will you do? Shoot them?'

'Not allowed to kill them. Cruelty to animals.'

'So then?'

'We'll let them loose in the jungle—down near Rajpur.'

'But they'll start biting people there.'

'Problem for Rajpur.' He smiled disarmingly—canines like a wolf's.

'If they are mad they'll die anyway,' I said. 'But don't you have a vet—an animal doctor—in this place?'

'Not in Fosterganj. Only in Rajpur. That's why we leave them there.'

Defeated by this logic, I picked up my two suitcases and crossed the empty street to Hassan's bakery. The taxi sped away; no business in Fosterganj.

Over the next few days, several people were bitten and had to go down to Dehra for anti-rabies treatment. The cobbler's wife refused to go, and was dead within the month. There were many cases in Rajpur, due no doubt to the sudden influx of mad dogs expelled from Fosterganj.

In due course, life returned to normal, as it always does in India, post earthquakes, cyclones, riots, epidemics and cricket controversies. Apathy, or lethargy, or a combination of the two, soon casts a spell over everything and the most traumatic events are quickly forgotten.

'Sab chalta hai,' Hassan, my philosophical landlord, would say, speaking for everyone.

It did not take me long to settle down in my little room above the bakery. Recent showers had brought out the sheen on new leaves, transformed the grass on the hillside from a faded yellow to an emerald green. A barbet atop a spruce tree was in full cry. It would keep up its monotonous chant all summer. And early morning, a whistling-thrush would render its interrupted melody, never quite finishing what it had to say.

It was good to hear the birds and laughing schoolchildren through my open window. But I soon learnt to shut it whenever I went out. Late one morning, on returning from my walk, I found a large rhesus monkey sitting on my bed, tearing up a loaf of bread that Hassan had baked for me. I tried to drive the fellow away, but he seemed reluctant to leave. He bared his teeth and swore at me in monkey language. Then he stuffed a piece of bread into his mouth and glared at me, daring me to do my worst. I recalled that monkeys carry rabies, and not wanting to join those who had recently been bitten by rabid dogs, I backed out of the room and called for help. One of Hassan's brood came running up the steps with a hockey stick, and chased the invader away.

'Always keep a mug of water handy,' he told me. 'Throw the water on him and he'll be off. They hate cold water.'

'You may be right,' I said. 'I've never seen a monkey taking a bath.'

'See how miserable they are when it rains,' said my rescuer. 'They huddle together as though it's the end of the world.'

'Strange, isn't it? Birds like bathing in the rain.'

'So do I. Wait till the monsoon comes. You can join me then.'

'Perhaps I will.'

On this friendly note we parted, and I cleaned up the mess made by my simian visitor, and then settled down to do some writing.

But there was something about the atmosphere of Fosterganj that discouraged any kind of serious work or effort. Tucked away in a fold of the hills, its inhabitants had begun to resemble their surroundings: one old man resembled a willow bent by rain and wind; an elderly lady with her umbrella reminded me of a colourful mushroom, quite possibly poisonous; my good baker-cum-landlord looked like a bit of the hillside, scarred and uneven but stable. The children were like young grass, coming up all over the place; but the adolescents were like nettles, you never knew if they would sting when touched. There was a young Tibetan lady whose smile was like the blue sky opening up. And there was no brighter blue than the sky as seen from Fosterganj on a clear day.

It took me some time to get to know all the inhabitants. But one of the first was Professor Lulla, recently retired, who came hurrying down the road like the White Rabbit in Alice in Wonderland, glancing at his watch and muttering to himself. If, like the White Rabbit, he was saying 'I'm late, I'm late!' I wouldn't have been at all surprised. I was standing outside the bakery, chatting to one of the children, when he came up to me, adjusted his spectacles, peered at me through murky lenses, and said, 'Welcome to Fosterganj, sir. I believe you've come to stay for the season.'

'I'm not sure how long I'll stay,' I said. 'But thank you for your welcome.'

'We must get together and have a cultural and cultured exchange,' he said, rather pompously. 'Not many intellectuals in Fosterganj, you know.'

'I was hoping there wouldn't be.'

'But we'll talk, we'll talk. Only can't stop now. I have a funeral to attend. Eleven o'clock at the Camel's Back cemetery. Poor woman. Dead. Quite dead. Would you care to join me?'

'Er—I'm not in the party mood,' I said. 'And I don't think I knew the deceased.'

'Old Miss Gamleh. Your landlord thought she was a flowerpot—would have been ninety next month. Wonderful woman. Hated chokra-boys.' He looked distastefully at the boy grinning up at him. 'Stole all her plums, if the monkeys didn't get them first. Spent all her life in the hill station. Never married. Jilted by a weedy British colonel, awful fellow, even made off with her savings. But she managed on her own. Kept poultry, sold eggs to the hotels.'

'What happens to the poultry?' I asked.

'Oh, hens can look after themselves,' he said airily. 'But I can't linger or I'll be late. It's a long walk to the cemetery.' And he set off in determined fashion, like Scott of the Antarctic about to brave a blizzard.

'Must have been a close friend, the old lady who passed away,' I remarked.

'Not at all,' said Hassan, who had been standing in his doorway listening to the conversation. 'I doubt if she ever spoke to him. But Professor Lulla never misses a funeral. He goes to all of them—cremations, burials—funerals of any well-known person, even strangers. It's a hobby with him.'

'Extraordinary,' I said. 'I thought collecting matchbox labels was sad enough as a hobby. Doesn't it depress him?'

'It seems to cheer him up, actually. But I must go too, sir. If you don't mind keeping an eye on the bakery for an hour or two, I'll hurry along to the funeral and see if I can get her poultry cheap. Miss Gamla's hens give good eggs, I'm told. Little Ali will look after the customers, sir. All you have to do is see that they don't make off with the buns and cream-rolls.'

I don't know if Hassan attended the funeral, but he came back with two baskets filled with cackling hens, and a rooster to keep them company.

ENTER A MAN-EATER

Did I say nothing ever happens in Fosterganj?

That is true in many ways. If you don't count the outbreak of rabies, that is, or the annual depredations of a man-eating leopard, or the drownings in the pool.

I suppose I should start with the leopard, since its activities commenced not long after I came to live in Fosterganj.

Its first victim was Professor Lulla, who was on his way to attend another funeral.

I don't remember who had died. But I remember the cremation was to take place in Rajpur, at the bottom of the hill, an hour's walk from Fosterganj. The professor was anxious not to miss it, although he had met the recipient of the honour only once. Before the sun was up, he was on his way down the mountain trail. At that early hour, the mist from the valley rises, and it obscured the view, so that he probably did not see the leopard as it followed silently behind him, waiting its opportunity, stalking its victim with pleasurable anticipation. The importunate professor might have heard the rattle of stones as the leopard charged; might have had a glimpse of it as it sprang at his throat; might even have uttered a cry, or screamed for help. But there was no one to hear, no witness of the attack.

The leopard dragged the dying man into the kingora bushes and began to gnaw at his flesh. He was still at his meal when, half an hour later, a group of Nepali labourers came down the path, singing and making merry, and frightened the beast away. They found the mangled remains of the professor; two of the party ran back to Fosterganj for help, while the rest stood guard over the half-eaten torso.

Help came in the form of half the population of Fosterganj. There was nothing they could do, as the leopard did not return. But next day they gave the professor a good funeral.

However, a couple of public-spirited citizens were determined to hunt down the leopard before it took a further toll of human life. One of them was our local bank manager, Vishaal, a friendly and amiable sort, who was also a self-confessed disciple of Jim Corbett, the great shikari who had disposed of dozens of man-eaters. Vishaal did not possess a gun, but the bank's chowkidar, a retired Gurkha soldier, did. He had an ancient 12-bore shotgun which he carried about with him wherever he was on duty. The gun hadn't been fired for years—not since it had gone off accidentally when being handled by an inquisitive customer.

Vishaal found a box of cartridges in the bank's safe. They had been there for several years and looked a little mouldy, as did almost everything in Fosterganj, including some of the older residents. 'Stay here more than three years,' philosophized Hassan, 'and unless you have God on your side, your hair goes white and your teeth get yellow. Everyone ends up looking like old Foster—descendent of the kings of Scotland!'

'It must be the water,' I said.

'No, it's the mist,' said Hassan. 'It hangs around Fosterganj even in good weather. It keeps the sun out. Look at my bread. Can't keep a loaf fresh for more than a day, the mould gets to it in no time. And the monsoon hasn't even begun!'

In spite of his bad teeth and ragged appearance, however, Foster—or Bonnie Prince Charlie, as the older residents called him—was fairly active, and it was he who set up a rough machaan in an old oak tree overlooking the stream at the bottom of the hill. He even sold Vishaal an old goat, to be used as bait for the leopard.

Vishaal persuaded me to keep him company on the machaan, and produced a bottle of brandy that he said would see us through the night.

Our vigil began at eight, and by midnight the brandy bottle was empty. No leopard, although the goat made its presence apparent by bleating without a break.

'If the leopard has developed a taste for humans,' I said, 'why should it come for a silly old goat?'

I dozed off for some time, only to be awakened by a nudge from Vishaal, who whispered, 'Something's out there. I think it's the leopard! Shine the torch on it!'

I shone the torch on the terrified goat, and at the same moment a leopard sprang out of the bushes and seized its victim. There was a click from Vishaal's gun. The cartridge had failed to go off.

'Fire the other barrel!' I urged.

The second cartridge went off. There was a tremendous bang. But by then both leopard and goat had vanished into the night.

'I thought you said it only liked humans,' said Vishaal.

'Must be another leopard,' I said.

We trudged back to his rooms, and opened another bottle of brandy.

In the morning a villager came to the bank and demanded a hundred rupees for his goat.

'But it was Foster's goat,' protested Vishaal. 'I've already paid him for it.'

'Not Foster Sahib's goat,' said the villager. 'He only borrowed it for the night.'

A MAGIC OIL

A day or two later I was in the bank, run by Vishaal (manager), Negi (cashier), and Suresh (peon). I was sitting opposite Vishaal, who was at his desk, taken up by two handsome paperweights but no papers. Suresh had brought me a cup of tea from the teashop across the road. There was just one customer in the bank, Hassan, who was making a deposit. A cosy summer morning in Fosterganj: not much happening, but life going on just the same.

In walked Foster. He'd made an attempt at shaving, but appeared to have given up at a crucial stage, because now he looked like a wasted cricketer finally on his way out. The effect was enhanced by the fact that he was wearing flannel trousers that had once been white but were now greenish yellow; the previous monsoon was to blame. He had found an old tie, and this was strung round his neck, or rather his unbuttoned shirt collar. The said shirt had seen many summers and winters in Fosterganj, and was frayed at the cuffs. Even so, Foster looked quite spry, as compared to when I had last seen him.

'Come in, come in!' said Vishaal, always polite to his customers, even those who had no savings. 'How is your gladioli farm?'

'Coming up nicely,' said Foster. 'I'm growing potatoes too.'

'Very nice. But watch out for the porcupines, they love potatoes.'

'Shot one last night. Cut my hands getting the quills out. But porcupine meat is great. I'll send you some the next time I shoot one.'

'Well, keep some ammunition for the leopard. We've got to get it before it kills someone else.'

'It won't be around for two or three weeks. They keep moving, do leopards. He'll circle the mountain, then be back in these parts. But that's not what I came to see you about, Mr Vishaal. I was hoping for a small loan.'

'Small loan, big loan, that's what we are here for. In what way can we help you, sir?'

'I want to start a chicken farm.'

'Most original.'

'There's a great shortage of eggs in Mussoorie. The hotels want eggs, the schools want eggs, the restaurants want eggs. And they have to get them from Rajpur or Dehradun.'

'Hassan has a few hens,' I put in.

'Only enough for home consumption. I'm thinking in terms of hundreds of eggs—and broiler chickens for the table. I want to make Fosterganj the chicken capital of India. It will be like old times, when my ancestor planted the first potatoes here, brought all the way from Scotland!'

'I thought they came from Ireland,' I said. 'Captain Young, up at Landour.'

'Oh well, we brought other things. Like Scotch whisky.'

'Actually, Irish whisky got here first. Captain Kennedy, up in Simla.' I wasn't Irish, but I was in a combative frame of mind, which is the same as being Irish.

To mollify Foster, I said, 'You did bring the bagpipe.' And when he perked up, I added: 'But the Gurkha is better at playing it.'

This contretemps over, Vishaal got Foster to sign a couple of forms and told him that the loan would be processed in due course and that we'd all celebrate over a bottle of Scotch whisky. Foster left the room with something of a swagger. The prospect of some money coming in—even if it is someone else's—will put any man in an optimistic frame of mind. And for Foster the prospect of losing it was as yet far distant.

I wanted to make a phone call to my bank in Delhi, so that I could have some of my savings sent to me, and Vishaal kindly allowed me to use his phone.

There were only four phones in all of Fosterganj, and there didn't seem to be any necessity for more. The bank had one. So did Dr Bisht. So did Brigadier Bakshi, retired. And there was one in the police station, but it was usually out of order.

The police station, a one-room affair, was manned by a Daroga and a constable. If the Daroga felt like a nap, the constable took charge. And if the constable took the afternoon off, the Daroga would run the place. This worked quite well, as there wasn't much crime in Fosterganj—if you didn't count Foster's illicit still at the bottom of the hill (Scottish hooch, he called the stuff he distilled); or a charming young delinquent called Sunil, who picked pockets for a living (though not in Fosterganj); or the barber who supplemented his income by supplying charas to his agents at some of the boarding schools; or the man who sold the secretions of certain lizards, said to increase sexual potency— except that it was only linseed oil, used for oiling cricket bats.

I found the last mentioned, a man called Rattan Lal, sitting on a stool outside my door when I returned from the bank.

'Saande-ka-tel,' he declared abruptly, holding up a small bottle containing a vitreous yellow fluid. 'Just one application, sahib, and the size and strength of your valuable member will increase dramatically. It will break down doors, should doors be shut against you. No chains will hold it down. You will be as a stallion, rampant in a field full of fillies. Sahib, you will rule the roost! Memsahibs and beautiful women will fall at your feet.'

'It will get me into trouble, for certain,' I demurred. 'It's great stuff, I'm sure. But wasted here in Fosterganj.'

Rattan Lal would not be deterred. 'Sahib, every time you try it, you will notice an increase in dimensions, guaranteed!'

'Like Pinocchio's nose,' I said in English. He looked puzzled. He understood the word 'nose', but had no idea what I meant.

'Naak?' he said. 'No, sahib, you don't rub it on your nose. Here, down between the legs,' and he made as if to give a demonstration. I held a hand up to restrain him.

'There was a boy named Pinocchio in a far-off country,' I explained, switching back to Hindi. 'His nose grew longer every time he told a lie.'

'I tell no lies, sahib. Look, my nose is normal. Rest is very big. You want to see?'

'Another day,' I said.

'Only ten rupees.'

'The bottle or the rest of you?'

'You joke, sahib,' and he thrust a bottle into my unwilling hands and removed a ten-rupee note from my shirt pocket; all done very simply.

'I will come after a month and check up,' he said. 'Next time I will bring the saanda itself! You are in the prime of your life, it will make you a bull among men.' And away he went.

~

The little bottle of oil stood unopened on the bathroom shelf for weeks. I was too scared to use it. It was like the bottle in Alice in Wonderland with the label DRINK ME. Alice drank it, and shot up to the ceiling. I wasn't sure I wanted to grow that high.

I did wonder what would happen if I applied some of it to my scalp. Would it stimulate hair growth? Would it stimulate my thought processes? Put an end to writer's block?

Well, I never did find out. One afternoon I heard a clatter in the bathroom and looked in to see a large and sheepish-looking monkey jump out of the window with the bottle.

But to return to Rattan Lal—some hours after I had been sold the aphrodisiac, I was walking up to town to get a newspaper when I met him on his way down.

'Any luck with the magic oil?' I asked.

'All sold out!' he said, beaming with pleasure. 'Ten bottles sold at the Savoy, and six at Hakman's. What a night it's going to be for them.' And he rubbed his hands at the prospect.

'A very busy night,' I said. 'Either that, or they'll be looking for you to get their money back.'

'I come next month. If you are still here, I'll keep another bottle for you. Look there!' He took me by the arm and pointed at a large rock lizard that was sunning itself on the parapet. 'You catch me some of those, and I'll pay you for them. Be my partner. Bring me lizards—not small ones, only big fellows—and I will buy!'

'How do you extract the tel?' I asked.

'Ah, that's a trade secret. But I will show you when you bring me some saandas. Now I must go. My good wife waits for me with impatience.'

And off he went, down the bridle path to Rajpur.

The rock lizard was still on the wall, enjoying its afternoon siesta.

It did occur to me that I might make a living from breeding rock lizards. Perhaps Vishaal would give me a loan. I wasn't making much as a writer.

FAIRY GLEN PALACE

The old bridle path from Rajpur to Mussoorie passed through Fosterganj at a height of about five thousand feet. In the old days, before the motor road was built, this was the only road to the hill station. You could ride up on a pony, or walk, or be carried in a basket (if you were a child) or in a doolie (if you were a lady or an invalid). The doolie was a cross between a hammock, a stretcher and a sedan chair, if you can imagine such a contraption. It was borne aloft by two perspiring partners. Sometimes they sat down to rest, and dropped you unceremoniously. I have a picture of my grandmother being borne uphill in a doolie, and she looks petrified. There was an incident in which a doolie, its occupant and two bearers, all went over a cliff just before Fosterganj, and perished in the fall. Sometimes you can see the ghost of this poor lady being borne uphill by two phantom bearers.

Fosterganj has its ghosts, of course. And they are something of a distraction.

Writing is my vocation, and I have always tried to follow the apostolic maxim: 'Study to be quiet and to mind your own business.' But in small-town India one is constantly drawn into other people's business, just as they are drawn towards yours. In Fosterganj it was quiet enough, there were few people; there was no excuse for shirking work. But tales of haunted houses and fairy-infested forests have always intrigued me, and when I heard that the ruined palace half way down to Rajpur was a place to be avoided after dark, it was natural for me to start taking my evening walks in its direction.

Fairy Glen was its name. It had been built on the lines of a Swiss or French chalet, with numerous turrets decorating its many wings—a huge, rambling building, two-storeyed, with numerous balconies and cornices and windows; a hodge-podge of architectural styles, a wedding-cake of a palace, built to satisfy the whims and fancies of its late owner, the Raja of Ranipur, a small state near the Nepal border. Maintaining this ornate edifice must have been something of a nightmare; and the present heirs had quite given up on it, for bits of the roof were missing, some windows were without panes, doors had developed cracks, and what had once been a garden was now a small jungle. Apparently there was no one living there anymore; no sign of a caretaker. I had walked past the wrought-iron gate several times without seeing any signs of life, apart from a large grey cat sunning itself outside a broken window.

Then one evening, walking up from Rajpur, I was caught in a storm.

A wind had sprung up, bringing with it dark, over-burdened clouds. Heavy drops of rain were followed by hailstones bouncing off the stony path. Gusts of wind rushed through the oaks, and leaves and small branches were soon swirling through the air. I was still a couple of miles from the Fosterganj bazaar, and I did not fancy sheltering under a tree, as flashes of lightning were beginning to light up the darkening sky. Then I found myself outside the gate of the abandoned palace.

Outside the gate stood an old sentry box. No one had stood sentry in it for years. It was a good place in which to shelter. But I hesitated because a large bird was perched on the gate, seemingly oblivious to the rain that was still falling.

It looked like a crow or a raven, but it was much bigger than either—in fact, twice the size of a crow, but having all the features of one—and when a flash of lightning lit up the gate, it gave a squawk, opened its enormous wings and took off, flying in the direction of the oak forest. I hadn't seen such a bird before; there was something dark and malevolent and almost supernatural about it. But it had gone, and I darted into the sentry box without further delay.

I had been standing there some ten minutes, wondering when the rain was going to stop, when I heard someone running down the road. As he approached, I could see that he was just a boy, probably eleven or twelve; but in the dark I could not make out his features. He came up to the gate, lifted the latch, and was about to go in when he saw me in the sentry box.

'Kaun? Who are you?' he asked, first in Hindi then in English. He did not appear to be in any way anxious or alarmed.

'Just sheltering from the rain,' I said. 'I live in the bazaar.' He took a small torch from his pocket and shone it in my face.

'Yes, I have seen you there. A tourist.'

'A writer. I stay in places, I don't just pass through.'

'Do you want to come in?'

I hesitated. It was still raining and the roof of the sentry box was leaking badly.

'Do you live here?' I asked.

'Yes, I am the raja's nephew. I live here with my mother. Come in.' He took me by the hand and led me through the gate. His hand was quite rough and heavy for an eleven- or twelve-year-old. Instead of walking with me to the front steps and entrance of the old palace, he led me around to the rear of the building, where a faint light glowed in a mullioned window, and in its light I saw that he had a very fresh and pleasant face—a face as yet untouched by the trials of life.

Instead of knocking on the door, he tapped on the window.

'Only strangers knock on the door,' he said. 'When I tap on the window, my mother knows it's me.'

'That's clever of you,' I said.

He tapped again, and the door was opened by an unusually tall woman wearing a kind of loose, flowing gown that looked strange in that place, and on her. The light was behind her, and I couldn't see her face until we had entered the room. When she turned to me, I saw that she had a long reddish scar running down one side of her face. Even so, there was a certain, hard beauty in her appearance.

'Make some tea, Mother,' said the boy rather brusquely. 'And something to eat. I'm hungry. Sir, will you have something?' He looked enquiringly at me. The light from a kerosene lamp fell full on his face. He was wide-eyed, full- lipped, smiling; only his voice seemed rather mature for one so young. And he spoke like someone much older, and with an almost unsettling sophistication.

'Sit down, sir.' He led me to a chair, made me comfortable.

'You are not too wet, I hope?'

'No, I took shelter before the rain came down too heavily. But you are wet, you'd better change.'

'It doesn't bother me.' And after a pause, 'Sorry there is no electricity. Bills haven't been paid for years.'

'Is this your place?'

'No, we are only caretakers. Poor relations, you might say. The palace has been in dispute for many years. The raja and his brothers keep fighting over it, and meanwhile it is slowly falling down. The lawyers are happy. Perhaps I should study and become a lawyer some day.'

'Do you go to school?'

'Sometimes.'

'How old are you?'

'Quite old, I'm not sure. Mother, how old am I?' he asked, as the tall woman returned with cups of tea and a plate full of biscuits.

She hesitated, gave him a puzzled look. 'Don't you know? It's on your certificate.'

'I've lost the certificate.'

'No, I've kept it safely.' She looked at him intently, placed a hand on his shoulder, then turned to me and said, 'He is twelve,' with a certain finality.

We finished our tea. It was still raining.

'It will rain all night,' said the boy. 'You had better stay here.'

'It will inconvenience you.'

'No, it won't. There are many rooms. If you do not mind the darkness. Come, I will show you everything. And meanwhile my mother will make some dinner. Very simple food, I hope you won't mind.'

The boy took me around the old palace, if you could still call it that. He led the way with a candle-holder from which a large candle threw our exaggerated shadows on the walls.

'What's your name?' I asked, as he led me into what must have been a reception room, still crowded with ornate furniture and bric-a-brac.

'Bhim,' he said. 'But everyone calls me Lucky.'

'And are you lucky?'

He shrugged. 'Don't know...' Then he smiled up at me.

'Maybe you'll bring me luck.'

We walked further into the room. Large oil paintings hung from the walls, gathering mould. Some were portraits of royalty, kings and queens of another era, wearing decorative headgear, strange uniforms, the women wrapped in jewellery—more jewels than garments, it seemed—and sometimes accompanied by children who were also weighed down by excessive clothing. A young man sat on a throne, his lips curled in a sardonic smile.

'My grandfather,' said Bhim.

He led me into a large bedroom taken up by a four-poster bed which had probably seen several royal couples copulating upon it. It looked cold and uninviting, but Bhim produced a voluminous razai from a cupboard and assured me that it would be warm and quite luxurious, as it had been his grandfather's.

'And when did your grandfather die?' I asked.

'Oh, fifty-sixty years ago, it must have been.'

'In this bed, I suppose.'

'No, he was shot accidentally while out hunting. They said it was an accident. But he had enemies.'

'Kings have enemies... And this was the royal bed?'

He gave me a sly smile; not so innocent after all. 'Many women slept in it. He had many queens.'

'And concubines.'

'What are concubines?'

'Unofficial queens.'

'Yes, those too.'

A worldly-wise boy of twelve.

A BIG BLACK BIRD

I did not feel like sleeping in that room, with its musty old draperies and paint peeling off the walls. A trickle of water from the ceiling fell down the back of my shirt and made me shiver.

'The roof is leaking,' I said. 'Maybe I'd better go home.'

'You can't go now, it's very late. And that leopard has been seen again.'

He fetched a china bowl from the dressing-table and placed it on the floor to catch the trickle from the ceiling. In another corner of the room a metal bucket was receiving a steady patter from another leak.

'The palace is leaking everywhere,' said Bhim cheerfully. 'This is the only dry room.' He took me by the hand and led me back to his own quarters. I was surprised, again, by how heavy and rough his hand was for a boy, and presumed that he did a certain amount of manual work such as chopping wood for a daily fire. In winter the building would be unbearably cold.

His mother gave us a satisfying meal, considering the ingredients at her disposal were somewhat limited. Once again, I tried to get away. But only half-heartedly. The boy intrigued me; so did his mother; so did the rambling old palace; and the rain persisted.

Bhim the Lucky took me to my room; waited with the guttering candle till I had removed my shoes; handed me a pair of very large pyjamas.

'Royal pyjamas,' he said with a smile. I got into them and floated around.

'Before you go,' I said. 'I might want to visit the bathroom in the night.'

'Of course, sir. It's close by.' He opened a door, and beyond it I saw a dark passage. 'Go a little way, and there's a door on the left. I'm leaving an extra candle and matches on the dressing table.'

He put the lighted candle he was carrying on the table, and left the room without a light. Obviously he knew his way about in the dark. His footsteps receded, and I was left alone with the sound of raindrops pattering on the roof and a loose sheet of corrugated tin roofing flapping away in a wind that had now sprung up.

It was a summer's night, and I had no need of blankets; so I removed my shoes and jacket and lay down on the capacious bed, wondering if I should blow the candle out or allow it to burn as long as it lasted.

Had I been in my own room, I would have been reading— a Conrad or a Chekhov or some other classic—because at night I turn to the classics—but here there was no light and nothing to read.

I got up and blew the candle out. I might need it later on.

Restless, I prowled around the room in the dark, banging into chairs and footstools. I made my way to the window and drew the curtains aside. Some light filtered into the room because behind the clouds there was a moon, and it had been a full moon the night before.

I lay back on the bed. It wasn't very comfortable. It was a box-bed, of the sort that had only just begun to become popular in households with small bedrooms. This one had been around for some time—no doubt a very early version of its type—and although it was covered with a couple of thick mattresses, the woodwork appeared to have warped because it creaked loudly whenever I shifted my position. The boards no longer fitted properly. Either that, or the box-bed had been overstuffed with all sorts of things.

After some time I settled into one position and dozed off for a while, only to be awakened by the sound of someone screaming somewhere in the building. My hair stood on end. The screaming continued, and I wondered if I should get up to investigate. Then suddenly it stopped—broke off in the middle as though it had been muffled by a hand or piece of cloth.

There was a tapping at the pane of the big French window in front of the bed. Probably the branch of a tree, swaying in the wind. But then there was a screech, and I sat up in bed. Another screech, and I was out of it.

I went to the window and pressed my face to the glass. The big black bird—the bird I had seen when taking shelter in the sentry box—was sitting, or rather squatting, on the boundary wall, facing me. The moon, now visible through the clouds, fell full upon it. I had never seen a bird like it before. Crow-like, but heavily built, like a turkey, its beak that of a bird of prey, its talons those of a vulture. I stepped back, and closed the heavy curtains, shutting out the light but also shutting out the image of that menacing bird.

Returning to the bed, I just sat there for a while, wondering if I should get up and leave. The rain had lessened. But the luminous dial of my watch showed it was two in the morning. No time for a stroll in the dark—not with a man-eating leopard in the vicinity.

Then I heard the shriek again. It seemed to echo through the building. It may have been the bird, but to me it sounded all too human. There was silence for a long while after that. I lay back on the bed and tried to sleep. But it was even more uncomfortable than before. Perhaps the wood had warped too much during the monsoon, I thought, and the lid of the old box-bed did not fit properly. Maybe I could push it back into its correct position; then perhaps I could get some sleep.

So I got up again, and after fumbling around in the dark for a few minutes, found the matches and lit the candle. Then I removed the sheets from the bed and pulled away the two mattresses. The cover of the box-bed lay exposed. And a hand protruded from beneath the lid.

It was not a living hand. It was a skeletal hand, fleshless, brittle. But there was a ring on one finger, an opal still clinging to the bone of a small index finger. It glowed faintly in the candlelight.

Shaking a little (for I am really something of a coward, though an inquisitive one), I lifted the lid of the box-bed. Laid out on a pretty counterpane was a skeleton. A bundle of bones, but still clothed in expensive-looking garments. One hand gripped the side of the box-bed; the hand that had kept it from shutting properly.

I dropped the lid of the box-bed and ran from the room— only to blunder into a locked door. Someone, presumably the boy, had locked me into the bedroom.

I banged on the door and shouted, but no one heard me. No one came running. I went to the large French window, but it was firmly fastened; it probably hadn't been opened for many years.

Then I remembered the passageway leading to the bathroom. The boy had pointed it out to me. Possibly there was a way out from there.

There was. It was an old door that opened easily, and I stepped out into the darkness, finding myself entangled in a creeper that grew against the wall. From its cloying fragrance I recognized it as wisteria.

A narrow path led to a wicket-gate at the end of the building. I found my way out of the grounds and back on the familiar public road. The old palace loomed out of the darkness. I turned my back on it and set off for home, my little room above Hassan's bakery.

Nothing happens in Fosterganj, I told myself. But something had happened in that old palace.

THE STREET OF LOST HOMES

'What did you want to go there for?' asked Hassan, when I knocked on his door at the crack of dawn.

'It was raining heavily, and I stopped near the gate to take shelter. A boy invited me in, his mother gave me something to eat, and I ended up spending the night in the raja's bedroom.' I said nothing about screams in the night or the skeleton in the bed.

Hassan presented me with a bun and a glass of hot sweet tea.

'Nobody goes there,' he said. 'The place has a bad name.'

'And why's that?'

'The old raja was a bad man. Tortured his wives, or so it was said.'

'And what happened to him?'

'Got killed in a hunting accident, in the jungles next to Bijnor. He went after a tiger, but the tiger got to him first. Bit his head off! Everyone was pleased. His younger brother inherited the palace, but he never comes here. I think he still lives somewhere near the Nepal border.'

'And the people who still live in the palace?'

'Poor relations, I think. Offspring from one of the raja's wives or concubines—no one quite knows, or even cares. We don't see much of them, and they keep to themselves. But people avoid the place, they say it is still full of evil, haunted by the old scoundrel whose cruelty has left its mark on the walls… It should be pulled down!'

'It's falling down of its own accord,' I said. 'Most of it is already a ruin.'

~

Later that morning I found Hassan closing the doors of the bakery.

'Are you off somewhere?' I asked.

He nodded. 'Down to Rajpur. My boys are at school and my daughter is too small to look after the place.'

'It's urgent, then?'

'That fool of a youth, Sunil, has got into trouble. Picking someone's pocket, no doubt. They are holding him at the Rajpur thana.'

'But why do you have to go? Doesn't he have any relatives?'

'None of any use. His father died some time back. He did me a favour once. More than a favour—he saved my life. So I must help the boy, even if he is a badmash.'

'I'll come with you,' I said on an impulse. 'Is it very far?'

'Rajpur is at the bottom of the hill. About an hour's walk down the footpath. Quicker than walking up to Mussoorie and waiting for a bus.'

I joined him on the road, and together we set off down the old path.

We passed Fairy Glen—the ruin where I had passed the night. It looked quite peaceful in the April sunshine. The gate was closed. There was no sign of the boy or his mother, my hosts of the previous night. It would have been embarrassing to meet them, for I had left in an almighty hurry. There was no sign of the big black bird, either. Only a couple of mynas squabbling on the wall, and a black-faced langur swinging from the branch of an oak.

I had some difficulty in keeping up with Hassan. Although he was over forty and had the beginnings of a paunch, he was a sturdy fellow, and he had the confident, even stride of someone who had spent most of his life in the hills.

The path was a steep one, and it began to level out only when it entered the foothills hamlet of Rajpur. At that time Rajpur was something of a ghost town. Some sixteen years earlier, most of its inhabitants, Muslims like Hassan, had fled or been killed by mobs during the communal strife that followed the partition of the country.

Rajpur had yet to recover. We passed empty, gutted buildings, some roofless, some without doors and windows. Weeds and small bushes grew out of the floors of abandoned houses. Successive monsoons had removed the mud or cement plaster from the walls, leaving behind bare brickwork which was beginning to crumble. The entire length of the street, where once there had been a hundred homes pulsating with life and human endeavour, now stood empty, homes only to jackals, snakes, and huge rock lizards.

Hassan stopped before an empty doorway. Behind it an empty courtyard. Behind it a wall with empty windows.

'I lived here once,' he said. 'My parents, younger brother, sister, my first wife…all of us worked together, making bread and buns and pastries for the rich folk in the houses along the Dehra road.

And in one night I lost everyone, everything—parents, brother, sister, wife…The fire swept through the mohalla, and those who ran out of their houses were cut down by swords and kirpans.'

I stopped and put a hand on his shoulder.

'It's hard for me to talk about it. Later, perhaps…' And he moved on.

The street of lost homes gave way to a small bazaar, the only visible sign of some sort of recovery. A young man from a nearby village ran the small dhaba where we stopped for tea and pakoras. He was too young to have any memories of 1947. And in India, town and countryside often appear to have completely different histories.

Hassan asked me to wait at the dhaba while he walked down to the local thana to enquire after Sunil.

'A thana is no place for a respectable person like you,' he said.

'In Delhi, the prisons are full of respectable people,' I said.

'But not respected anymore?'

'Well, some of them don't seem to be too bothered. They get bail, come out with a swagger, and drive home in their cars.'

'And what are their crimes?'

'The same as Sunil's. They pick pockets, but in a big way. You don't see them doing it. But carry on, I'll wait here for you.'

The dhak, or flame of the forest, was in flower, and I sat on a bench taking in the sights and sounds of summer's arrival in the valley. Scarlet bougainvillea cascaded over a low wall, and a flock of parrots flung themselves from one tall mango tree to another, sampling the young unripe fruit.

'Will there be a good crop this year?' I asked the young dhabawala.

'Should be, if the parrots and monkeys leave any for us.'

'You need a chowkidar,' I said, and thought of recommending Sunil. But Hassan came back without him.

'No magistrate in court today. We'll try again tomorrow. In the meantime he gets board and lodging at government expense. He doesn't have to pick any pockets.'

'He will, if he gets a chance. It's an incurable disease.'

EYE OF THE LEOPARD

We did not return by way of the ruined and deserted township. Hassan wished to avoid it. 'Bad memories,' he said.

We cut across a couple of fields until we reached a small stream which came down the ravine below Fosterganj. Hassan knew it well. He went there to bathe from time to time. A narrow path took us upstream.

'How did you escape?' I asked, still curious about the events of 1947.

Hassan continued to walk, looking straight ahead. He did not turn his face to me as he spoke. 'I was late returning from Mussoorie. The houses were already ablaze. I began running towards ours, but the mob cut me off. Most of them Sikhs, wanting revenge—they had lost homes and loved ones in the Punjab—there was madness everywhere—hate and greed and madness. Gandhi couldn't stop it. Several men caught hold of me and flung me to the ground. One stood over me with his sword raised. That's when Bhai Saheb—Sunil's father—appeared as if out of nowhere. "What are you doing?" he cried. "That's my nephew. Don't touch him, or my entire village will be up in arms against you!" The attackers left me and moved on to other targets. Of course it was all over with my people. Sunil's father kept me in his village, not far from here, until the killing stopped. Sooner or later it had to stop. It exhausts itself. A few hours of madness and we spend years counting the cost.'

∽

After almost an hour of walking upstream, slipping on moss-covered boulders and struggling up the little-used pathway, we came to a pool, a catchment area where the water was still and deep.

'We'll rest here awhile,' said Hassan. 'Would you like to bathe?'

It was a warm day, and down there in the ravine there was no breeze. I stripped to my underwear and slipped into the pool.

After some time Hassan joined me. He was a well-built man. Birthing and raising so many children had worn out his consumptive wife, but he was in fine shape—strong in the chest and thighs; he had the build of a wrestler.

I was enjoying the water, swimming around, but Hassan was restless, continually looking up at the hillside and the overhanging branches of the trees that grew near the water. Presently he left the pool and began striding up a grassy knoll as though in search of something—as though he sensed the presence of danger. If you have faced danger once, you will know when it comes again.

'What are you looking for?' I called.

'Nothing,' he replied. 'Just looking around.' And he went further up the path.

I swam around a little, then pulled myself up on a flat boulder, and sat there in the sun, contemplating a thicket of ferns. A long-tailed magpie squawked and flew away in a hurry. The sun was in my eyes. I turned my back to it, and looked up into the yellow eyes of a leopard crouching on the rocks above me.

I wanted to shout, but couldn't. And perhaps it was better that I remained silent. Was it the man-eater? There was no way of knowing, but it seemed likely.

For what seemed an age, I looked at the leopard and the leopard stared at me. In fact, it was only a matter of seconds; but each second was an hour to me.

The leopard came forward a little and snarled. Perhaps he was puzzled that I made no sound and did not run. But he sank down, his forepaws spreading to get a grip on the rocks. His tail began to twitch—a sure signal that he was about to spring. His lips drew back and the sun shone on his canines and the dark pink of his gums.

Then I saw Hassan appear just behind the crouching beast. He held a large rock in his hands—it was bigger than a football. He raised his arms and brought the rock down with all his might on the leopard's head.

The leopard seemed to sag. Its paws scrabbled in the dust. Blood trickled from its ears. Hassan appeared again, with an even bigger rock, and he brought it down with such force that I heard the animal's skull crack. There was a convulsive movement, and then it was still.

∽

We returned to Fosterganj and told everyone that the man- eater was dead. A number of people went down to the stream to fetch the carcass. But Hassan did not join them. He was behind with his work, and had to bake twenty to thirty loaves of bread for delivery the next morning. I tried to help him, but I am not much good at baking bread, and he told me to go to bed early.

Everyone was pleased that the leopard had been killed. Everyone, that is, except Vishaal, the bank manager, who had been hoping to vanquish it himself.

AN EVENING WITH FOSTER

Keep right on to the end of the road,
Keep right on to the end.
If your way be long
Let your heart be strong,
And keep right on to the end.
If you're tired and weary
Still carry on,
Till you come to your happy abode.
And then all you love
And are dreaming of,
Will be there—
At the end of the road!

The voice of Sir Harry Lauder, Scottish troubadour of the 1930s, singing one of his favourites, came drifting across the hillside as I took the winding path to Foster's cottage.

On one of my morning walks, I had helped him round up some runaway hens, and he had been suitably grateful.

'Ah, it's a fowl subject, trying to run a poultry farm,' he quipped. 'I've already lost a few to jackals and foxes. Hard to keep them in their pens. They jump over the netting and wander all over the place. But thank you for your help. It's good to be young. Once the knees go, you'll never be young again. Why don't you come over in the evening and split a bottle with me? It's a home-made brew, can't hurt you.'

I'd heard of Foster's home-made brew. More than one person had tumbled down the khad after partaking of the stuff. But I did not want to appear standoffish, and besides, I was curious about the man and his history. So towards sunset one summer's evening, I took the path down to his cottage, following the strains of Harry Lauder.

The music grew louder as I approached, and I had to knock on the door several times before it was opened by my bleary-eyed host. He had already been at the stuff he drank, and at first he failed to recognize me.

'Nice old song you have there,' I said. 'My father used to sing it when I was a boy.'

Recognition dawned, and he invited me in. 'Come in, laddie, come in. I've been expecting you. Have a seat!'

The seat he referred to was an old sofa and it was occupied by three cackling hens. With a magnificent sweep of the arm Foster swept them away, and they joined two other hens and a cock-bird on a book-rack at the other end of the room. I made sure there were no droppings on the sofa before subsiding into it.

'Birds are finding it too hot out in the yard,' he explained.

'Keep wanting to come indoors.'

The gramophone record had run its course, and Foster switched off the old record player.

'Used to have a real gramophone,' he said, 'but can't get the needles any more. These electric players aren't any good. But I still have all the old records.' He indicated a pile of 78 rpm gramophone records, and I stretched across and sifted through some of them. Gracie Fields, George Formby, The Street Singer…music hall favourites from the 1930s and 40s. Foster hadn't added to his collection for twenty years.

He must have been close to eighty, almost twice my age. Like his stubble (a permanent feature), the few wisps of hair on his sunburnt head were also grey. Mud had dried on his hands. His old patched-up trousers were held up by braces. There were buttons missing from his shirt, laces missing from his shoes.

'What will you have to drink, laddie? Tea, cocoa or whisky?'

'Er—not cocoa. Tea, maybe—oh, anything will do.'

'That's the spirit. Go for what you like. I make my own whisky, of course. Real Scotch from the Himalaya. I get the best barley from yonder village.' He gestured towards the next mountain, then turned to a sagging mantelpiece, fetched a bottle that contained an oily yellow liquid, and poured a generous amount into a cracked china mug. He poured a similar amount into a dirty glass tumbler, handed it to me, and said, 'Cheers! Bottoms up!'

'Bottoms up!' I said, and took a gulp.

It wasn't bad. I drank some more and asked Foster how the poultry farm was doing.

'Well, I had fifty birds to start with. But they keep wandering off, and the boys from the village make off with them. I'm down to forty. Sold a few eggs, though. Gave the bank manager the first lot. He seemed pleased. Would you like a few eggs? There's a couple on that cushion, newly laid.'

The said cushion was on a stool a few feet from me. Two large hens' eggs were supported upon it.

'Don't sit on 'em,' said Foster, letting out a cackle which was meant to be laughter. 'They might hatch!'

I took another gulp of Foster's whisky and considered the eggs again. They looked much larger now, more like goose eggs.

Everything was looking larger.

I emptied the glass and stood up to leave.

'Don't go yet,' said Foster. 'You haven't had a proper drink. And there's dinner to follow. Sausages and mash! I make my own sausages, did you know? My sausages were famous all over Mussoorie. I supplied the Savoy, Hakman's, the schools.'

'Why did you stop?' I was back on the sofa, holding another glass of Himalayan Scotch.

'Somebody started spreading a nasty rumour that I was using dog's meat. Now why would I do that when pork was cheap? Of course, during the war years a lot of rubbish went into sausages—stuff you'd normally throw away. That's why they were called "sweet mysteries". You remember the old song? "Ah! Sweet Mystery of Life!" Nebon Eddy and Jeanette Macdonald. Well, the troops used to sing it whenever they were given sausages for breakfast. You never knew what went into them—cats, dogs, camels, scorpions. If you survived those sausages, you survived the war!'

'And your sausages, what goes into them?'

'Good, healthy chicken meat. Not crow's meat, as some jealous rivals tried to make out.'

He frowned into his china mug. It was suddenly quieter inside. The hens had joined their sisters in the backyard; they were settling down for the night, sheltering in cardboard cartons and old mango-wood boxes. Quck-quck-quck. Another day nearer to having their sad necks wrung.

I looked around the room. A threadbare carpet. Walls that hadn't received a coat of paint for many years. A couple of loose rafters letting in a blast of cold air. Some pictures here and there—mostly racing scenes. Foster must have been a betting man. Perhaps that was how he ran out of money.

He noticed my interest in the pictures and said, 'Owned a racehorse once. A beauty, she was. That was in Meerut, just before the war. Meerut had a great racecourse. Races every Saturday. Punters came from Delhi. There was money to be made!'

'Did you win any?' I asked.

'Won a couple of races hands down. Then unexpectedly she came in last, and folks lost a lot of money. I had to leave town in a hurry. All my jockey's fault—he was hand in glove with the bookies. They made a killing, of course! Anyway, I sold the horse to a sporting Parsi gentleman and went into the canteen business with my Uncle Fred in Roorkee. That's Uncle Fred, up there.'

Foster gestured towards the mantelpiece. I expected to see a photograph of his Uncle Fred but instead of a photo I found myself staring at a naked skull. It was a well-polished skull and it glistened in the candlelight.

'That's Uncle Fred,' said Foster proudly.

'That skull? Where's the rest of him?'

'In his grave, back in Roorkee.'

'You mean you kept the skull but not the skeleton?'

'Well, it's a long story,' said Foster, 'but to keep it short, Uncle Fred died suddenly of a mysterious malady—a combination of brain fever, blood-pressure and Housemaid's Knee.'

'Housemaid's Knee!'

'Yes, swollen kneecaps, brought about by being beaten too frequently with police lathis. He wasn't really a criminal, but he'd get into trouble from time to time, harmless little swindles such as printing his own lottery tickets or passing forged banknotes. Spent some time in various district jails until his health broke down. Got a pauper's funeral—but his cadaver was in demand. The students from the local medical college got into the cemetery one night and made off with his cranium! Not that he had much by way of a brain, but he had a handsome, well-formed skull, as you can see.'

I did see. And the skull appeared to be listening to the yarn, because its toothless jaws were extended in a grin, or so I fancied.

'And how did you get it back?' I asked.

'Broke into their demonstration room, naturally. I was younger then, and pretty agile. There it was on a shelf, among a lot of glass containers of alcohol, preserving everything from giant tapeworms to Ghulam Qadir's penis and testicles.'

'Ghulam Qadir?'

'Don't you know your history? He was the fellow who blinded the Emperor Shah Alam. They caught up with him near Saharanpur and cut his balls off. Preserved them for posterity. Waste of alcohol, though. Have another drink, laddie. And then for a sausage. Ah! Sweet Mystery of Life!'

After another drink and several 'mystery' sausages, I made my getaway and stumbled homewards up a narrow path along an open ridge. A jackal slunk ahead of me, and a screech-owl screeched, but I got home safely, none the worse for an evening with the descendant of Bonnie Prince Charlie.

WHO'S BEEN SLEEPING IN MY BED?

There was a break in the rains, the clouds parted, and the moon appeared—a full moon, bathing the mountains in a pollen-yellow light. Little Fosterganj, straddling the slopes of the Ganga-Yamuna watershed, basked in the moonlight, each lighted dwelling a firefly in the night.

Only the Fairy Glen palace was unlit, brooding in the darkness. I was returning from an evening show at the Realto in Mussoorie. It had been a long walk, but a lovely one. I stopped outside the palace gate, wondering about its lonely inhabitants and all that might have happened within its walls. I wanted to see them again, but not at night—not with strange birds flapping around and skeletons hidden in the box-beds. Old skeletons, maybe; but what were they doing there?

I reached Hassan's bakery around midnight, and mounted the steps to my room. My door was open. It was never locked, as I had absolutely nothing that anyone would want to take away. The typewriter, which I had hired from a shop in Dehradun, was a heavy machine, designed for office use; no one was going to carry it off.

But someone was in my bed.

Fast asleep. Snoring peacefully. Not Goldilocks. Nor a bear. I switched on the light, shook the recumbent figure. He started up. It was Sunil. After giving him a beating, the police had let him go.

'Uncle, you frightened me!' he exclaimed.

He called me 'Uncle', although I was only some fifteen or sixteen years older than him. Call a tiger 'Uncle', and he won't harm you; or so the forest-dwellers say. Not quite how it works out with people approaching middle age. Being addressed as 'Uncle' didn't make me very fond of Sunil.

'I'm the one who should be frightened,' I said. 'A pickpocket in my bed!'

'I don't pick pockets any more, Uncle. I've turned a new leaf. Don't you know that expression?' Sunil had studied up to Class 8 in a 'convent school'.

'Well, you can turn out of my bed,' I said. 'And return that watch you took off me before you got into trouble.'

'You lent me the watch, Uncle. Don't you remember? Here!' He held out his arm. 'Take it back.' There were two watches on his wrist; my modest HMT, and something far more expensive.

I removed the HMT and returned it to my own wrist.

'Now can I have my bed back?' I asked.

'There's room for both of us.'

'No, there isn't, it's only a khatiya. It will collapse under our combined weight. But there's this nice easy chair here, and in the morning, when I get up, you can have the bed.'

Reluctantly, Sunil got off the bed and moved over to the cane chair. Perhaps I'd made a mistake. It meant that Sunil would be awake all night, and that he'd want to talk. Nothing can be more irritating than a room companion who talks all night.

I switched off the light and stretched out on the cot. It was a bit wobbly. Perhaps the floor would have been better. Sunil sat in the chair, whistling and singing film songs—something about a red dupatta blowing in the wind, and telephone calls from Rangoon to Dehradun. A romantic soul, Sunil, when he wasn't picking pockets. Did I say there's nothing worse than a companion who talks all night? I was wrong. Even worse is a companion who sings all night.

'You can sing in the morning,' I said. 'When the sun comes out. Now go to sleep.'

There was silence for about two minutes. Then: 'Uncle?'

'What is it?'

'I have to turn over a new leaf.'

'In the morning, Sunil,' I turned over and tried to sleep.

'Uncle, I have a project.'

'Well, don't involve me in it.'

'It's all seedha-saadha, and very interesting. You know that old man who sells saande-ka-tel—the oil that doubles your manhood?'

'I haven't tried it. It's an oil taken from a lizard, isn't it?'

'A big lizard.'

'So?'

'Well, he's old now and can't go hunting for these lizards. You can only find them in certain places.'

'Maybe he should retire and do something else, then. Grow marigolds. Their oil is also said to be good for lovers.'

'Not as good as lizard oil.'

'So what's your project?' He was succeeding in keeping me awake. 'Are you going to gather lizards for him?'

'Exactly, Uncle. Why don't you join me?'

~

Next morning Sunil elaborated on his scheme. I was to finance the tour. We would trek, or use a bus where there were roads, and visit the wooded heights and rocky slopes above the Bhagirathi river, on its descent from the Gangotri glacier. We would stay in rest-houses, dharamsalas, or small hotels. We would locate those areas where the monitors, or large rock lizards, were plentiful, catch as many as possible and bring them back alive to Fosterganj, where our gracious mentor would reward us to the tune of two hundred rupees per reptile. Sunil and I would share this bonanza.

The project, if any, did not interest me. I was extremely skeptical of the entire scheme. But I was bored, and it sounded like it could be fun, even an adventure of sorts, and I would have Sunil as guide, philosopher and friend. He could be a lovely and happy-go-lucky companion—provided he kept his hands out of other people's pockets and did not sing at night.

Hassan was equally skeptical about the success of the project. For one thing, he did not believe in the magical properties of saande-ka-tel (never having felt the need for it); and for another, he did not think those lizards would be caught so easily. But he thought it would be a good thing for Sunil, something different from what he was used to doing. The young man might benefit from my 'intellectual' company. And in the hills, not many folks had money in their pockets.

And so, with the blessings of Hassan, and a modest overdraft from Vishaal, our friendly bank manager, I packed a haversack with essentials (including my favourite ginger biscuits as prepared by Hassan) and set out with Sunil on the old pilgrim road to Tehri and beyond.

Sunil had brought along two large baskets, as receptacles for the lizards when captured. But as he had no intention of carrying them himself—and wisely refrained from asking me to do so—he had brought along a twelve-year-old youth from the bazaar—a squint-eyed, hare-lipped, one-eared character called Buddhoo, whose intelligence and confidence made up for his looks. Buddhoo was to act as our porter and general factotum. On our outward journey he had only to carry the two empty baskets; Sunil hadn't told him what their eventual contents might be.

It was late July, still monsoon time, when we set out on the Tehri road.

In those days it was still a mule-track, meandering over several spurs and ridges, before descending to the big river. It was about forty miles to Tehri. From there we could get a bus, at least up to Pratap Nagar, the old summer capital of the hill state.

ON THE TRAIL OF THE LIZARD

That first day on the road was rather trying. I had done a certain amount of walking in the hills, and I was reasonably fit. Sunil, for all his youth, had never walked further than Mussoorie's cinemas or Dehra's railway station, where the pickings for his agile fingers had always been good. Buddhoo, on the other hand, belied his short stature by being so swift of foot that he was constantly leaving us for behind. Every time we rounded a corner, expecting to find him waiting for us, he would be about a hundred yards ahead, never tiring, never resting.

To keep myself going I would sing either Harry Lauder's 'Keep right on to the end of the road,' or Nelson Eddy's 'Tramp, tramp, tramp'.

Tramp, tramp, tramp, along the highway,
Tramp, tramp, tramp, the road is free!
Blazing trails along the byways...

Sunil did not appreciate my singing.

'You don't sing well,' he said. 'Even those mules are getting nervous.' He gestured at a mule-train that was passing us on the narrow path. A couple of mules were trying to break away from the formation.

'Nothing to do with my singing,' I said. 'All they want are those young bamboo shoots coming up on the hillside.'

Sunil asked one of the mule-drivers if he could take a ride on a mule; anything to avoid trudging along the stony path. The mule-driver agreeing, Sunil managed to mount one of the beasts, and went cantering down the road, leaving us far behind.

Buddhoo waited for me to catch up. He pointed at a large rock to the side of road, and sure enough, there, resting at ease, basking in the morning sunshine, was an ungainly monitor lizard about the length of my forearm.

'Too small,' said Buddhoo, who seemed to know something about lizards. 'Bigger ones higher up.'

The lizard did not move. It stared at us with a beady eye; a contemptuous sort of stare, almost as if it did not think very highly of humans. I wasn't going to touch it. Its leathery skin looked uninviting; its feet and tail reminded me of a dinosaur; its head was almost serpent like. Who would want to use its body secretions, I wondered. Certainly not if they had seen the creature. But human beings, men especially, will do almost anything to appease their vanity. Tiger's whiskers or saande-ka-tel—anything to improve their sagging manhood.

We did not attempt to catch the lizard. Sunil was supposed to be the expert. And he was already a mile away, enjoying his mule-ride.

An hour later he was sitting on the grassy verge, nursing a sore backside. Riding a mule can take the skin off the backside of an inexperienced rider.

'I'm in pain,' he complained. 'I can't get up.'

'Use saande-ka-tel,' I suggested.

Buddhoo went sauntering up the road, laughing to himself.

'He's mad,' said Sunil.

'That makes three of us, then.'

COMPANIONS OF THE ROAD

By noon we were hungry. Hassan had provided us with buns and biscuits, but these were soon finished, and we were longing for a real meal. Late afternoon we trudged into Dhanolti, a scenic spot with great views of the snow peaks; but we were in no mood for scenery. Who can eat sunsets? A forest rest-house was the only habitation, and had food been available we could have spent the night there. But the caretaker was missing. A large black dog frightened us off.

So on we tramped, three small dots on a big mountain, mere specks, beings of no importance. In creating this world, God showed that he was a Great Mathematician; but in creating man, he got his algebra wrong. Puffed up with self-importance, we are in fact the most dispensable of all his creatures.

On a long journey, the best companion is usually the one who talks the least, and in that way Buddhoo was a comforting presence. But I wanted to know him better.

'How did you lose your ear?' I asked.

'Bear tore it off,' he said, without elaborating. Brevity is the soul of wit, or so they say.

'Must have been painful,' I ventured.

'Bled a lot.'

'I wouldn't care to meet a bear.'

'Lots of them out here. If you meet one, run downhill. They don't like running downhill.'

'I'll try to remember that,' I said, grateful for his shared wisdom. We trudged on in silence. To the south, the hills were bleak and windswept; to the north, moist and well-forested. The road ran along the crest of the ridge, and the panorama it afforded, with the mountains striding away in one direction and the valleys with their gleaming rivers snaking their way towards the plains, gave me an immense feeling of freedom. I doubt if Sunil felt the same way. He was preoccupied with tired legs and a sore backside. And for Buddhoo it was a familiar scene.

A brief twilight, and then, suddenly, it grew very dark. No moon; the stars just beginning to appear. We rounded a bend, and a light shone from a kerosene lamp swinging outside a small roadside hut.

It was not the pilgrim season, but the owner of the hut was ready to take in the odd traveller. He was a grizzled old man. Over the years the wind had dug trenches in his cheeks and forehead. A pair of spectacles, full of scratches, almost opaque, balanced on a nose long since broken. He'd lived a hard life. A survivor.

'Have you anything to eat?' demanded Sunil.

'I can make you dal-bhaat,' said the shopkeeper. Dal and rice was the staple diet of the hills; it seldom varied.

'Fine,' I said. 'But first some tea.'

The tea was soon ready, hot and strong, the way I liked it. The meal took some time to prepare, but in the meantime we made ourselves comfortable in a corner of the shop, the owner having said we could spend the night there. It would take us two hours to reach the township of Chamba, he said. Buddhoo concurred. He knew the road.

We had no bedding, but the sleeping area was covered with old sheepskins stitched together, and they looked comfortable enough. Sunil produced a small bottle of rum from his shoulder bag, unscrewed the cap, took a swig, and passed it around. The old man declined. Buddhoo drank a little; so did I. Sunil polished off the rest. His eyes become glassy and unfocused.

'Where did you get it?' I asked.

'Hassan Uncle gave it to me.'

'Hassan doesn't drink—he doesn't keep it, either.'

'Actually, I picked it up in the police station, just before they let me go. Found it in the havildar's coat pocket.'

'Congratulations,' I said. 'He'll be looking forward to seeing you again.'

The dal-bhaat was simple but substantial.

'Could do with some pickle,' grumbled Sunil, and then fell asleep before he could complain any further.

~

We were all asleep before long. The sheepskin rug was reasonably comfortable. But we were unaware that it harboured a life of its own—a miniscule but active population of fleas and bugs—dormant when undisturbed, but springing into activity at the proximity of human flesh and blood.

Within an hour of lying down we were wide awake. When God, the Great Mathematician, discovered that in making man he had overdone things a bit, he created the bedbug to even things out.

Soon I was scratching. Buddhoo was up and scratching. Sunil came out of his stupor and was soon cursing and scratching. The fleas had got into our clothes, the bugs were feasting on our blood.

When the world as we know it comes to an end, these will be the ultimate survivors.

Within a short time we were stomping around like Kathakali dancers. There was no relief from the exquisite torture of being seized upon by hundreds of tiny insects thirsting for blood or body fluids.

The teashop owner was highly amused. He had never seen such a performance—three men cavorting around the room, scratching, yelling, hopping around.

And then it began to rain. We heard the first heavy raindrops pattering a rhythm on the tin roof. They increased in volume, beating against the only window and bouncing off the banana fronds in the little courtyard. We needed no urging. Stripping off our clothes, we dashed outside, naked in the wind and rain, embracing the elements. What relief! We danced in the rain until it stopped, and then, getting back into our clothes with some reluctance, we decided to be on our way, no matter how dark or forbidding the night.

We paid for our meal—or rather, I paid for it, being the only one with funds—and bid goodnight and goodbye to our host. Actually, it was morning, about 2 a.m., but we had no intention of bedding down again; not on those sheepskin rugs.

A half-moon was now riding the sky. The rain had refreshed us. We were no longer hungry. We set out with renewed vigour.

Great lizards, beware!

TAIL OF THE LIZARD

At daybreak we tramped into the little township of Chamba, where Buddhoo proudly pointed out a memorial to soldiers from the area who had fallen fighting in the trenches in France during the First World War. His grandfather had been one of them. Young men from the hills had traditionally gone into the army; it was the only way they could support their families; but times were changing, albeit slowly. The towns now had several hopeful college students. If they did not find jobs they could go into politics.

The motor road from Rishikesh passed through Chamba, and we were able to catch a country bus which deposited us at Pratap Nagar later that day.

Pratap Nagar is not on the map, but it used to exist once upon a time. It may still be there, for all I know. Back in the days of the old Tehri Raj it had been the raja's summer capital. There had even been a British resident and a tiny European population—just a handful of British officials and their families. But after Independence, the raja no longer had any use for the place. The state had been poor and backward, and over the years he had spent more time in Dehradun and Mussoorie.

We were there purely by accident, having got into the wrong bus at Chamba.

The wrong bus or the wrong train can often result in interesting consequences. It's called the charm of the unexpected.

Not that Pratap Nagar was oozing with charm. A dilapidated palace, an abandoned courthouse, a dispensary without a doctor, a school with a scatter of students and no teachers, and a marketplace selling sad-looking cabbages and cucumbers—these were the sights and chief attractions of the town. But I have always been drawn to decadent, decaying, forgotten places—Fosterganj being one of them—and while Sunil and Buddhoo passed the time chatting to some of the locals at the bus stand—which appeared to be the centre of all activity—I wandered off along the narrow, cobbled lanes until I came to a broken wall.

Passing through the break in the wall I found myself in a small cemetery. It contained a few old graves. The inscriptions had worn away from most of the tombstones, and on others the statuary had been damaged. Obviously no one had been buried there for many years.

In one corner I found a grave that was better preserved than the others, by virtue of the fact that the lettering had been cut into an upright stone rather than a flat slab. It read:

Dr Robert Hutchinson
Physician to His Highness
Died July 13, 1933
of Typhus Fever
May his soul rest in peace.

Typhus fever! I had read all about it in an old medical dictionary published half a century ago by The Statesman of Calcutta and passed on to me by a fond aunt. Not to be confused with typhoid, typhus fever is rare today but sometimes occurs in overcrowded, unsanitary conditions and is definitely spread by lice, ticks, fleas, mites and other micro-organisms thriving in filthy conditions—such as old sheepskin rugs which have remained unwashed for years.

I began to scratch at the very thought of it.

I remembered more: 'Attacks of melancholia and mania sometimes complicate the condition, which is often fatal.'

Needless to say, I now found myself overcome by a profound feeling of melancholy. No doubt the mania would follow.

I examined the other graves, and found one more victim of typhus fever. There must have been an epidemic. Fortunately for my peace of mind, the only other decipherable epitaph told of the missionary lady who had fallen victim to an earthquake in 1905. Somehow, an earthquake seemed less sinister than a disease brought on by bloodthirsty bugs.

While I was standing there, ruminating on matters of life and death, my companions turned up, and Sunil exclaimed:

'Well done, Uncle, you've already found one!'

I hadn't found anything, being somewhat short-sighted, but Sunil was pointing across to the far wall, where a great fat lizard sat basking in the sun.

Its tail was as long as my arm. Its legs were spread sideways, like a goalkeeper's. Its head moved from side to side, and suddenly its tongue shot out and seized a passing dragonfly. In seconds the beautiful insect was imprisoned in a pair of strong jaws.

The giant lizard consumed his lunch, then glanced at us standing a few feet away.

'Plenty of fat around that fellow,' observed Sunil. 'Full of that precious oil!'

The lizard let out a croak, as though it had something to say on the matter. But Sunil wasn't listening. He lunged forward and grabbed the lizard by its tail. Miraculously, the tail came away in his hands.

Away went lizard, minus its tail.

Buddhoo was doubled up with laughter. 'The tail's no use,' he said. 'Nothing in the tail!'

Sunil flung the tail away in disgust.

'Never mind,' I said. 'Catch a lizard by its tail—make a wish, it cannot fail!'

'Is that true?' asked Sunil, who had a superstitious streak.

'Nursery rhyme from Brazil,' I said.

The lizard had disappeared, but a white-bearded patriarch was looking at us from over the wall.

'You need a net,' he said. 'Catching them by hand isn't easy. Too slippery.'

We thanked him for his advice; said we'd go looking for a net.

'Maybe a bedsheet will do,' Sunil said.

The patriarch smiled, stroked his flowing white beard, and asked: 'But what will you do with these lizards? Put them in a zoo?'

'It's their oil we want,' said Sunil, and made a sales pitch for the miraculous properties of saande-ka-tel.

'Oh, that,' said the patriarch, looking amused. 'It will irritate the membranes and cause some inflammation. I know—I'm a nature therapist. All superstition, my friends. You'll get the same effect, even better, with machine oil. Try sewing-machine oil. At least it's harmless. Leave the poor lizards alone.'

And the barefoot mendicant hitched up his dhoti, gave us a friendly wave, and disappeared in the monsoon mist.

TREMORS IN THE NIGHT

Not to be discouraged, we left the ghost town and continued our journey upriver, as far as the bus would take us. The road ended at Uttarkashi, for the simple reason that the bridge over the Bhagirathi had been washed away in a flash flood. The glaciers had been melting, and that, combined with torrential rain in the upper reaches, had brought torrents of muddy water rushing down the swollen river. Anything that came in its way vanished downstream.

We spent the night in a pilgrim shelter, built on a rocky ledge overlooking the river. All night we could hear the water roaring past below us. After a while, we became used to the unchanging sound; it became like a deep silence, and made our sleep deeper. Sometime before dawn, however, a sudden tremor had us trembling out of our cots.

'Earthquake!' shouted Sunil, making for the doorway and banging into the wall instead.

'Don't panic,' I said, feeling panicky.

'It will pass,' said Buddhoo.

The tremor did pass, but not before everyone in the shelter had rushed outside. There was the sound of rocks falling, and everyone rushed back again. 'Landslide!' someone shouted. Was it safer outside or inside? No one could be sure.

'It will pass,' said Buddhoo again, and went to sleep. Sunil began singing at the top of his voice: 'Pyar kiya to darna kya—Why be afraid when we have loved'. I doubt Sunil had ever been in love, but it was a rousing song with which to meet death.

'Chup, beta!' admonished an old lady on her last pilgrimage to the abode of the gods. 'Say your prayers instead.'

The room fell silent. Outside, a dog started howling. Other dogs followed his example. No serenade this, but a mournful anticipation of things to come; for birds and beasts are more sensitive to the earth's tremors and inner convulsions than humans, who are no longer sensitive to nature's warnings.

A couple of jackals joined the chorus. Then a bird, probably a nightjar, set up a monotonous croak. I looked at my watch. It was 4 a.m, a little too early for birds to be greeting the break of day. But suddenly there was a twittering and cawing and chattering as all the birds in the vicinity passed on the message that something was amiss.

There was a rush of air and a window banged open.

The mountain shuddered. The building shook, rocked to and fro.

People began screaming and making for the door.

The door was flung open, but only a few escaped into the darkness.

Across the length of the room a chasm opened up. The lady saying her prayers fell into it. So did one or two others. Then the room and the people in it—those who were on the other side of the chasm—suddenly vanished.

There was the roar of falling masonry as half the building slid down the side of the mountain.

We were left dangling in space.

'Let's get out of here quickly!' shouted Sunil.

We scrambled out of the door. In front of us, an empty void. I couldn't see a thing. Then Buddhoo took me by the hand and led me away from the crumbling building and on to the rocky ledge above the river.

The earth had stopped quaking, but the mountain had been shaken to its foundations, and rocks and trees were tumbling into the swollen river. The town was in darkness, the power station having shut down after the first tremor. Here and there a torch or lantern shone out of the darkness, and people could be heard wailing and shouting to each other as they roamed the streets in the rain. Somewhere a siren went off. It only seemed to add to the panic.

At 5 a.m, the rain stopped and the sky lightened. At six it was daybreak. A little later the sun came up. A beautiful morning, except for the devastation below.

THE MOUNTAINS ARE MOVING

'I think I'll join the army,' announced Sunil three days later, when we were back in Fosterganj. 'Do you think they'll take me?' Sunil had been impressed by the rescue work carried out by the army after the Uttarkashi earthquake.

'Like a flash,' I said. 'Provided you keep your fingers out of the brigadier's pockets.'

~

In those early hours of the morning, confusion had prevailed in and around Uttarkashi. Houses had crumbled from the tremors and aftershocks, or been buried under the earth and rocks of a number of landslides. Survivors were wandering around in a daze. Many lay crushed or trapped under debris. It would take days, weeks for the town to recover.

At first there were disorganized attempts at rescue, and Sunil,

Buddhoo and I made clumsy attempts to extricate people from the ruins of their homes. A township built between two steep mountains, and teetering along the banks of a moody river, was always going to be at risk. It had happened before, it would happen again.

A little girl, dusty but unhurt, ran to me and asked, 'Will there be school today?'

'I don't think so,' I said.

A small boy was looking for his mother; a mother was searching for her children; several men were digging in the rubble, trying to extricate friends or family members.

And then a couple of army trucks arrived, and the rescue work moved more swiftly, took on a certain momentum. The jawans made all the difference. Many were rescued who would otherwise have perished.

But the town presented a sad spectacle. A busy marketplace had vanished; a school building lay in ruins; a temple had been swallowed up by a gaping wound in the earth.

On the road we met the bearded patriarch, the one we had encountered two days earlier.

'Did you find your lizards?' he asked. But we had forgotten about lizards.

'What we need now are kitchen utensils,' he said. 'Then we can prepare some food for those who need it.'

He was, it appeared, the head of a social service organization, and we followed him to his centre, a shed near the bus stand, and tried to make ourselves useful. A doctor and nurse were at work on the injured.

I have no idea how many perished, or were badly injured in that earthquake, I was never any good at statistics. Old residents told me that the area was prone to such upheavals.

'Men come and go,' I said, 'but the mountains remain.'

'Not so,' said an old-timer. 'Out here, the mountains are still on the move.'

∽

As soon as the buses were running again, Sunil and I returned to

Fosterganj. Buddhoo remained behind, having decided to join the patriarch's aid centre. We missed his good-natured company, even his funny hare-teeth smile. He promised to meet us again. But till the time I left Fosterganj, we were still waiting for him to turn up. I wonder what became of him. Some of the moving forces of our lives are meant to touch us briefly and then go their way.

A GHOST VILLAGE

On our way back, the bus broke down, as buses were in the habit of doing in those good old days. It was shake, rattle and roll for most of the journey, or at least part of the journey, until something gave way. Occasionally a bus went out of control and plunged over a cliff, taking everyone with it; a common enough occurrence on those hill roads.

We were lucky. Our bus simply broke its axle and came to rest against a friendly deodar tree.

So we were walking again.

Sunil said he knew of a short cut, and as a result we got lost, just the two of us, everyone else having kept to the main road.

We wandered over hill and dale, through a forest of oak and rhododendron, and then through some terraced fields (with nothing in them) and into a small village which appeared to be inhabited entirely by monkeys. An unfriendly lot of the short-tailed rhesus clan, baring their teeth at us, making guttural sounds and more or less telling us to be off.

There were about fifteen houses in the village, and all of them were empty—except for the monkeys and a colony of field rats. Where were all the people?

Going from house to house, we finally found an old couple barricaded inside a small hut on the outskirts of the village. They were happy to see us. They hadn't seen another human for over a month.

Prem Singh and his wife Chandni Devi were the only people still living in the village. The others had gone away—most of them to towns or cities in the plains, in search of employment, or to stay with friends or relatives; for there was nothing to sustain them in the village. The monkeys by day and the wild boars by night had ravaged the fields. Not a leaf, nor an edible root, remained. Prem Singh and his wife were living on their small store of rice and lentils. Even so, the wife made us tea and apologized that there was no milk or sugar.

'We too will leave soon,' she said. 'We will go to our son in Ludhiana. He works in a factory there.'

And that was what the others had done—gone wherever an earning member of the family had settled.

As it was growing dark, and the couple had offered us the occupancy of a spare room, we decided to stay the night.

An eerie silence enveloped the hillside. No dogs barked. They were no match for the monkeys. But we were comfortable on our charpais.

Just before daybreak Sunil had to go outside to relieve himself. The nearest field would do, he said; they were all empty anyway. I was still asleep, dreaming of romantic encounters in a rose garden, when I was woken by shouts and a banging of the door, and Sunil rushed in bare-bottomed and out of breath.

'What happened?' I asked, somewhat disoriented by this ridiculous interruption of my love dream.

'A wild pig came after me!' he gasped. 'One of those with tusks. I got up just in time!'

'But it got your pants, it seems,' I said.

When the sun came up, we both ventured into the field but there was no sign of a wild pig. By now the monkeys were up and about, and I had a feeling that they had made off with Sunil's pants. Prem Singh came to the rescue by giving him an old pair of pyjamas, but they were much too tight and robbed Sunil of his usual jaunty ebullience. But he had to make to do with them.

The whole situation had provided Prem Singh and his wife with much needed comic relief. In their hopeless predicament they could still find something to laugh at. Sunil invited them to visit his village, and we parted on friendly terms.

And so we limped back to Fosterganj without any lizards, and Sunil without pants; but we had learnt something during the week's events. Life in the hills and remote regions of the country was very different from life in the large towns and cities. And already the drift towards the cities had begun. Would the empty spaces be taken over again by the apes, reptiles and wild creatures? It was too early to tell, but the signs were there.

Meanwhile, Sunil was still intent on joining the army, and no sooner were we back in Fosterganj than he was off to the recruiting centre in Lansdowne. Would they take him, I wondered. He wasn't exactly army material. But then, neither was Beetle Bailey.

SOME PEOPLE DON'T AGE

As usual, nothing was happening in Fosterganj. Even the earthquake had barely touched it. True, part of Foster's old cottage had collapsed, but it was going to do that anyway. He simply moved into the remaining rooms without bothering about the damaged portion. In any case, there was no money for repairs.

Passing that way a couple of times, I heard the strains of Sir Harry Lauder again. At least the gramophone was still intact!

Hassan had a Murphy radio and had heard about the Uttarkashi earthquake and its aftermath, so he was relieved to see that I was back.

There was a rumour going around that Fairy Glen had been sold, and that it was going to be pulled down to make way for a grand hotel. I wondered what would happen to its occupants, the young-old boy and his equally intriguing mother. And would skeletons be turning up all over the place, now that it was to be dismantled? Or had I imagined that skeletal hand in the box-bed? In retrospect, it seemed more and more like a nightmare.

I dropped in at the bank and asked Vishaal if the rumours were true.

'There's something going on,' he admitted. 'Nothing certain as yet, because there's more than one owner—a claimant in Nepal, another in Calcutta and a third in Mauritius! But if they come to some agreement there's a hotel group that's interested.'

'Who would want to come to Fosterganj?' I mused.

'Oh, you never know. They say the water here has healing properties.'

'Well, I certainly get diarrhoea pretty frequently.'

'That's because it's pumped up from the dhobi ghat. Don't drink the tap water. Drink the water from upstream.'

'I walked upstream,' I said, 'and I arrived at the burning ghat.'

'Oh, that. But it isn't used much,' said Vishaal. 'Only one or two deaths a year in Fosterganj.'

'They can put that in the brochure, when they build that hotel. But tell me—what will happen to those people living in the palace? They're caretakers, aren't they?

'The boy and his mother? Poor relatives. They'll be given some money. They'll go away.'

I thought it would be charitable on my part to warn the boy and his mother of the impending sale—if they did not know about it already. Quixotic rather than charitable. Or perhaps I just needed an excuse to see them again.

But unwilling to meet skeleton or big black bird, I went there during the day.

It was early September, and the monsoon was beginning to recede. While the foliage on the hillside was still quite lush, autumn hues were beginning to appear. The Virginia creepers, suspended from the oak trees, were turning red. Wild dahlias reared their heads from overhanging rocky outcrops. In the bank manager's garden, chrysanthemums flounced around like haughty maharanis. In the grounds of Fairy Glen, the cosmos had spread all over the place and was just beginning to flower. In the late monsoon light, the old palace looked almost beautiful in its decadence; a pity it would have to go. We need these reminders of history, even though they be haunted, or too grand for their own good.

The boy was out somewhere, but the mother—if, indeed, she was his mother—was at the back of the building, putting out clothes to dry. She smiled when she saw me. The smile spread slowly across her face, like the sun chasing away a shadow, but it also lit up the scar on her cheek.

She asked me to sit down, offered me tea. I declined the tea but sat down on the steps, a bench and a couple of old chairs being festooned with garments.

'At last I can dry some clothes. After so many days the sun has finally come out.'

Although the boy usually spoke in English, she was obviously more at home in Hindi. She spoke it with a distinct Nepali lilt.

'Well, you haven't seen the sun for days,' I said, 'and I haven't seen the dhobi for weeks. I'm down to my last shirt.'

She laughed. 'You should get married.'

It was my turn to laugh. 'You mean marry a washerwoman? Wives don't wash clothes anymore.'

'But mothers do.' And then she surprised me by adding, 'Wives can also be mothers.'

'There are washing machines now, in England and America,' I said. 'They'll be here soon enough. Expensive, of course. But new things are always expensive. We'll also have television soon.'

'What's that?'

'Radio with pictures. It's in Delhi already. A bit boring but it might catch on. Then you won't have to go to the cinema.'

'I don't go to the cinema. Not since my husband died. He took me once—six or seven years ago. I forget the name of the film, but an actress called Madhubala was in it. She was very pretty.'

'Just like you,' I said.

She looked away. 'I'm not young.'

'Some people don't age. Your son—some say that he's much older than he looks.'

She did not reply, and just then the boy himself appeared, whistling cheerfully and bowing to me as he approached.

'It is good to see you again,' he said. 'The last time you were here, you left in a hurry.'

'I'm sorry, but that was a very creepy room you put me in. There was something in the box-bed. My imagination, probably.'

'A skeleton, probably. Grandfather stored them all over the palace. He didn't like burial grounds or cremations. And in the old days, if you were rich and powerful you could do as you liked.'

'It's the same today,' I said. 'Although not so openly. But I heard the property is being sold, to be pulled down—a hotel will come up. Did you know?'

'If it's true—' a shadow crossed his face, and for a few seconds he looked much older. 'If it's true, then…' He did not complete what he wanted to say.

'If it happens,' said his mother, 'then we will have to leave. To Nepal, perhaps. Or to Nabha. I have a cousin there. We are Sirmauris on my mother's side.'

'We are not going anywhere,' said the boy, glowering. The brightness had gone from his face. No one likes the thought of being thrown out of a house which has been a home for most of one's life. When I was a boy, my mother and stepfather were constantly being evicted from one house after another. Their fault, no doubt, but I grew up feeling that the world was a hostile place full of rapacious landlords.

'I'll try to find out more,' I said, getting up to leave.

'Vishaal, the bank manager, will know.'

MORNING AT THE BANK

When I called on Vishaal at the bank a day or two later, he was busy with a couple of customers. This was unusual. Busy days in the bank, let alone in Fosterganj, were rare indeed.

The cashier brought in another chair, and I joined the tea party in Vishaal's office. No secrets in Fosterganj. Everyone knew what everyone else had in their accounts, savings or otherwise.

One of the clients was Mr Foster.

He had first presented Vishaal with a basket of eggs, with the proviso that they be distributed among the staff.

'I should have brought sweets,' said Foster, 'but for sweets I'd have to trudge up to Mussoorie, while the eggs are courtesy my hens. Courtesy your bank, of course.'

'We appreciate them,' said Vishaal. 'We'll have omelettes in the lunch break. So how are the hens doing?'

'Well, a fox got two of them, and a jackal got three, and your guard got my rooster.'

Vishaal looked up at the guard who was standing just outside the door, looking rather stupid.

'Gun went off by mistake,' said the guard.

'It's not supposed to go off at all,' said Vishaal. 'You could kill somebody. It's only for show. If someone holds up the bank, we give them the money. It's all insured.'

The second customer looked interested. A lean, swarthy man in his sixties, he played with the knob of his walnut-wood walking stick and said, 'Talking of insurance, do you know if the Fairy Glen was insured?'

'Don't think so,' said Vishaal. 'It's just a ruin. What is there to insure?'

'It's full of interesting artifacts, I'm told. Old pictures, furniture, antiques... I'm going there today. The owners have asked me to list anything that may be valuable, worth removing, before they hand over the place to the hotel people.

'So it's really going?' I asked.

'That's right,' he said. 'The deal is all but sealed.'

'And the present occupants?'

'Just caretakers. Poor relatives. I believe the woman was the old raja's keep—or one of them, anyway. They'll have to go.'

'Perhaps the hotel can find some work for them.'

'They want vacant possession.' He got up, twirling his walking stick. 'Well, I must go. Calls to make.'

'You can use our phone,' said Vishaal. 'The only other public phone is at the police outpost, and it's usually out of order. And if you like, I can send for the local taxi.'

'No, I'll call from Mussoorie. I shall enjoy walking back to town. But I might want that taxi later.'

He strode out of the bank, walking purposefully through the late monsoon mist. He was one of the world's middlemen, a successful commission agent, fixing things for busy people. After some time they make themselves indispensable.

Mr Foster was quite the opposite. No one really needed him. But he needed another loan.

'No more chickens,' said Vishaal. 'And you haven't built your poultry shed.'

'Someone stole the wire netting. But never mind the chickens, I've another proposition. Mr Vishaal, sir, what about aromatherapy?'

'What about it? Never heard of such a thing.'

'It's all the rage in France, I hear. You treat different ailments or diseases with different aromas. Calendula for headaches, roses for nervous disorders, gladioli for piles—'

'Gladioli don't have an aroma,' I said.

'Mine do!' exclaimed Foster, full of enthusiasm. 'I can cover the hillside with gladioli. And dahlias too!'

'Dahlias don't have an aroma, either.' I was being Irish again.

'Well then, nasturtiums,' said Foster, not in the least put out. 'Nasturtiums are good for the heart.'

'All right, go ahead,' said Vishaal. 'What's stopping you? You don't need a loan to grow flowers.'

'Ah, but I have to distil the aroma from them.'

'You need a distillery?'

'Something like that.'

'You already have one. That rhododendron wine you made last year wasn't bad. Forget about aromas. Stick to wine and spirits, Mr Foster, and you'll make a fortune. Now I'm off for lunch.'

The bank shut its doors for lunch, and we went our different ways: Vishaal to his rented cottage, Foster to his dilapidated house and poultry farm, and I to Fairy Glen to warn my friends of trouble that lay in store for them.

MORNING AT THE POOL

Over the next two days the assessor, let's call him Mr Middleman, was busy at Fairy Glen, notebook in hand, listing everything that looked as though it might have some value: paintings, furnishings, glassware, chinaware, rugs, carpets, desks, cupboards, antique inkwells, an old grandfather clock (home to a colony of mice, now evicted), and a nude statue of Venus minus an arm. Two or three rooms had been locked for years. These were opened up by Mr Middleman who proceeded to explore them with enthusiasm. Small objects, like silver hand-bowls and cutglass salt cellars, went into his capacious pockets.

The boy and his mother watched all this activity in silence. They had been told to pack and go, but in reality they had very little to pack. The boy had handed over a bunch of keys; he wasn't obliged to do any more.

On the second day, when he had finished his inventory, Mr Middleman said he would be back the next day with a truck and some workmen to help remove all that he had listed—box-beds included. The boy simply shrugged and walked away; his mother set about preparing dinner, the kitchen still her domain. They were in no hurry.

It was almost dark when Mr Middleman set out on his walk back to town. The clouds had parted, and a full moon was coming up over Pari Tibba, Fairy Hill. In the moonlight a big black bird swooped low over the ravished building.

Pockets bulging with mementos, Mr Middleman strode confidently through the pine forest, his walking stick swinging at his side. A village postman, on his way home, passed him in the gathering darkness. That was the last time Mr Middleman was seen alive.

His body was discovered early next morning by some girls on their way to school. It lay at the edge of the pond, where the boys sometimes came for a swim. But Mr Middleman hadn't been swimming. He was still in his clothes and his pockets were still bulging with the previous day's spoils. He had been struck over the head several times with the clubbed head of his walking stick. Apparently it had been wrenched from his hands by a stronger person, who had then laid into him with a fury of blows to the head. The walking stick lay a few feet away, covered with blood.

AN INSPECTOR CALLS

From then on, events moved quickly.

A jeepful of policemen roamed up and down Fosterganj's only motorable road, looking for potential killers. The bank, the bakery and the post office were centres of information and speculation.

Fosterganj might have had its mad dogs and professor-eating leopards; old skeletons might pop up here and there; but it was a long time since there'd been a proper murder. It was reported in the Dehradun papers (both Hindi and English) and even got mentioned in the news bulletin from All India Radio, Najibabad.

When I walked into Vishaal's small office in the bank, I found him chatting to a police inspector who had come down from Mussoorie to investigate the crime. One of his suspects was Sunil, but Sunil was far away in Lansdowne, making an earnest attempt to enlist in the Garhwal Rifles. And Sunil would have cleaned out the victim's pockets, the only possible motivation being robbery.

The same for Mr Foster, who was also one of the inspector's suspects. He wouldn't have left behind those valuable little antiques. And in any case, he was a feeble old man; he would not have been able to overcome someone as robust as Mr Middleman.

The talk turned to the occupants of Fairy Glen. But the inspector dismissed them as possible suspects: the woman could never have overpowered the assessor; and her son was just a boy.

I could have told him that the boy was much stronger than he looked, but I did not wish to point the finger of suspicion in his direction; or in any direction, for that matter. Mr Middleman was an outsider; his enemies were probably outsiders too.

After the inspector had gone, Vishaal asked: 'So—who do you think did it?'

'I, said the sparrow, with my bow and arrow, I killed Cock Robin!'

'Seriously, though.'

'I, said the fly, with my little eye, I saw him die.'

Vishaal raised his hands in exasperation. I decided to be serious.

'We'll know only if there was a witness,' I said. 'Someone who saw him being attacked. But that's unlikely, if it happened after dark. Not many people use that path at night.'

'True. More than one person has fallen into that pond.' Indeed, before the day was over, the inspector had fallen into the pond. He had been looking for clues at the water's edge, peering down at a tangle of reeds, when he heard an unusually loud flapping of wings. Looking up, he saw a big black bird hovering above him. He had never seen such a bird before. Startled, he had lost his footing and fallen into the water.

A constable dragged him out, spluttering and cursing. Along with the reeds and water weeds that clung to him was a mask made of cloth. It was a small mask, made for a boy.

The inspector threw it away in disgust, along with a drowned rat and a broken cricket bat that had come to the surface with him. Empty a village pond, and you will come up with a lot of local history; but the inspector did not have time for history.

The only person who seemed unperturbed by the murder was Hassan; he had seen people being killed out of feelings of hate or revenge. But here the reasons seemed more obscure.

'Such men make enemies,' he said. 'The go-betweens, the fixers. Someone must have been waiting for him.' He shrugged and went back to his work.

Hassan, a man who loved his work. He loved baking, just as some of us love writing or painting or making things. Most of the children were off to school in the morning, and his wife would be busy washing clothes or cleaning up the mess that children make. The older boys would take turns making deliveries, although sometimes Hassan did the rounds himself. But he was happiest in the bakery, fashioning loaves of bread, buns, biscuits and other savouries.

The first condition of happiness is that a man must find joy in his work. Unless the work brings joy, the tedium of an aimless life can be soul-destroying.

Something that I had to remember.

A FIRE IN THE NIGHT

It was late evening the same day when I encountered the boy from the palace.

I was strolling through the forest, admiring the mushrooms that had sprung up in damp, shady places. Poisoned, no doubt, but very colourful. Beware of nature's show-offs: the banded krait, the scarlet scorpion, the beautiful belladonna, the ink-squirting octopus. Even so, history shows human beings to be the most dangerous of nature's show-offs. Inimical to each other, given over to greed and insatiable appetites. Nature strikes when roused; man, out of habit and a perverse nature.

The boy still had some of the animal in him, which was what made him appealing.

'I've been looking for you, sir,' he said, as he stepped out of the shadows.

'I did not see you,' I said, startled.

'They've been looking for me. The police. Ever since that fellow was killed.'

'Did you kill him?'

I could see him smile even though it was dark. 'Such a big man? And why bother? They will take the palace anyway.'

He fell into step with me, holding my hand, leading the way; he knew the path and the forest better than I did. They would not find him easily in these hills.

'My mother has a favour to ask of you, sir.'

'Yes?'

'Will you keep something for her?'

'If it's not too big. I can't carry trunks and furniture around. I'm a one-suitcase person.'

'It's not heavy. I have it with me.' He was carrying a small wooden case wrapped in cloth. 'I can't open it here. It contains her jewellery. A number of things. They are all hers, but they will take them from us if they get a chance.'

'They?'

'The owners. The old king's family. Or their friends.'

'So you are going away?'

'We have to. But not before—.' He did not finish what he was going to say. 'You will keep them for us?'

'For how long? I may leave Fosterganj before the end of the year. I will run out of money by then. I'll have to return to Delhi and take up a job.'

'We will get in touch with you. We won't be far.'

'All right, then. Give me the case. I'll have to look inside later.'

'Of course. But don't let anyone else see it. I'll go now. I don't want to be seen.'

He put the wrapped-up box in my hands, embraced me—it was more of a bear hug, surprising me with its intensity—and made off into the darkness.

I returned to my room with the box, but I did not open it immediately. The door of my room did not fasten properly, and anyone could have walked in. It was only eight o'clock. So I placed the box on a shelf and covered it with my books. No one was going to touch them. Books gather dust in Fosterganj.

Vishaal had asked me over for a drink, and it was past ten when I started walking back to my room again.

Hassan and family were out on the road, along with some other locals. They were speculating on the cause of a bright rosy glow over the next ridge.

'What's happening?' I asked.

'Looks like a fire,' said Hassan. 'Down the Rajpur road.'

'It may be the Fairy Glen palace,' I said.

'Yes, it's in that direction. Let's go and take a look. They might need help.'

Fosterganj did not have a fire engine, and in those days Mussoorie did not have one either, so there was little that anyone could do to put out a major fire.

And this was a major fire.

One section of the palace was already ablaze, and a strong wind was helping the fire to spread rapidly. There was no sign of the boy and his mother. I could only hope that they were safe somewhere, probably on the other side of the building, away from the wind-driven flames.

A small crowd had gathered on the road, and before long half the residents of Fosterganj were watching the blaze.

'How could it have started?' asked someone.

'Probably an electrical fault. It's such an old building.'

'It didn't have electricity. Bills haven't been paid for years.'

'Then maybe an oil lamp fell over. In this wind anything is possible.'

'Could have been deliberate. For the insurance.'

'It wasn't insured. Nothing to insure.'

'Plenty to insure, the place was full of valuables and antiques. Furniture, mostly. All gone now.'

'What about the occupants—that woman and her boy?'

'Might be gone too, if they were sleeping.'

'Perhaps they did it.'

'But why?'

'They were being forced out, I heard.'

And so the speculation continued, everyone expressing an opinion, and in the meantime the fire had engulfed the entire building, consuming everything within—furniture, paintings, box-beds, skeletons, carpets, curtains, grandfather clock, a century's accumulated finery, all reduced to ashes. Most of the stuff had already outlived its original owner, who had himself been long since reduced to ashes. His heirs had wished to add to their own possessions, but possession is always a fleeting, temporary thing, and now there was nothing.

Towards dawn the fire burnt itself out and the crowd melted away. Only a shell of the palace remained, with here and there some woodwork still smouldering among the blackened walls. I wandered around the property and the hillside, looking for the boy and his mother, but I did not really expect to find them.

As I set out for home, something screeched in the tallest tree, and the big black bird flew across the road and over the burnt-out palace before disappearing into the forest below.

A HANDFUL OF GEMS

After an early breakfast with Hassan, I returned to my room and threw myself down on my bed. Then I remembered the case that the boy had left with me. I got up to see if it was still where I had hidden it. My books were undisturbed.

So I took the case down from the shelf, placed it on the bed, and prepared to open it. Then I realized I had no key. There was a keyhole just below the lid, and I tried inserting the pointed end of a pair of small scissors, but to no avail; then a piece of wire from the wire netting of the window, but did no better with that. Finally I tried the open end of a safety pin which I had been using on my pyjama jacket; no use. Obviously I was not meant to be a locksmith, or a thief.

Eventually, in sheer frustration, I flung the box across the room.

It bounced off the opposite wall, hit the floor, and burst open.

Gemstones and jewellery cascaded across the floor of the room.

When I had recovered from my astonishment and confusion, I made sure the door was shut, then set about collecting the scattered gems.

There were a number of beautiful translucent red rubies, all aglow in the sun that streamed through the open window. I spread them out on my counterpane. I did not know much about gemstones, but they looked genuine enough to me. Presumably they had come from the ruby mines of Burma.

There was a gold bracelet studded with several very pretty bright green emeralds. Where did emeralds come from? South America, mostly. Supposedly my birthstone; but I'd never been able to afford one.

A sapphire, azure, sparkling in a silver neck-chain. A sapphire from Sri Lanka? And a garnet in a ring of gold. I could recognize a garnet because my grandmother had one. When I was small and asked her what it was, she said it was a pomegranate seed.

So there I was, with a small fortune in my hands. Or may be a large fortune. I had never bothered with gemstones before, but I was beginning to get interested. Having them in your hands makes all the difference.

Where should I hide them? Sooner or later someone would disturb my books. I looked around the room; very few places of concealment. But on my desk was a round biscuit tin. One of Hassan's boys used to keep his marbles in it; I had given him more marbles in exchange for the tin, because it made a handy receptacle for my paper-clips, rubber bands, erasers and such like. These I now emptied into a drawer. The jewels went into the biscuit tin—rubies, emeralds, sapphire, garnet—just like marbles, only prettier.

But I couldn't leave that biscuit tin lying around. One of the boys might come back for it.

On the balcony were several flowerpots; two were empty; one was home to a neglected geranium, another to a money- plant that didn't seem interested in going anywhere. I put the biscuit tin in an empty pot, and covered it with the geranium, earth, roots and all, and gave it a light watering. It seemed to perk up immediately! Nothing like having a fortune behind you.

I brought the pot into my room, where I could keep an eye on it. The plant would flourish better indoors.

All this activity had sharpened my appetite, and I went down to the bakery and had a second breakfast.

FOSTER MAKES A SALE

In our dear country sensational events come and go, and excitement soon gives way to ennui.

And so it was in Fosterganj. Interest in the murder and the fire died down soon enough, although of course the police and the palace owners continued to make their enquiries.

Vishaal tried to liven up the hillside, spotting another leopard in his back garden. But it was only a dog-lifter, not a man-eater, and since there were very few dogs to be found in Fosterganj after the last rabies scare, the leopard soon moved on.

A milkman brought me a message from Foster one morning, asking me to come and see him.

'Is he ill?' I asked.

'Looks all right,' said the milkman. 'He owes me for two months' supply of milk.'

'He'll give you a laying hen instead,' I said. 'The world's economy should be based on exchange.'

'That's all right,' said the milkman. 'But his hens are dying, one by one. Soon he won't have any left.'

This didn't sound too good, so I made my way over to Foster's and found him sitting in his small patch of garden, contemplating his onions and a few late gladioli.

'No one's buying my gladioli, and my hens are dying,' he said gloomily. An empty rum bottle lay in the grass beside his wobbly cane chair. 'Sorry I can't offer you anything to drink. I've run out of booze.'

'That's all right,' I said. 'I don't drink in the daytime. But why don't you sell onions? They'll fetch a better price than your gladioli.'

'They've all rotted away,' he said. 'Too much rain. And the

porcupines take the good ones. But sit down—sit down, I haven't been out for days. Can't leave the hens alone too long, and the gout is killing me.' He removed a slipper and displayed a dirty bare foot swollen at the ankles. 'But tell me—how's the murder investigation going?'

'It doesn't seem to be going anywhere.'

'Probably that boy,' said Foster. 'He's older than he looks. A strange couple, those two.'

'Well, they are missing. Disappeared after the fire.'

'Probably started it. Well, good luck to them. We don't want a flashy hotel in the middle of Fosterganj.'

'Why not? They might buy your eggs—and your gladioli.'

'No, they'd go to town for their supplies.'

'You never know... By the way, when did Fosterganj last have a murder? Or was this the first?'

'Not the first by any means. We've had a few over the years. Mostly unsolved.'

'The ones in the palace?'

'The disappearing maharanis—or mistresses. Very mysterious. No one really knows what happened to them, except they disappeared. Any remains probably went in that fire. But no one really bothered. The raja's life was his own business, and in those days they did much as they wanted. A law unto themselves.'

A large white butterfly came fluttering up to Foster and sat on his ear. He carried on speaking.

'Then there was that school principal, down near Rajpur. Fanthorne, I think his name was. Suspected his wife of infidelity. Shot her, and then shot himself. Nice and simple. Made it easy for the police and everyone concerned. A good example to all who contemplate murder. Carry out the deed and then turn yourself in or blow your brains out. Why leave a mess behind?'

'Why, indeed. Apart from your brains.'

'Of course you can also hang yourself, if you want to keep it clean. Like poor old Kapoor, who owned the Empire. It went downhill after Independence. No one coming to Mussoorie, no takers for the hotel. He was heavily in debt. He tried setting fire to it for the insurance, but it was such a sturdy old building, built with stones from the riverbed, that it wouldn't burn properly! A few days later old Kapoor was found hanging from a chandelier in the ballroom.'

'Who got the hotel?'

'Nobody. It passed into the Receiver's hand. It's still there, if you want to look at it. Full of squatters and the ghost of old Kapoor. You can see him in the early hours, wandering about with a can of petrol, trying to set fire to the place.'

'Suicide appears to have been popular.'

'Yes, it's that kind of place. Suicidal. I've thought of it once or twice myself.'

'And how would you go about it?'

'Oh, just keep boozing until I pass out permanently.'

'Nice thought. But don't do it today—not while I'm here.'

'I was coming to that—why I asked you to come over. I was wondering if you could lend me a small sum—just to tide me over the weekend. I'm all out of rations and the water supply has been cut too. Have to fill my bucket at the public tap, after all those washerwomen. Very demeaning for a sahib!'

'Well, I'm a little short myself,' I said. 'Not a good time for writers. But I can send you something from the bakery, I have credit there.'

'Don't bother, don't bother. You wouldn't care to buy a couple of hens, would you? I'm down to just three or four birds.'

'Where would I keep them? But I'll ask Hassan to take them off you. He'll give you a fair price.'

'Fine, fine. And there's my furniture. I could part with one or two pieces. That fine old rocking chair—been in the family for a century.'

I had seen the rocking chair on my previous visit, and had refrained from sitting in it, as it had looked rather precarious.

'I would laze in it all day and get no work done,' I said.

'What about Uncle Fred's skull? It's a real museum piece.'

'No, thanks. It's hardly the thing to cheer me up on a lonely winter's evening. Unlike your gramophone, which is very jolly.'

'Gramophone! Would you like the gramophone?' The white butterfly jumped up a little, as excited as Foster, then settled back on his ear.

'Well, it only just occurred to me—but you wouldn't want to part with it.'

'I might, if you made me a good offer. It's a solid HMV 1942 model. Portable, too. You can play it on a beach in Goa or a mountaintop in Sikkim. Springs are in good condition. So's the handle. Four hundred rupees, and you get the records free. It's a bargain!'

How do you bargain with a Scotsman? Foster's urgent need of money overrode his affection for the ballads of Sir Harry Lauder. I offered him two hundred, which was all the money I had on me. After a good deal of haggling we settled on three hundred. I gave him two and promised to pay the rest later.

In good spirits now, Forster suddenly remembered he had some booze stashed away somewhere after all. We celebrated over a bottle of his best hooch, and I stumbled home two hours later, the gramophone under one arm and a box of records under the other.

That night I treated myself to Sir Harry Lauder singing 'Loch Lomond', Dame Clara Buck singing 'Comin' through the Rye', and Arthur Askey singing 'We have no bananas today'. Hassan's children attended the concert, and various passers-by stopped in the road, some to listen, others to ask why I couldn't play something more pleasing to the ear. But everyone seemed to enjoy the diversion.

TREASURE HUNT

The nights were getting chilly, and I needed another blanket. The rains were over, and a rainbow arched across the valley, linking Fosterganj to the Mussoorie ridge. A strong wind came down from Tibet, rattling the rooftops.

I decided to stay another month, then move down to Rajpur.

∽

Someone had slipped a letter under my door. I found it there early one morning. Inside a plain envelope was a slip of paper with a few words on it. All it said was: 'Chakrata. Hotel Peak View. Next Sunday'.

I presumed the note was from the boy or his mother. Next Sunday was just three days away, but I could get to Chakrata in a day. It was a small military cantonment half way between Mussoorie and Simla. I had been there as a boy, but not in recent years; it was still a little off the beaten track.

I did not tell Hassan where I was going, just said I'd be back in a day or two; he wasn't the sort to pry into my affairs. I stuffed a change of clothes into a travel bag, along with the little box containing the jewels. Before hiding it, I had taped the lid town with Sellotape. It was still under the geranium, and I removed it carefully and returned the plant to its receptacle, where it would now have a little more freedom to spread its roots.

I took a bus down to Dehradun, and after hanging around the bus station for a couple of hours, found one that was going to Chakrata. It was half empty. Only a few village folk were going in my direction.

A meandering road took us through field and forest, and then we crossed the Yamuna just where it emerged from its mountain fastness, still pure and unpolluted in its upper reaches. The road grew steeper, more winding, ascending through pine and deodar forest, and finally we alighted at a small bus stop, where an old bus and two or three ponies appeared to be stranded. A deserted church and a few old graves told me that the British had once been present here.

There was only one hotel on the outskirts of the town, and it took me about twenty minutes to get to it, as I had to walk all the way. It stood in a forest glade, but it did provide a view of the peaks, the snow-capped Chor range being the most prominent.

It was a small hotel, little more than a guesthouse, and I did not notice any other residents. There was no sign of a manager, either; but a gardener or handyman led me to the small reception desk and produced a register. I entered my name and my former Delhi address. He then took me to a small room and asked me if I'd like some tea.

'Please,' I said. 'And something to eat.'

'No cook,' he said. 'But I'll bring you something from the market.' And he disappeared, leaving me to settle down in my room.

I needed a wash, and went into the bathroom. It had a nice view, but there was no water in the tap. There was a bucket half filled with water, but it looked rather murky. I postponed the wash.

I settled down in an armchair, and finding it quite comfortable, immediately fell asleep. Being a man with an easy conscience I've never had any difficulty in falling asleep.

I woke up about an hour later, to find the cook-gardener-caretaker hovering over me with a plate of hot pakoras and a pot of tea. He had only one eye, which, strangely, I hadn't noticed before. I recalled the old proverb: 'In the country of the blind the one-eyed man is king.' But I'd always thought the antithetical was true, and a more likely outcome, in the country of the blind, would be the one-eyed man being stoned to death. How dare he be different.

My one-eyed man seemed happy to talk. Not many tourists came to Chakrata; the intelligence department took a strong interest in visitors. In fact, I could expect a visit from them before the day was out.

'Has anyone been asking for me?' I asked. 'A young man accompanied by his mother?'

'They were here last week. Said they were from Nepal. But they left in a hurry. They did not take your name.'

'Perhaps they'll be back. I'll stay tonight—leave in the morning. Will that be all right?'

'Stay as long as you like. It's ten rupees a day for the room and two rupees for a bucket of water. Water shortage.'

'And it's been raining for three months.'

'But we are far from the river,' he said. And then he left me to my own devices.

It was late evening when he appeared again to inform me that there were people in the hall who wanted to see me. Assuming that the boy and his mother had arrived, I said,

'Oh, show them in,' and got up from the armchair to receive them.

Three men stepped into the room. They were total strangers.

One of them asked to see my passport.

'I don't have one,' I said. 'Never left the country.'

'Any identification?'

I shook my head. I'd never been asked for identification. This was 1961, and border wars, invasions, insurrections and terrorist attacks were all in the future. We were free to travel all over the country without any questions being asked.

One of the three was in uniform, a police inspector. The second, the man who had spoken to me, was a civilian but clearly an official. The third person had some personal interest in the proceedings.

'I think you have something to deliver,' he said. 'Some stones belonging to the royal family.'

'You represent the royal family?' I asked.

'That is correct.'

'And the people who looked after the property?'

'They were servants. They have gone missing since the fire. Are you here to meet them?'

'No,' I said. 'I'm a travel writer. I'm writing a book on our hill stations. Chakrata is one of them.'

'But not for tourists,' said the official. 'This is purely a military station now.'

'Well, I have yet to see a soldier. Very well camouflaged.'

'Soldiers are not deployed here. It is a scientific establishment.'

I thought it better to leave it at that. I had come to the place simply to deliver some gemstones, and not as a spy; I said as much.

'Then may we have the stones?' said the third party. 'You will then be free to leave, or to enjoy the hospitality of this hotel.'

'And if I don't hand them over?'

'Then we may have to take you into custody,' said the inspector. 'For being in possession of stolen property.' And without further ado, he picked up my travel bag, placed it on a table, and rummaged through the contents. With three men standing over me, and the gardener in the background, there was no point in trying to be a hero.

The biscuit tin was soon in his hands. He shook it appreciatively, and it responded with a pleasing rattle. He tore off the tape, pressed open the lid and emptied the contents on the table.

Some thirty or forty colourful marbles streamed across the table, some rolling to the ground, others into the hands of the inspector, who held them up to the light and exclaimed, 'But these are not rubies!'

'My marble collection,' I said. 'And just as pretty as rubies.'

THE GREAT TRUCK RIDE

What had happened, quite obviously, was that Hassan's children, or at least one of them, had seen me secrete the box in the geranium pot. Wanting it back, they had unearthed it while I was out, removed the gemstones and replaced them with their store of marbles.

But what on earth had they done with the jewels? Hidden them elsewhere, perhaps. Or more likely, being still innocent children, they had seen the gems as mere rubbish and thrown them out of my window, into the ravine.

If I got back safely, I'd have to search the ravine.

But I was still in Chakrata, and my interlocutors had told me not to leave before morning. They were still hoping that the boy and his mother, or someone on their behalf, might have followed me to Chakrata.

The three gentlemen left me, saying they'd be back in the morning. I was left with the one-eyed gardener.

'When does the first bus leave for Dehradun?' I asked.

'At ten tomorrow.'

'Are there no taxis here?'

'Who would want a taxi? There is nothing to see. The best view is from your window.'

I gave him five rupees and asked him to bring me some food. He came back with some puris and a potato curry, and I shared it with him. He became quite chatty, and told me the town hadn't been off-bounds in the past, but security had been tightened since some border intrusions by the Chinese. Relations with China had soured ever since the Dalai Lama and his followers had fled to India two years previously. The Dalai Lama was still living in Mussoorie. Chakrata was, in a way, a lookout point; from here, the passes to the north could be better monitored. I'd come to the wrong place at the wrong time.

'I'm no spy,' I said. 'I'll come some other time to enjoy the scenery. I'll be off in the morning.'

'If they let you go.'

That sounded ominous.

The gardener-caretaker left me in order to lock up for the night, and I lay down on my bed in my clothes, wondering what I should do next. I was never much good in an emergency, and I was feeling quite helpless. Without friends, the world can seem a hostile place.

After some time I heard the door being bolted from outside. I'd been locked in.

I hate being locked into rooms. Once, as a small boy, I broke an expensive vase, and as punishment my grandmother locked me in the bathroom. I tried kicking the door open, and when that didn't work, I got hold of a water jug, smashed open a window, and climbed out; only to receive further punishment, by way of being sent to bed without any dinner.

And now I did more or less the same thing, but I waited for an hour or two, to give the gardener time to retire for the night. Then I unlatched the window—no need to break any glass—and peered out into the night.

The moon was a melon, just coming up over the next mountain. There was a vegetable patch just below the window. A cluster of cucumbers stood out in the mellow light. As I did not want to be encumbered with things to carry, I abandoned my travel bag and its meagre contents; I would survive without pyjamas and a tattered old sweater. I climbed out on the window ledge and dropped into the vegetable patch, avoiding the cucumbers but pitching forward into a clump of nettles.

The nettles stung me viciously on the hands and face, and I cursed in my best Hindustani. The European languages have their strengths, but for the purposes of cursing out loud you can't beat some of the Indian languages for range and originality.

It took about twenty minutes for the pain of the nettle stings to subside, and by then my linguistic abilities were exhausted. But the nettles had given greater urgency to my flight, and I was soon on the motor road, trudging along at a good pace. I was beginning to feel like a character in a John Buchan novel, always on the move and often in the wrong direction. All my life had been a little like that. But I wouldn't have known any other way to live.

I knew I had to go downhill, because that was the way to the river. After walking for an hour, I was hoping someone would come along and give me a lift. But there would be few travellers at that late hour. Jackals bayed, and an owl made enquiring sounds, but that was all…

And then I heard the approach of heavy vehicles—not one, but several—and a convoy of army trucks came down the road, their headlights penetrating the gloom and leaving no corner of the road in shadow.

I left the road and stood behind a walnut tree until they had passed. I had no intention of taking a lift in an army truck; I could end up at some high-altitude border post, abandoned there in sub-zero temperatures.

So I returned to the road only when the last truck had gone round the bend, then continued to tramp along the highway, sore of foot but strong of heart. Harry Lauder would have approved.

Something else was coming down the road. Another truck. An old one, rattling away and groaning as it changed gear on a sudden incline. The army wouldn't be using an old wreck. So I stood in the middle of the road and waved it to a stop. An elderly Sardarji, older than the truck, looked out of his cabin window and asked me where I was headed.

'Anywhere,' I said. 'Wherever you're going.'

'Herbertpur,' he said. 'Get in the back.'

Herbertpur was a small township near the Timli Pass, on the old route to Dehradun. Herbert had been a tea-planter back in the 1860s or thereabouts. The family had died out, but the name remained.

I would have liked to sit up front, but Sardarji already had a companion, his assistant, about half my age and fair of face, who showed no signs of making way for me. So I made my way to the back of the truck and climbed into its open body, expecting to find it loaded with farm produce. Instead, I found myself landing in the midst of a herd of goats.

There must have been about twenty of them, all crammed into

the back of the truck. Before I could get out, the truck started, and I found myself a fellow traveller with a party of goats destined for a butcher's shop in Herbertpur.

I must say they tried to make me welcome. As the truck lurched along the winding road, we were thrown about a good deal, and I found myself in close contact with those friendly but highly odorous creatures.

Why do we eat them, I wonder. There can be nothing tougher than the meat of a muscular mountain goat. We should instead use them as weapons of offence, driving herds of goats into enemy territory, where they will soon consume every bit of greenery—grass, crops, leaves—in a matter of minutes. Sometimes I wonder why the Great Mathematician created the goat; hardly one of nature's balancing factors.

But I was the intruder, I had no right to any of their space. So I could not complain when a kid mistook me for its mother and snuggled up to me, searching for an udder. When I thrust it away, a billy goat got annoyed and started butting me on the rump. Fortunately for me, two female goats came to my rescue, coming between me and the aggressive male.

By the time we reached Herbertpur it was two in the morning, and I was feeling like a serving of rogan josh or mutton keema, two dishes that I resolved to avoid if ever I saw a menu again.

When I scrambled out of that truck, I was smelling to high heaven. The goats were bleating, as though they missed me. I thanked Sardarji for the lift, and he offered to take me further—all the way to Saharanpur. The goats, he said, would soon be unloaded, and replaced by a pair of buffaloes.

I decided to walk.

There was a small canal running by the side of the road. There was just one thing I wanted in life. A bath.

I jumped into the canal, clothes and all, and wallowed there until daylight.

RUBIES IN THE DUST

I was back in Fosterganj that same evening, but I waited near the pool until it was dark before returning to my room. My clothes were in a mess, and I must have looked like the Creature from the Black Lagoon or an explorer who had lost his way in the jungle. After another bath, this time with good old Lifebuoy soap, I changed into my last pair of pyjamas, and slept all through the night and most of the next day, only emerging from my room because hunger had overcome lassitude. Hassan fed me on buns, biscuits and boiled eggs while I gave him an edited account of my excursion. He did not ask any questions, simply told me to avoid areas which were in any way under surveillance. Sage advice.

Over the next week, nothing much happened, except that the days grew shorter and the nights longer and I needed a razai at night.

I inspected all the flowerpots, emptying them one by one, just in case the marble players had switched the hiding place of the gemstones. The children watched me with some amusement, and I had to pretend that I was simply repotting the geraniums and begonias. It was the season for begonias; they flamed scarlet and red and bright orange, challenging the autumn hues of dahlias and chrysanthemums. Early October was a good time for flowers in Fosterganj. Vishaal's wife had created a patch of garden in front of the bank; the post office verandah had been brightened up; and even Foster's broken-down cottage was surrounded by cosmos gone wild.

I searched the ravine below the bakery, in case the gems had been thrown down from my window. I found broken bottles, cricket balls, old slippers, chicken bones, the detritus that accumulates on the fringes of human habitations; but nothing resembling jewellery.

And then one morning, as I was returning from a walk in the woods, I encountered the poor woman who was sweeping the road. This chore was usually carried out by her husband, but he had been ill for some time and she had taken over his duties. She was a sturdy woman, plain-looking, and dressed in a faded sari. Even when sweeping the road she had a certain dignity—an effortless, no-fuss dignity that few of us possess.

When I approached, she was holding something up to the light. And when she saw me, she held it out on her palm, and asked,

'What is this stone, Babuji? It was lying here in the dust. It is very pretty, is it not?'

I looked closely at the stone. It was not a pebble, but a ruby, of that I was certain.

'Is it valuable?' she asked. 'Can I keep it?'

'It may be worth something,' I said. 'But don't show it to everyone. Just keep it carefully. You found it, you keep it.'

'Finders keepers', the philosophy of my school days. And whom did it belong to, anyway? Who were the rightful owners of those stones? There was no way of telling.

And what was their real worth? We put an artificial value on pretty pebbles found in remote places. Just bits of crystals, poor substitutes for marbles. Innocent children know their true worth. Nothing more than the dust at their feet.

The good lady tied the stone in a corner of her sari and lumbered off, happy with her find. And I hoped she'd find more. Better in her hands than in the hands of princes.

SUNIL IS BACK

Out of the blue, Sunil arrived. There he was, lean and languid, sitting on the bakery steps, waiting for me to return from my walk.

'I thought you'd joined the army,' I said.

'They wouldn't take me. I couldn't pass the physical. You have to be an acrobat to do some of those things, like climbing ropes or swinging from trees like Tarzan.'

'All out of date,' I said. 'They need less brawn and more brain.'

He followed me up the steps to my room and stretched himself out on the cot. He reminded me of a cat, sleek and utterly self-satisfied.

'So what else happened?' I asked.

'Well, the colonel was a nice chap. He couldn't enlist me, but he gave me a job in the mess room. You know, keeping the place tidy, polishing the silver, helping at the bar. It wasn't hard work, and sometimes I was able to give myself a rum or a vodka on the quiet. Lots of silver trophies on the shelves. Very tempting, but you can't do much with those things, they are mostly for show.'

'What made you leave?'

'Ivory. There were these elephant's tusks mounted on the wall, you see. Huge tusks. They'd been there for years. The elephant had been shot by a colonel-shikari about fifty years ago, and the tusks put on display in the mess. All that ivory! Very tempting.'

'You can't just pocket elephant tusks.'

'Not pocket them, but you can carry them off. And I knew how to get into that mess room in the middle of the night without anyone seeing me.'

'So did you get away with them?'

'Perfectly. I had a rug in which I hid the tusks, and I'd tied them up with a couple of good army belts. I took the bus down to Kotdwar without any problem. No one was going to miss those tusks—not for a day or two, anyway.'

'So what went wrong?'

'Things went wrong at the Kotdwar railway station. I was walking along the platform with the rug on my shoulder, looking for an empty compartment, when a luggage trolley bumped into me. I dropped the rug and it burst open. The tusks were there for all to see. A couple of railway police were coming down the platform, so I took off like lightning. Ran down the platform until it ended, then crossed the railway lines and hid in a sugarcane field. Later, I took a ride on a bullock-cart until I was well away from the town. Then I borrowed a bicycle and rode all the way to Najibabad.'

'Where's the cycle?'

'Left it outside the police station just in case the owner came looking for it.'

'Very thoughtful of you. So here you are.'

He smiled at me. He was a rogue. But at least he'd stopped calling me uncle.

~

It was only later that day—towards evening, in fact—that Sunil spotted the gramophone in a corner of my room.

'What's this you've got?' he asked.

'Mr Foster's gramophone. It plays music.'

'I know that. My grandfather has one. He plays old Saigal records.'

'Well, this one has old English records. You won't care for them. I bought the gramophone and the records came with it.'

Sunil lost no time in placing the gramophone on the table, opening it, and putting a record on the turntable. But the table was stuck.

'It's fully wound,' said Sunil. 'There's something jammed inside.'

'It was all right when I went away. The kids must have been fooling around with it.'

'Have you a screwdriver?'

'No, but Hassan will have one. I'll go and borrow it.'

I left Sunil fiddling about with the gramophone, and went downstairs, and came back five minutes later with a small screwdriver. Sunil took it and began unscrewing the upper portion of the gramophone. He opened it up; revealing the springs, inner machinery, the emerald bracelet, garnet broach and sapphire ring.

Sunil immediately slipped the ring on to a finger and said,

'Very beautiful. Did it come with the gramophone?'

SAPPHIRES ARE UNLUCKY

'Sapphires are unlucky,' I told him. 'You have to be very special to wear a sapphire.'

'I'm lucky,' he said, holding his hands to the light and admiring the azure stone in its finely crafted ring. 'It suits me, don't you think? And where did all this treasure come from?'

There was no point in making up a story. I told him how the jewels had come into my possession. Even as I did, I wondered who had put the jewellery in the gramophone. One of the children, I presumed—only a child would recognize the value of jewels but not of gemstones. I thought it best not to tell Sunil this. I did not mention the rubies, either. I did not want him hunting all over Fosterganj for them, and interrupting games of marbles to check if the children were playing with rubies.

'Those two won't be back,' he said, referring to the palace boy and his mother. 'They will be wanted for theft, arson and murder. But others may be after these pretty pebbles.'

'I know,' I said, and told him about my visitors in Chakrata.

'And you will get visitors here as well. I think we should go away for some time. Come to my village. Not the one near Rajpur. I mean my mother's village in Bijnor, on the other side of the Ganga. It's an out-of-the-way place, far from the main highways. Strangers won't be welcome.'

'Will I be welcome?'

'With me, you will always be welcome.'

I allowed Sunil to take over. I wasn't really interested in the stones, they were more trouble than they were worth. All I wanted was a quiet life, a writing pad, books to read, flowers to gaze upon, and sometimes a little love, a little kiss... But Sunil was fascinated with the gems. Like a magpie, he was attracted to all that glittered.

He transferred the jewels to a small tin suitcase, the kind that barbers and masseurs used to carry around. It was seldom out of his sight. He told me to pack a few things, but to leave my books and the gramophone behind; we did not want any heavy stuff with us.

'You can't carry a palace around,' he said. 'But you can carry the king's jewels.'

'Take that sapphire off,' I said. 'Unless it's your birthstone, it will prove to be unlucky.'

'Well, I don't know my date of birth. So I can wear anything I like.'

'It doesn't suit you. It makes you look too prosperous.'

'Seeing it, people won't suspect that I'm after their pockets.' He had a point there. And he wasn't going to change his ways.

You have to accept people as they are, if you want to live with them. You can't really change people. Only a chameleon can change colour, and then only in order to deceive you.

If, like Sunil, you have a tendency to pick pockets, that tendency will always be there, even if one day you become a big corporate boss. If, like Foster, you have spent most of your life living on the edge of financial disaster, you will always be living on the edge. If, like Hassan, you are a single-minded baker of bread and maker of children, you won't stop doing either. If, like Vishaal, you are obsessed with leopards, you won't stop looking for them. And if, like me, you are something of a dreamer, you won't stop dreaming.

GANGA TAKES ALL

'Ganga-maiki jai!'

The boat carrying pilgrims across the sacred river was ready to leave. Sunil and I scrambled down the river bank and tumbled into it. It was already overloaded, but we squeezed in amongst the pilgrims, mostly rural folk who had come to Hardwar to visit the temples and take home bottles of Ganga water—in much the same way that the faithful come to Lourdes, in France, and carry away the healing waters of a sacred stream. People are the same everywhere.

In those days there was no road bridge across the Ganga, and the train took one to Bijnor by a long and circuitous route. Sunil's village was off the beaten track, some thirty miles from the nearest station. The easiest way to get there was to cross the river by boat and then take an ekka, or pony- cart, to get to the village.

The boat was meant to take about a dozen people, but for a few rupees more the boatmen would usually take in more than the permitted number. When we set off, there must have been at least twenty in the boat—men, women and children.

'Ganga-maiki jai!' they chanted, as the two oarsmen swung into the current.

For a time, all went well. In spite of its load, the boat made headway, being carried a little downstream but in the general direction of its landing place. Then halfway across the river, where the water was deep and strong, the boat began to wobble about and water slopped in over the sides.

The singing stopped, and a few called out in dismay. There was little one could do, except urge the oarsmen on.

They did their best, straining at the oars, the sweat pouring down their bare bodies. We made some progress, although we were now drifting with the current.

'It doesn't matter where we land,' I said, 'as long as we don't take in water.'

I had always been nervous in small boats. The fear of drowning had been with me since childhood: I'd seen a dhow go down off the Kathiawar coast, and bodies washed ashore the next day.

'Ganga-maiki jai!' called one or two hardy souls, and we were about two-thirds across the river when water began to fill the boat. The women screamed, the children cried out.

'Don't panic!' I yelled, though filled with panic. 'It's not so deep here, we can get ashore.'

The boat struck a sandbank, tipped over. We were in the water.

I was waist-deep in water, but the current was strong, taking me along. The menfolk picked up the smaller children and struggled to reach the shore. The women struggled to follow them.

Two of the older women were carried downstream; I have no idea what happened to them.

Sunil was splashing about near the capsized boat. 'Where's my suitcase?' he yelled.

I saw it bobbing about on the water, just out of his reach. He made a grab for it, but it was swept away. I saw it disappearing downstream. It might float for a while, then sink to the bottom of the river. No one would find it there. Or some day the suitcase would burst open, its contents carried further downstream, and the emerald bracelet be washed up among the pebbles of the riverbed. A fisherman might find it. In older times he would have taken it to his king. In present times he would keep it.

We struggled ashore with the others and sank down on the sand, exhausted but happy to be alive.

Those who still had some strength left sang out: 'Ganga- maiki jai!' And so did I.

Sunil still had the sapphire ring on his hand, but it hadn't done him much good.

END OF THE ROAD

We stayed in Sunil's village for almost a month. I have to say I enjoyed the experience, in spite of the absence of modern conveniences. Electricity had come to the village—which was surprising for that time—and in our room there was a ceiling fan and an old radio. But sanitation was basic, and early in the morning one had to visit a thicket of thorn bushes, which provided more privacy than the

toilets at the bus stop. Water came from an old well. It was good sweet water. There were pigeons nesting in the walls of the well, and whenever we drew up a bucket of water the pigeons would erupt into the air, circle above us, and then settle down again.
There were other birds. Parrots, green and gold, settled in the guava trees and proceeded to decimate the young fruit. The children would chase them away, but they would return after an hour or two.
Herons looked for fish among the hyacinths clogging up the village pond. Kingfishers swooped low over the water. A pair of Sarus cranes, inseparable, treaded gingerly through the reeds. All on fishing expeditions.

The outskirts of an Indian village are a great place for birds. You will see twenty to thirty species in the course of a day. Bluejays doing their acrobatics, sky-diving high above the open fields; cheeky bulbuls in the courtyard; seven sisters everywhere; mynas quarrelling on the verandah steps; scarlet minivets and rosy pastors in the banyan tree; and at night, the hawk cuckoo or brain fever bird shouting at us from the mango-tope.

Almost every village has its mango-tope, its banyan tree, its small temple, its irrigation canal. Old men smoking hookahs; the able-bodied in the fields; children playing gulli-danda or cricket. An idyllic setting, but I did not envy my hosts. They toiled from morn till night—ploughing, sowing, reaping, always with an eye on the clouds—and then having to sell, in order to buy…

Sunil's uncle urged him to stay, to help them on the farm; but he was too lazy for any work that required physical exertion. Towns and cities were his milieu. He was fidgety all the time we were in the village. And when I told him it was time for me to start working, looking for a job in Delhi, he did not object to my leaving but instead insisted on joining me. He too would find a job in Delhi, he said. He could work in a hotel or a shop or even start his own business.

And so I found myself back in my old room in dusty Shahdara in Delhi, and within a short time I'd found work with a Daryaganj publisher, polishing up the English of professors who were writing guides to Shakespeare, Chaucer and Thomas Hardy.

Sunil had friends in Delhi, and he disappeared for long periods, turning up only occasionally, when he was out of pocket or in need of somewhere to spend the night.

And then one of his friends came by to tell me he'd been arrested at the New Delhi railway station. He'd been back to his old ways, relieving careless travellers of their cash or wristwatches. He was a skilful practitioner of his art, but he'd grown careless.

The police took away the sapphire ring, and of course he never saw it again. It must have brought a little affluence but not much joy to whoever flaunted it next.

Denied bail, Sunil finally found himself lodged in a new, modern jail that had come up at a village called Tihar, on the old Najafgarh road. As a boy I'd gone fishing in the extensive Najafgarh Jheel, but now much of it had been filled in and built over. The herons and kingfishers had moved on, the convicts had moved in.

Sunil had been there a few months when at last I was able to see him. He was looking quite cheerful, not in the least depressed; but then, he was never the despondent type. He was working in the pharmacy, helping out the prison doctor. He had become popular with the inmates, largely due to his lively renderings of Hindi film songs.

Our paths had crossed briefly, and now diverged. I knew we would probably not see each other again. And we didn't. What became of him? Perhaps he spent many more months in jail, making up prescriptions for ailing dacoits, murderers, embezzlers, fraudsters and sexual offenders; and perhaps when he came out, he was able to start a chemist's shop. Unlikely, but possible. In any case, he would have made Delhi his home. The big city would have suited him.

Fosterganj was a far cry from all this, and I was too busy to give it much thought. And then one Sunday, when I was at home, I had a visitor.

It was Hassan.

He had come to Delhi to attend a relative's marriage and he had got my address from the publisher in Daryaganj. Having given up any hope of seeing me again in Fosterganj, he'd brought along my books, typewriter, and the gramophone.

He spent all morning with me, bringing me up to date on

happenings in Fosterganj.

Vishaal had been transferred, getting a promotion, and taking over a branch in the heart of Madhya Pradesh. Mowgli country! Leopard country! Vishaal would be happy there.

'And how's old Foster?' I asked.

'Not too good. He says he won't last long, and he may be right. He wants to know if you'll accept his uncle's skull as a gift.'

'Tell him to gift it to the Mussoorie municipality. I believe they are starting a museum in the Clock Tower. But thanks for bringing the gramophone down. I could do with a little music.'

Hassan then told me that the hotel was now coming up on the site of the old palace. It would be a posh sort of place, very expensive.

'What are they calling it?' I asked.

'Lake View Hotel.'

'But there isn't a lake.'

'They plan to make one. Extend the old pool, and feed it with water from the dhobi ghat. Fosterganj is changing fast.'

'Well, as long as it's good for business. Should be good for the bakery.'

'Oh, they'll have their own bakery. But I'll manage. So many workers and labourers around now. Population is going up. So when will you visit us again?'

'Next year, perhaps. But I can't afford Lake View palaces.'

'You don't need to. Your room is still there.'

'Then I'll come.'

∽

Over the next three or four years I lost touch with Fosterganj. My life changed a little. I found companionship when I was least expecting it, and I became a freelance writer for a travel magazine. It was funded by a Parsi gentleman who was rumoured to own half of Bombay. I saw no evidence of the wealth in the cheques I received for my stories, but at least I got to travel a lot, zipping around the country by train, bus and, on one occasion, a dilapidated old Dakota of the Indian Airlines.

The forests of Coonoor; the surge of the sea at Gopalpur; old settlements on the Hooghly; the ghats of Banaras; the butterflies of the Western Ghats; the forts of Gwalior; the sacred birds of Mathura; the gardens of Kashmir—all were grist to my mill, or rather to the portable typewriter which had taken the place of the clumsy old office machine. How could Fosterganj's modest charms compare with the splendours that were on offer elsewhere in the land?

So Fosterganj was far from my thoughts—until one day I picked up a newspaper and came across a news item that caught my attention.

On the outskirts of the hill station of Nahan a crime had been committed. An elderly couple living alone in a sprawling bungalow had been strangled to death. The police had been clueless for several weeks, and the case was almost forgotten, until a lady turned up with information about the killer. She led them to a spot among the pines behind the bungalow, where a boy was digging up what looked like a small wooden chest. It contained a collection of valuable gemstones. The murdered man had been a well-known jeweller with an establishment in Simla.

The accused claimed that he was a minor, barely fifteen. And certainly he had looked no older to the police. But the woman told them he was only a few years younger than her, and that she was nearly fifty. She confessed to being his accomplice in similar crimes in the past; it was always gems and jewellery he was after. He had been her lover, she said. She had been under his domination for too long.

I looked at the photograph of the man-boy that accompanied the report. A bit fuzzy, but it certainly looked like Bhim the Lucky. Who else could it have been?

The next few mornings I scanned the papers for more information on the case. There was a small update, which said that a medical test had confirmed the accused was in his forties. And the woman had disappeared.

Then there was nothing. The newspapers had moved on to other scandals and disasters.

I felt sorry for the woman. We had met only twice, but I had sensed in her a fellow feeling, a shared loneliness that was on the verge of finding relief. But for her it was not to be. I wondered where she was, and what she would do to forget she had given many years of her life for a love that had never truly existed.

I never saw her again.

∽

Not the happiest memory to have of Fosterganj. When I look back on that year, I prefer to think of Hassan and Sunil and Vishaal, and even old Foster (long gone), and the long-tailed magpies flitting among the oak trees, and the children playing on the dusty road.

And last winter, when I was spending a few weeks in a bungalow by the sea—far from my Himalayan haunts—I remembered Fosterganj and thought: I have written about moonlight bathing the Taj and the sun beating down on the Coromandel Coast—and so have others—but who will celebrate little Fosterganj?

And so I decided to write this account of the friends I made there—a baker, a banker, a pickpocket, a hare-lipped youth, an old boozer of royal descent, and a few others—to remind myself that there had been such a place, and that it had once been a part of my life.

AFTERWORD

A Long Walk with Ruskin

One of the great pleasures of my life as a reader has been the walks I have taken with Ruskin Bond. Not literally, for although I have known Ruskin for over thirty years now, I cannot remember strolling with him through his beloved mountains, or a small town that time forgot. But here's the thing, even though we haven't tramped the streets together, I have been walking with him practically my entire adult life, through my reading of his books, and that is what I'd like to talk about in this brief afterword.

Ruskin has been a walker all his life. He explains his fondness for walking, and how it has influenced his outlook on life as well as his writing in one of his lesser known books, *Roads to Mussoorie*, 'I have never been a fast walker, or a conqueror of mountain peaks, but I can plod along for miles. And that's what I have been doing all my life—plodding along, singing my song, telling my tales in my own unhurried way. I have lived my life at my own gentle pace, and if as a result I have failed to get to the top of the mountain (or of anything else), it doesn't matter, the long walk has brought its own sweet rewards; buttercups and butterflies along the way.' The unhurried pace of the long distance walker invests all his work but is seen to best effect in his novellas because it gives him the scope to meander, to pursue the 'zig-zag way' that allows for the unexpected bon mot, the felicitous insight or just the pause to take in the mountains.

The stories in this book, among the finest he has created in the course of his distinguished career, speak of a world that has long vanished from our country, but it is a world that has lost none of its power to enchant. Whether we are accompanying Sita on her perilous journey down the angry river or Bisnu as he gets the better of a dangerous leopard, whether we delight in Binya's joy at owning her blue umbrella or are saddened by the fate of the last tiger, whether we laugh uproariously at the antics of the eccentric guests at the 'hotel' in Shamli, get involved in the adventures of the boys in Pipalnagar or plunge into the various goings-on in the 'backwater' of Fosterganj, we are always entertained, always surprised by the gifts that our generous companion on our long journey, the creator of these marvellous stories, has for us. All the stories unwind in an unhurried way, even those that are filled with death-defying thrills and spills, and it is this quality that enables us to sink into them and experience to its fullest the magic of the fiction that Ruskin Bond has spun out of the hills and small towns of India for over sixty years. A long walk with Ruskin does not ever pall.

D. D.

ACKNOWLEDGEMENTS

Grateful acknowledgement is made to Penguin Books India for permission to use *Time Stops at Shamli* and *Bus Stop, Pipalnagar*; to Rupa Publications India for granting permission to use the following stories: *Angry River*; *The Blue Umbrella*; and *Night of the Leopard*.

The Last Tiger first appeared in the *Illustrated Weekly of India*.